D0908057

Above the Fold

by
Rachel Scott McDaniel

SMITTEN
HISTORICAL ROMANCE
LIGHTHOUSE PUBLISHING OF THE CAROLINAS

ABOVE THE FOLD BY RACHEL SCOTT MCDANIEL
Published by Smitten Historical Romance
an imprint of Lighthouse Publishing of the Carolinas
2333 Barton Oaks Dr., Raleigh, NC 27614

ISBN: 978-1-64526-064-6
Copyright © 2019 by Rachel Scott McDaniel
Cover design by Elaina Lee
Interior design by Karthick Srinivasan

Available in print from your local bookstore, online, or from the publisher at:
ShopLPC.com

For more information on this book and the author visit:
https://rachelscottmcdaniel.com/

Brought to you by the creative team at Lighthouse Publishing of the Carolinas (LPCBooks.com): Eddie Jones, Shonda Savage, Pegg Thomas, Denise Weimer, Stephen Mathisen, Emily Fromke, Jenny Leo

Library of Congress Cataloging-in-Publication Data
McDaniel, Rachel Scott.
Above the Fold, Rachel Scott McDaniel. 1st ed.

Printed in the United States of America

Praise for *Above the Fold*

What a blast! In *Above the Fold*, the Roaring Twenties in Pittsburgh comes to life, from the sooty streets to the speakeasies to the raucous world of journalism. Both Cole and Elissa are appealing—strong and sassy, but deeply vulnerable—and their romance is swoon-worthy. Rachel Scott McDaniel's debut novel will keep you flipping pages to the end!

~**Sarah Sundin**
Bestselling and award-winning author of *The Land Beneath Us*

What a fantastic debut! Rachel McDaniel brings a wonderful combination of romance, suspense, and historical delights in her 1920s-era novel, *Above the Fold*. And while the spunky and innovative heroine is a joy to read, the hero steals the show with his loyal heart, protectiveness, and ability to give Elissa space, encouragement, and love to expand the expectations of women in the newspaper world of the early 1900s. From speakeasies to murder to a renewed romance from the past, *Above the Fold* is right on the mark for a great read!

~**Pepper Basham**
Author of *My Heart Belongs in the Blue Ridge*

With a determined heroine, a beautifully crafted mystery, and a love story that sizzles off the page, *Above the Fold* is a joy to read! Rachel McDaniel has captured to perfection the roaring culture of the 1920's newspaper business and the intricacies of two hearts yearning for a second chance at love. I couldn't put it down.

~**Abigail Wilson**
Author of *In the Shadow of Croft Towers*

Acknowledgments

The writing journey is never a solo effort. I'd like to thank those who've supported me, put up with my endless story musings, and supplied me with chocolate. To my critique partner and dearest friend, Rebekah Millet, I'm so grateful God has teamed us together! You've been an immense help, not only enriching this story, but my life as well. Thanks to Julie Gwinn, my awesome agent, for championing this story from the start. It's a fabulous thing to have your support! Special thanks to my early readers, Amy, Crissy, Joy, and Robyn, your encouragement meant the world to me. To my very first launch team, The Newsies, you guys are the best ever.

I'd like to thank Pegg Thomas and the rest of the team at Smitten Historical Romance/Lighthouse Publishing of the Carolinas for taking a chance on me. I'm grateful for the opportunity to share this story. A special thanks to my editor, Denise Weimer. You've been so patient and gracious, and I truly appreciate how you made this book shine.

Most of all, thanks to my family. Scott, you've spent your past few vacations showing your support by driving me to writing conferences, but you've spent the past seventeen years showing your devotion by loving me so much. Thank you. Drew and Meg, thank you for being awesome and accompanying your mama to all the bookish places, research excursions, and museum visits. See, even grown-ups need field trips! I'm thankful to be your mom.

And above all, to God. You are the ultimate storyteller. Your words have brought me life eternal. Thank You.

DEDICATION

To my first and only hero, Scott.
For your faith in me, your support through all my tears,
and most of all, for your love.

CHAPTER 1

March 10, 1922
Pittsburgh, Pennsylvania

Soot-stained windows filtered the morning light, casting an ashen shadow on the crowded courtroom and darkening the sting of judgment. Elissa Tillman couldn't help but stare at the man accused of murder. With his shoulders curled forward and face buried in his palms, Franco Cartelli didn't resemble the arrogant crime boss his reputation once boasted.

She pulled her elbows into her sides to keep from touching the stout men who bookended her in the congested space. If the trolley hadn't been delayed this morning, she would've arrived early enough to claim a seat. Though lingering in the back gave her a direct route to the exit should things grow riotous.

Press photographers lined the right side of the room. Some crouched behind box cameras, while others stood tall clutching portable ones. Bartek, the *Review*'s cameraman, cradled the new Graflex to his chest, a smug smile visible beneath his thick mustache. Maybe she shouldn't have pressed her father to spend the extra money for the latest model—heaven knew they needed every penny they could scrape together—but with ten other newspapers contesting for Pittsburgh's attention, staying ahead in the industry wasn't a luxury.

"Will the foreman please rise." The judge's authoritative voice filled the room, and a hundred pairs of eyes locked on the head juror. "Has the jury come to a unanimous decision?"

"Yes." The man slid his glasses up the bridge of his nose with a shaky knuckle. "We find the defendant ..."

The ticking clock on the wall punctuated the silence.

"Guilty."

Camera shutters clicked. Benches skidded and rocked as the horde sprang from their seats, their raised voices clashing. A cluster of men dashed to the window, hollering the verdict to bystanders on Fifth Avenue. Guards escorted the condemned man out of the room to the "bridge of sighs" which connected the courthouse and the jail.

An odd blend of satisfaction and compassion swirled in Elissa's gut. She'd proofread dozens of editorials for her father over the past four months. Sordid details about Cartelli's bribery and embezzlements. The graphic retelling of his murderous act toward the private detective who had exposed him.

Oh, yes. Her journalistic mind had invested ample hours on this case. To prove it, she had a desk drawer crammed with notes and drafts of articles which, sadly, no one knew—or cared—about except her.

The judge pounded his gavel, slowly reestablishing order. "The jury is thanked and excused. Sentencing is scheduled for Friday at three in the afternoon. Adjourned."

Elissa shrank against the wood-paneled wall as men barreled past her toward the exit. Reporters from the *Gazette*.

The sight of journalists from the rival paper stoked the fire in her veins. But she'd been raised to outmaneuver, outdo, and grab the story before the rest could sharpen their pencils. Even though she'd been passed over to write the articles, she'd remained chained to her desk, ensuring what *was* printed by others on staff would obliterate their competitors. Today was no exception.

The press conference with the district attorney would start soon. She scanned the crowd for her father's assigned man. Surely, Alfred Tillman would send someone to cover this. Bartek stood unmatched when it came to photography, but being a Polish immigrant, he barely grasped the English language, let alone possessed the skill to craft a print-worthy article.

The notorious son of the Cartelli family convicted of murder? It was the biggest story of the year—possibly the decade. The *Review* couldn't lose out. Her breath caged in her lungs.

Should she cover this lead?

Exhilaration landed on a curl of hope. How long had she asked—no, begged—her father for a reporter assignment? Though her last name matched those of the previous two generations who'd provided leading voices in the *Review*, her gender did not. She couldn't fault her father or grandfather for society's disapproval of women in this male-dominant profession, but the injustice remained, mocking her. She glanced at her coat where she'd pinned the yellow rose—the emblem of women's equality. Maybe she didn't have to remain quiet any longer.

Sliding a gloved hand from her muff and into her pocket, she retrieved the notepad and pencil she'd tucked away this morning.

Determination lifted her head, pulsing blood in her ears. All she had to do was find the throng of men with press passes stuffed into their hatbands, but first she had to squeeze her way across the mass of people exiting the courtroom.

Never before had she been more thankful for this year's fashion. Those precious inches of raised hemline, from her ankle to her upper calf, meant she could move more easily, side-stepping the portly gentleman to her left and snaking through the rest of the group. Though the propensity to rush coursed through her, she wouldn't allow herself to regress into old habits.

With high granite walls and rounded archways, this place bore a greater likeness to a cathedral than a justice building. She passed a wiry old man with a newspaper wedged under his arm, the partially exposed masthead drawing her frown. *The New York Dispatch.* The image of its star reporter trespassed into her thoughts. Time hadn't siphoned the memories from her soul. Instead, they lingered, brimming. Draining all the false sentiments and painful remembrances proved as futile as emptying the Ohio River with a teaspoon.

But she couldn't be distracted by him—or his betrayal. She had a story to tackle.

A litter of newshounds surrounded the press gallery door. Stepping into the room, Elissa wrinkled her nose at the stench of cigar smoke and perspiration. She attracted a few glances and smirks, but what did she expect, being the only female? Her cranberry coat among the dozens of black and charcoal suits resembled a cardinal among crows.

Her gaze darted from reporter to reporter, making certain of her father's error. How could he have forgotten? Was the withdrawal of support from key advertisers distressing him more than he'd said?

A man a few feet ahead snagged her attention. She could only see the back of his dark head, but a strange familiarity tickled her brain. His attire distinguished him from the others. A tailored suit? Italian leather shoes? Admiration stole through her. Who was this breathing *Vanity Fair* ad?

The district attorney strode across the front of the room, and attendants pulled the doors closed, a click echoing off the walls. She lifted her shoulders with a solid breath and squeezed the notepad. At least her pencil tip hadn't dulled from its travel in her pocket, but still … she'd keep her ears sharp and her strokes light.

"I have only a few minutes to field your questions." Robert Jackson, their aggressive district attorney, settled behind the wooden podium.

A tall gentleman in the front shot his hand in the air. "Julian Prove from the *Gazette*. Do you think Mr. Cartelli will receive the chair?"

"We're confident Judge Garner will rightly sentence Mr. Cartelli," the D.A. said. "We stand behind his ruling."

No need to shorthand his response. If that wasn't skirting the question, she didn't know what was. Shouldn't she ask something? Maybe about the national attention this had received or—

"Jim Brown. *Allegheny Times*." A mustached man to her left lifted his notepad, his lighted cigar flopping in his mouth as he spoke. "Will the court honor an appeal if Mr. Cartelli chooses to fight?"

The D.A. smirked. "We'll cross that bridge when we come to it."

Clever, that one. At least the ruling itself would make for a great headline. A headline she'd get to manufacture instead of proofread. But would her father allow her name on the byline? Her toes curled in her black pumps. She'd received accolades for her tribute honoring the brave women who'd battled for the right to vote. But would the other newspapers have reprinted her article had she not assumed a masculine moniker?

Maybe it was crucial for her to ask a question, and by that, to prove she hadn't come here to be an idle spectator, but to work. As an equal. Her spine straightened, and her lungs pulled in a scrape of air.

Movement ahead caught her eye. Mr. *Vanity Fair* waved two fingers in the air, his head slightly tilted to the left. A sudden desperation to see his face seized her because his mannerisms reminded her of—

"Cole Parker from the *Review*."

Her pencil tip snapped on her notepad.

The circus of newsmen hushed into awed whispers. At least Cole hoped it was awe. If they knew why he was really here, the murmurs would evolve into heckling. A feminine gasp pricked his ears.

He glanced over his shoulder.

Elissa.

Arresting blue eyes swallowed the gulf of five years. The reality of her presence rushed through him, throttling the air from his chest.

Her shock seemed to linger only a second before she closed her mouth into a firm line, and the surprise in her eyes turned stormy.

The D.A. cleared his throat. "Nice to have you back in Pittsburgh, Mr. Parker. What's your question?"

Ah, his question. Right. He pushed back the throbbing ache to go to her and scrounged for his voice. "Thank you for the welcome, sir. It's public knowledge the Cartellis are leaders in organized crime, second only to the Salvastano family. It's also evident that the law has been struggling to find ways to subdue their illegal activity. Are you aware of the rumors circulating from the Cartelli camp that you have been pressuring the jurors behind closed doors to supply a favorable verdict? And if so, do you think this supposition will affect your chances of reelection?"

The D.A. straightened and nodded. "I didn't expect any less from you, Cole." He jutted his chin as if to accept the challenge. "I am conscious of the lies that have been invented and spread—if I may be so bold—by newspapers represented in this very room. It's natural for those who dally on the wrong side of justice, like crime bosses, to want to sully the honorable workings of the judicial system. This case has been handled with the utmost caution. As for my reelection, I've proven myself through my dedication over the years, and I trust the hearts of voters." He raised a brow along with one side of his mouth. "Does that satisfy your curiosity?"

"Quite."

Jackson released the podium sides in an exaggerated motion and took a step back. "Have a good day, people of the press." He shot them what looked like a forced smile and bounded out of the room.

Cole tipped his hat to the vacant spot where the D.A. once stood. A slight nudge of what he could only guess was invigoration shifted in his heart. Was it too late to hope he'd begun to feel again?

The sorry lot of newsmen filed for the exit, but he aimed to find—

"What are you doing?" Her unmistakable voice carried over his shoulder along with the sweet fragrance of wildflowers.

He turned on his heel, almost knocking into her. His breath caught upon the discovery that her likeness in his imagination had been a lousy substitute compared to the brilliancy of the original. He swallowed so hard he could've choked on a tonsil. "It's a pleasure to see you again too."

"I can't express such a formality, Mr. Parker, because it's not a pleasure seeing you."

He glanced at the notepad in her hand, and she slipped it into her side pocket. "Mr. Parker, huh? Since when were we strangers?" But perhaps they were. Because on closer inspection, the woman standing before him seemed hard and polished, unlike the carefree spirit who'd entranced him years ago. No hairpin dangling from the nape of her neck. No rumples in her collar or stains on her sleeves. Though to be fair, his wardrobe had changed significantly since the last time they'd seen each other. Growing up together, what a pair they'd made, he with patches in his trousers and she with tears in her stockings. His gaze lowered. No gaping holes today, just some nice, shapely—

She huffed, and the yellow petals of the rose fixed to her coat trembled.

His lips twitched before he could stop them.

Elissa's chin snapped up, her narrowed eyes informing him she'd misunderstood his reaction. "Five years without any association can affect a woman's memory. So, yes, strangers."

No excuse, not even the wretched truth, could pacify the tempest swirling in the blue depths of her eyes.

"Shall we become acquainted, then?" He stuck out his hand, and she took a step back, arms folded.

Despite the rigid angles of her face matching the stiff line of her shoulders, Cole couldn't venture past how striking she was. From the delicate slope of her nose to the tender turn of her chin and fixed so perfectly in between—the mouth that had lured him in more times than he could count.

"Since I answered your question, I suppose you should return the favor." She tugged the hem of her glove. "What were you doing?"

He smiled his most dashing grin, and she gave him a glare so heated it could boil ice water. "Your father assigned me. I'm covering the Cartelli story."

"I gathered." Her lashes lowered for a second, and he could've sworn a sigh escaped her lips. "I'm referring to the way you treated the D.A. How dare you claim ties to my paper and then act in such a scoundrel fashion?"

He couldn't control the chuckle rising from his chest. "I'm proud of that. Didn't you catch how he was tiptoeing around all the questions? I cornered him, making him speak more words to me than his wife can probably get out of him in a week."

"We've worked hard to gain his favor." The golden ringlets framing her face swayed as she spoke. "And we can't lose it. Not now."

Her marked fury and contained desperation nipped his light humor and reminded him of the conversation he'd had with her father earlier in the week. The *Review* was struggling. "Spark, I'm sorry. I just—"

"Please refrain from familiarities." She turned away but glanced back with glacial regard. "You forfeited that right. And now my heart is wedded elsewhere." The sharp click of her heels faded as she glided out the room, but the word punctured his heart. Wedded.

Elissa Tillman was married.

CHAPTER 2

Tobacco smoke sparred with coffee vapors, punching Cole's senses as he stepped into the *Review*'s newsroom, but the heavy scents were insignificant compared to nostalgia's pang. He scanned the area that once had been his second home. Uneven rows of desks filled the center space. Maps of Pittsburgh and lists of possible leads were pinned to the wall edging the entrance, and floor-to-ceiling windows allowed in the light slanting past the Oakland Social Hall next door.

Jackets draped chairs occupied by men hunched over their typewriters, too engaged to notice Cole. With a deep exhale, he strode down the main aisle, passing several vacant stations, not abnormal, considering most of the staff could be out on a story or an early lunch.

"Who do I see here?" Frank Gosher eased back in his chair, patting a stomach which had significantly rounded since the last time Cole'd seen him. "I knew you'd be back."

Cole shook Frank's plump hand. "Nice to see a familiar face 'round here."

"You'll find a lot has changed." The seasoned wire editor jerked a thumb toward an empty desk behind him. "The princess mostly."

The secretarial station must be Elissa's. Cole didn't need Frank to point out the difference in Elissa. He'd seen it himself. And he hadn't fully recovered. While time had sculpted her face and curved her frame, it'd also darkened her sunny personality. Even her sparkling blue eyes had dimmed yet remained entrancing.

Married. She's married.

Cole swallowed. "I best go see the boss." He gave a quick nod and resumed his trek toward the office. He rapped the wooden frame of the open door.

"Parker, 'bout time you showed your face. You know we don't keep banking hours." Alfred Tillman, wielding a pencil over a stack of editorials, didn't spare a glance, but he sported his signature smirk—one side hitched up, making his cheek pucker. "Step in and shut the door."

"Got it, sir." Things felt like they'd never changed. Checking in with the publisher of the *Review* had forged his daily routine for a good portion of his adolescence. Back then, his fingers hadn't been typing an article but clutching, selling, or delivering bundles of newspapers.

The wood-paneled space remained the same, but the man in the leather chair had aged remarkably over the past half-decade. The salt-and-pepper hair Tillman once sported now thinned and grayed.

Cole adjusted the hem of his vest. "A golden article will be in your hands, er, as soon as you tell me where a vacant typewriter is."

The words tugged the older man's gaze from his work and also pulled out a hearty chuckle. "Suppose you might need one." He stood, the chair screeching against the planked floor. "Glad you're back, son."

"Thank you, sir."

His chin dipped. "Just glad you knew where to turn for help. But be aware you may not receive a friendly reception from—"

"I saw her."

"Elissa?" His dulled eyes widened, and his gaze darted to the clock on the wall. "Already?"

"Yes. At the courthouse." All five-foot-four of her trimmed in the latest fashion but possessing a coldness he could never blame her for.

Tillman scratched his scalp, the lines in his forehead wrinkling with his furrowed brow. "At the Cartelli trial?"

"Yes, sir. I came across her in the gallery." Which, looking back, seemed odd. Why had she attended the press conference? And what about the notepad she'd hidden from him? As if she had planned to cover the … His chest tightened. "She didn't know I was coming, did she?"

"Well …" Tillman palmed the back of his neck and stared at his shoes.

Heat seared his throat. Cole yanked loose his tie knot, ignoring decorum. It all made sense now. She hadn't expected to see him this morning any more than she would've Josephine Dodge. Though Elissa probably would've treated the anti-suffrage leader with more cordiality than she'd served Cole.

His boss picked up a folder and rummaged through the pages inside. "I never imagined her going to the Cartelli trial, or I would've told her yesterday. I planned on telling her at breakfast, but she was already gone."

"Breakfast?" Cole straightened. "Both she and her husband live with you?"

Tillman dropped the folder on his desk, barely missing his coffee mug. "Huh?"

"Elissa mentioned her heart being wedded. I took that as—"

"Nonsense."

"Marriage isn't nonsense to me."

He smiled. "It is when it's a falsehood. My daughter isn't married to flesh and blood but to ink and paper. The *Review* is her life. That, and the women's movement." Tillman took a swig of his coffee. "Did you see the rose?"

"I did."

"Almost two years since the womenfolk gained voting rights, but Elissa still wears the flower as a badge."

"Maybe she feels there's more to be accomplished, sir."

"Not you too." He grunted. "I just hope her zeal doesn't result in her becoming estranged from her friends. Adam is the only fellow who still has the nerve to approach her."

As in Adam Kendrew? Cole's hand clenched. Though who was he to say Kendrew hadn't changed? The rich kid who'd bullied his way through school could've become a general in the Salvation Army, for all Cole knew. Still, tension stiffened every muscle, and if the words sat any longer on his tongue, they'd burn a hole. "Is Kendrew courting Elissa?"

His boss guffawed. "Adam wishes. He's been persistent, but Lissie shows no more regard for him than anyone else. I think Adam works here only to be near her. He could have a higher salary at another place."

No. Not a Salvationist. But a *Review* correspondent. Cole wanted to pound his forehead on the mahogany desk.

"Come to the house for dinner this Friday." Tillman spoke the invitation as he had years ago when Cole had been twelve—full of kindness and without judgment.

In a pathetic irony, today was little different than the first day he'd walked into Mr. Tillman's office. Like then, he was looking for hope after his world had been shattered.

"You could come tonight, but I suspect your mother won't want to share you for a few days."

Guilt jabbed Cole's heart. He hadn't contacted his mother yet. He would have—if it weren't for the shame and disappointment. The two evils took turns sucker-punching Cole every time he thought about his failure. Which was often. How was he going to explain himself to her? Why he was here and not rubbing elbows with the elites. Not paying a visit but staying. For good. It still sounded foreign in his own head.

Tillman looked at him sideways. "I won't be bothered if you take a rain check. Considering it's been, what, five years since you've been in town?" His boss had never been one for subtlety, but Cole deserved it.

He hadn't meant to stay away ... well, yes. Yes, he had. But he'd written letters. Sent gifts. That had counted for something, right? Plus, his mother had visited New York the handful of times Cole could persuade her to leave her tenants. She ran that apartment complex like she had her household growing up—like a mother hen. "I can come this Friday. The Cartelli sentencing is at three, but I'm free after. What time would you like me to stop by? Still on the same routine?"

Smile lines fanned from the corners of his eyes. "The same. Grace is as strict with seven o'clock meal time as I am with my deadline." He gestured toward the door. "Speaking of which, you owe me an article. The desk right outside the door to the left is yours." His grin stretched longer than the train tracks Cole had traveled yesterday. "Right next to Lissie's."

Cole craned his neck, glimpsing the station—vacant only moments ago—through the narrow office door window. The lady herself now perched perfectly in her seat, holding the phone to her ear with her right hand, writing down something with her left.

"Things run somewhat differently nowadays." Tillman propped an elbow on a tall filing cabinet. "Turn your finished copy in to Elissa. She'll proofread it and deliver it to the composing room."

Cole's brow furrowed. What exactly was Elissa's role here? This morning, she'd appeared to be an eager reporter, but then Frank had implied she was the secretary. Now Elissa wore the hat of copyeditor too? Cole shook his head. "She seems to have her hands full."

Mr. Tillman sighed, his eyes half-lidded. "Henry Marshall has been our main copyeditor, but last August his daughter contracted polio. The stress of everything got to be too much for him, and Elissa stepped in, easing the load."

Of course, she would. Growing up, her heart had always been for the broken, the needy. Like Cole. An ache stretched behind his eyes. Was coming home a smart idea? Every day would be a brutal reminder of all he'd lost.

"Give her time, Parker. Your presence here will shift her world."

"Are you going to tell her why I returned?"

"That's all your department. She probably won't speak with me right now anyway. She'll be as cross with me as she is with you. She'll think we both betrayed her."

Cole winced. Would she ever trust him again? Since he couldn't have her heart, could their friendship be restored? It looked as attainable as winning a Pulitzer, but he had to try. Later. His boss was right. She needed time, and patience was a virtue he'd yet to master.

Now he had a job to complete. One he wasn't going to bungle. The last time had cost him.

Though maybe he could get Elissa to listen to him without him speaking a word. He smiled. Something for old times' sake.

Elissa stared at her shorthand, hoping she'd heard the information about the classified correctly. The lady had fed her information like a telegraph, but without the stops to give her brain time to catch up. And the awareness of Cole Parker ten feet behind her in Father's office hadn't helped any.

She rearranged her pencils and notepads for the third time since she'd sat down. Maybe she should've gone home. She'd never been one to cry into her pillow, but today her goose feathers beckoned.

How could Father have done this?

A soreness spread from her heart to her toes. Maybe she'd been overreacting. Maybe Cole was in town to visit his mother, and her father had heard about it. It was possible he'd offered Cole this particular article to promote the paper, like a guest reporter sort of thing. That had to be the situation here. Then Cole would simply turn in his piece and be on his way without another look back. Just like last time.

The creak of her father's door scraped in her ears, and it took all Elissa's willpower not to glance over her shoulder.

"Get to it, Parker." Her father's editor-voice had always made her laugh, but not this time.

Cole appeared in her peripheral. He pulled out the chair at the desk ... parallel to hers. Her stomach sank. Now she'd have to put up with him for however many minutes before he finished his article and left. Hopefully, forever.

The newsroom bustled, always in a hurried state, but the man beside her didn't move. Oh, she shouldn't glance over. She shoved her attention to the phone, wishing it to ring. Anything to keep from—

Smack.

She jumped, slapping a hand over her heart. Something had landed on her desk.

A fountain pen. His.

She recognized its abalone pearl barrel and fourteen-karat gold nib. The pen her father had given Cole for his high school graduation. "Quite an expensive pen to be tossing around." She allowed herself one quick peek.

He slid a paper from the drawer and rolled it into the carriage of the typewriter. Like every other male in this stuffy room, Cole had shed his jacket, but unlike every other man in here, Cole had corded muscles, flexing with his movements. "Hmm? Did you say something?" He tugged the bottom of his earlobe.

His onyx eyes sparkled, alerting her to his mischief. The raucous blend of ticking typewriters, ringing phones, and slamming file cabinet drawers could distract an amateur, but not him.

"What's this about?" She motioned to the pen.

He shifted in his seat, facing her with a broadening smile, his cleft chin amply exposed and dangerously appealing. "I'm resorting to my old methods. Hoping to get you to speak with me."

She squeezed her pencil hard enough to cramp her finger. Any verbal response would only satisfy his strategy. No, her best line of attack would be to remain silent.

Elissa fixed her attention on the billing list for next month's advertisers. Several businesses still owed payment from February.

Her brows pinched. Since when had Father allowed this? He'd always taught her to be sure to collect the money before ad placement. She should speak with him, but not now. Not until she could face him without emotion clogging her brain. Was he even aware of the distress he'd caused her today?

The familiar click-click of keys striking the paper stole her gaze without her mind's permission. Wouldn't Cole's schooling at Columbia and time at the *Dispatch* have forced him out of his self-taught typing style? Yet his forefinger and middle finger darted all over the keyboard while his left hand manipulated the shift key.

She'd once called his hunt-and-peck method silly and challenged him to a typing race. Her perfect eight-finger-and-one-thumb technique had finished last. Which was a lesson for her to remember—against Cole she'd always end up the loser.

The headache that had threatened earlier struck full force. She could finish this article later. As for the phone, her father could answer it.

She collected all the necessary paperwork to complete the assignment at home and pulled her handbag from the bottom drawer.

Cole's fingers stopped their maniacal dancing across the keys. "Going somewhere?"

Elissa mashed her lips together to quell the rising huff. "I don't see how that's any of your business."

"Aren't you going to check the pen?"

"We're not kids anymore."

"Please?" The deep rasp of his voice exposed a hint of hopefulness.

The hammering in her skull increased.

He eased back in his chair and barred his arms across his chest. "Just check the pen, Spark, and I'll leave you alone."

"Save your promises. They've proven hollow." She snatched the renegade writing utensil and unscrewed it. As expected, a sliver of paper wrapped around the ink cartridge. Oh, how she had loved this diversion after graduation when Cole had scribed romantic poems. Little had she known his flowery words would decay more quickly than the ink could dry.

A heavy aggravation wound tight in her chest. How could he think he could just step right back in like nothing had changed? He was well aware of her last words to him on the train station platform, and he hadn't cared.

Only abandoned her.

Elissa pulled out the note. With a smirk, she walked toward the exit, crumpling the paper in her hand and depositing it in Frank Gosher's spittoon.

CHAPTER 3

Cole swiped a thick finger under his collar. Elissa hadn't read his apology. She'd destroyed the note along with any confidence he had possessed.

Why had he returned?

All the rational reasons for his presence in this city had evaporated while the faint scent of wildflowers taunted his emotions for the long moments after Elissa left. He'd struggled to complete the article, but by God's grace, he had. A portion of him reveled in the slight hope he still had what it took. But a larger piece of him could sink into the cracks of the grooved floorboards.

She hated him.

He could see it in the fiery flecks of her eyes. Hear it in her icy tone. Such a vehemence wouldn't, couldn't, disappear. But then, what had he expected? For Elissa to fling herself into his arms?

Cole pressed a clammy palm against his neck and leaned back in his chair. His fingers itched for a bottle, a glass, anything to numb the intense craving building inside him. He ran his tongue along his teeth, keeping the dryness from settling in. It didn't work. His heart rate accelerated, and instinct swallowed reason. Just one sip. A taste of whiskey on his lips should be enough. His hand dove into his vest pocket where he'd kept his flask. The tips of his fingers grazed the smooth edges of his … New Testament.

Oh God.

The newsroom whirred around him, reporters and editors

unaware of his moment of weakness. Or maybe it was triumph. He patted the small Bible and thanked God for the strength to not succumb to alcohol's enticement.

A familiar sound floated in his ears, soothing as a lullaby.

The press.

How long had he been sitting here? He glanced at his pocket watch. Two-fifteen. The nagging thought to leave for the day tapped his mind, but he slid his eyes shut and took in the calming tones. When had he lost the zeal that made him scour the streets for the next big story?

Manhattan. He'd been on the fourth floor in New York, removed several stories from the pulse of the news world—the press. The giant contraption that bled black ink and birthed afternoon editions. Here in Pittsburgh, the iron monster's muted roar called from just below in the basement. The wooden floor beneath him quivered, sending a hum through his soles, reaching his heart. This was where he belonged. But secrets didn't remain buried for long. He prayed Elissa would never unearth his shame.

Cole slowed his pace on Wadsworth Street, guilt layering his heart thicker than the soot encrusting the buildings he passed. Only two blocks left to devise an excuse that would satisfy his curious mother.

He flicked his gaze to the smoke-filled skies. The iron works and steel factories had unleashed their poisons for decades, replacing sunny days with ashen clouds. Thick and bleak. The same would have been Cole's future if Tillman hadn't welcomed him back, giving him a second chance.

A stray cat darted past him into the garbage-strewn alley. Cole frowned. The outskirts of Oakland had always been a charming area—a great alternative for those who hadn't sufficient income to live in the swanky neighborhoods but had earned enough to escape from the slums. Had the adverse effects of Prohibition touched even these parts? He'd learned from Mom's letters that speakeasies had invaded Pittsburgh along with the flooding of immigrants who cherished their booze more than the law.

A band of tension stretched across Cole's back. Temptation so close to home.

He rolled his shoulders and prayed for strength. Rounding the bend, he eyed the Willow Courts Apartments—his home for a good portion of his life. Its brick walls had succumbed to the dominant smog, dulling the crimson shade. The low picket fence could stand another coat of white paint. He grabbed hold of a silvery-grimed slat and shook it, testing its sturdiness. When it wouldn't budge, he checked another.

"Are you going to check every one of them or come give your mama a hug?" Helen Parker called from the back doorway of the two-story structure, a dishtowel draped over her shoulder and a smile brighter than the sunniest days stretching across her face.

With a grin and nod, he jogged to meet her.

She stretched out her arms, welcoming. "So glad to see you, Cole."

"Hey, Mom." He pulled her into a hug, her hair the aroma of coffee and cinnamon. "You shouldn't keep the door open on a cold day like this. Lets all the heat out."

She swatted his shoulder and broke away. "My son hasn't stepped foot in Pittsburgh for over a thousand moons and is complaining about a little chill."

They crossed the threshold into the foyer, and Cole took in the different surroundings. The bones of the layout were the same, but the stale place had been freshened up. A lot. New wallpaper blanketed the halls, and stylish electric lamps lined the stairways leading to the apartments.

"Sterling's been my handyman these past few years." She stepped beside him and tucked her arm in his elbow. "By handyman, I mean everything from replacing creaky floorboards to installing fancy lighting. And he wouldn't let me pay a dime for any of it."

He'd been mildly sore with his older cousin, thinking he'd

taken advantage of free lodging, and all the while, Sterling had been improving the place. "Everything looks great."

His mother hadn't aged much since her visit to New York last summer. A few more gray hairs, but the spark of life and confidence shone brightly in her hazel eyes.

"Where are your bags?" She looked at his bare hands and scowled, tiny wrinkles framing her mouth. "I want to see you during your visit. Don't you tell me—"

"They're at the hotel." He forced more enthusiasm into his tone than he felt and strolled into the front parlor. Updated as well. The corner of the room boasted something he never dreamed would be sitting in the Willow Courts parlor—a piano. "Since when did you start playing an instrument?"

Her sharp glare revealed the previous conversation wasn't finished, but she humored him with a small smile. "Sterling bought it for Sophie."

He cocked a brow. "Sophie lives here too?" Might as well ask Uncle Wooly to take residence in the attic since this place had turned into a family affair. Well … future family, considering Sterling and Sophie weren't married yet.

"She lived here for a few months, but she's staying in the house Sterling purchased on Herron Ave. He's staying here until they get married." Mom wiped her hands on her apron, which looked like it had lost a fistfight with tomato sauce.

He smiled. The woman had always been a messy cook. But a good one. His years as a bachelor had consisted of meals at restaurants on his way home from his office, so Cole looked forward to some home-cooked dinners.

"Sophie gives music lessons here. And just happens to always leave a bit of money on the piano stand when she's finished."

Even Sterling's fiancée supported his mother. Cole was no doubt perceived as the callous prodigal son, but it wasn't his fault his mother never cashed the checks he sent.

"Now about your bags." She planted two fists on her rounded

hips and offered the look she'd use when he'd stayed out past curfew.

"I'm not living here."

"But it's just during your stay." The plea in her voice tore at his heart.

"That's the thing. I'm not returning to Manhattan."

"So you're not just here for Sterling's wedding next week? You're here for good?"

He nodded.

Her hands flew in the air, knocking the brim of his hat, and she did a jig. "Praise the Lord. You've come home."

He fixed his stare on a fresh scuff on his shoe. His heart couldn't rejoice. Failure skittered around his chest, its sharp claws slicing the tender surface of his confidence—what was left of it, anyway. "I took a job at the *Review*. I covered the Cartelli case today."

Her jaw slackened, and his tightened with guilt.

"I arrived last night. Late."

She wrung her apron into creases, but the wrinkles concerning him were the ones rippling her forehead. "A little notice would've been nice. It kind of makes me feel like I'm the last on your list."

"Never." His shoulders weighted at her pained expression. "This entire thing was a last-minute decision, well … kind of. I've been busy at the courthouse then at the newsroom." And he may have lingered while the presses ran, but his state of mind had required it. "Don't be cross with your only son. I came the first chance I got." He stooped and pressed a kiss to her temple.

A slow smile built, the hard lines framing her mouth softening. "You've always been impulsive."

Impulsive.

The word his dear mother meant as an endearment stabbed into his gut and blazed a fiery trail to his toes. He shuffled his foot on the tweed rug as if to brush away the sensation, but it welded into every nerve. Impulsive … like his father. "I'll stay here." The declaration ripped out like a bottle rocket—loud at first and then fizzling out.

His mother hugged his left arm, pressing her cheek into his shoulder. "The room across from Sterling's is vacant." Her fingers tapped a joyous cadence on his elbow, but his smile slipped into a frown as he noticed her reddened knuckles and cracked skin. She'd been working too hard.

"Here." He pulled an envelope from his pocket. "It's yours."

"I told ya once, I told you a million times." The stubborn woman shoved her hands into her apron pockets. "I won't take your money."

"But you take Sophie's for the use of the parlor for music lessons. Let Sterling purchase different things around the complex." He stepped closer, towering over her five-two frame. "This is all the money from the checks I sent that you didn't cash."

She raised her chin, but Cole laughed. "Were you blowing on the spoon again?"

"What?"

He got out his handkerchief and started gently wiping the tip of her nose. "Growing up, I'd watch you blow on a hot wooden spoon when tasting the sauce, and every time you wound up with tomato freckles." He showed her the glaring red offenders on the stark white cloth.

Her posture relaxed, and she gave a delicate smile. "I'm so glad you're home, Cole."

"Mom, please take this money. It's my way of caring for you."

A glassy sheen covered her rheumy eyes. "You've always had a good heart. But what am I going to do with all this cash?" She glanced at the envelope in the hollow of his hand.

"Hire a helper. Someone who can relieve the load of keeping up with this place."

"But I already have—" Her mouth locked tighter than the justification jaw on Tillman's press. A flick of horror flashed in her eyes before she lowered her gaze to her clasped hands.

Were there more repairs needing attention? Costly ones

Sterling couldn't afford? Cole might have wasted many things over the years, like relationships and his prestigious job, but he hadn't squandered money. It didn't matter if it was the roof, the plumbing, or anything else. He'd take care of it. "What aren't you telling me?"

The grooves between her brows deepened. "It's what I *am* telling you. What I've been telling you for years. I don't need your earnings."

"Just hire help with the cleaning and laundering." He handed over the money, and she took it with a heavy sigh. "But not the cooking because I've missed your meals."

The sparkle returned to her eyes. "Then take off your hat and go wash up." She shooed him along, the envelope flapping in her hand.

Cole stepped into the kitchen but stopped short at the sight of a faded sheet tacked over the window. "What happened?"

"Oh, that." Her voice pitched high, raising Cole's alarm. "Happened this morning. People on the hunt again."

He lifted the edge of the fabric and took in the shattered pane. "What do you mean, 'on the hunt'? For what?"

"Sterling had stored some leftover bottles of denatured wood alcohol from when he stripped the varnish off the stairs. A few weeks ago, someone broke into the cellar and stole it." She pulled the dishtowel from her shoulder and tossed it on the counter, avoiding Cole's heated glare.

"And you haven't told me about it?" Cole yanked his hat off and ran a hand through his hair. Mom's sheepish glances spoke more than words. She hadn't wanted to bother him. Her usual excuse. "What if you had been injured?"

She sighed and walked over to the stove. "Sterling investigated. Said it was probably some amateur bootlegger trying to make Pittsburgh scotch." She stirred the pot, the wooden spoon scraping against the bottom. "He's even had patrolmen swing by here on their rounds. So you see, all safe."

He glanced again at the damaged window. "Yeah, I see all right."

It didn't matter if the intruder had been a bootlegger needing to turn a profit or an alcoholic desiring to numb the cravings, both would be desperate to satisfy their compulsion. He was too aware of the brutal truth—addiction was dangerous.

"Hot off the press." Elissa grumbled, frowning at the *Review*'s newest edition. Cole's article glared at her from above the fold. For the fourth day in a row. Resignation sunk her hopes. Cole was staying in Pittsburgh.

She tossed the paper onto her bed with enough force, it slid off her quilt and onto the floor. Darcy scrambled over, nails clicking against the wood, and sniffed the pages.

"This time, gnaw the headline and not my new muff." Elissa moseyed to her vanity and plopped onto the stool.

Her cocker spaniel regarded her with innocent eyes. After nudging a sheet with his snout, he proceeded to traipse across the edition as if it were a welcome mat.

"Don't think Father would appreciate that, Darcy." At present, she didn't mind the actions of her loyal pup, but she did mind the decisions of her father.

How could he have done this? He'd known Cole had used her. Used him! Out of sheer decency, Father could have given her a warning.

Five years without a trace of Cole. Well, not exactly true. He'd haunted her Monday through Friday, his syndicated column in the *Review* laughing at her from page three.

But ... how long had it been since she'd spied his article before he'd come to Pittsburgh? A couple of weeks? A month? Maybe two? She ran her fingers along her forehead as if it'd help her think. She'd been too consumed in the Cartelli ordeal, too absorbed in coercing her father to give her a chance to prove herself. If anyone had known the hours she'd poured into the case, she'd be labeled obsessed. She preferred passionate. After all, justice was due. But if she scraped away a few layers of noble purpose, she'd have to stare at the core of her motivation—distraction from the nagging thoughts of Cole's betrayal which had grown in intensity as the days, years, slipped by.

And the diversion had worked. Until now. Yes, she'd gone from seeing Cole's name on the byline to seeing him in the flesh. Worse yet, his *flesh* looked good. Really good. By the way he filled his expensive suits, his previously slim build had thickened irritatingly well.

Thankfully, Cole had kept his feeble promise and had hardly bothered her for the past three days. She'd spoken less than a handful of sentences to him, but what about tonight when he came for dinner? While she was at lunch, Father had left a note on her desk with the displeasing news that Cole would be joining them this evening. She thumped the vanity top with her bent elbow and sank her cheek into her cupped hand. How could she avoid talking to him? How could she keep her eyes from straying his direction?

Same confident manner. Same dashing smile.

Once, she'd hungered for the taste of those lips, but now that she'd been made aware of his true nature, she'd lost all appetite for such a man.

Her pup's collar jingled as he circled in a spot to lie down.

"I should've kept my mouth shut that day, Darcy." Her dog regarded her with lazy eyes which then drooped shut. If only she could close off her memory and wish away the look on Cole's face that pivotal day she'd admitted her feelings for him.

"You decent, honey?" Her housekeeper's Welsh-accented voice snapped her to the present.

"Come in, Greta." She tightened her dressing robe around her waist and pasted on a smile.

Greta shuffled in, her plump arms loaded with a welcome distraction—Elissa's gala gown. "Picked it up from the dressmaker today. She fixed the bust so it shouldn't be snug. All ready for tomorrow night." Her smile filled with satisfaction as she lifted the dress high for Elissa to inspect. "Of course, you'd choose this color. So help me, young lady, you take this women's suffrage stance to a whole new level. Wearing yellow all the time?" She huffed, stirring her black bangs. "Is it really necessary, darling?"

Dear Greta couldn't be more tender-hearted or traditional-minded.

"There's no other option. I need to do my part." However small it seemed. She claimed the gown from Greta's hands, her gaze absorbing the rich golden satin. The neckline brimmed with crystal beads, tapering down the bodice like drips of sunshine.

She'd never understood why Mother insisted that the *Review*'s yearly anniversary party be formal, but Elissa loved it. Nothing like seeing those burly pressmen sporting tuxes, their hands still stained with ink from running the press only hours before.

"I have to say, it's stunning." The skin around the older woman's eyes bunched with her smile. "You in this dress will have men forgetting their own names."

"Greta!" The word came out more of a chortle than a rebuke. The humorous side of her longtime housekeeper always poked Elissa when she least expected it. But Elissa didn't want to think about men, especially one with an enamoring grin and a habit of taking advantage of devoted hearts.

"By the way, Miss Lissie, the telephone is for you."

"And you waited this long to mention it?" She hustled to her closet, nearly tripping over Darcy as he skittered out the room. Careful not to snag the gown on the doorknob, she slid it in the spot she'd cleared earlier. "The person has most likely hung up by now."

"Not him."

Him. Three little letters, but they held the power to suck the air from her lungs. Wasn't it horrific enough she'd see Cole in less than two hours? Must she now be forced to talk to him on the phone? No. Nobody was forcing her to do anything. She was a woman and not a child. Though sometimes the adolescent feelings swamped her like the newsboys on payday. "Tell him I'm busy. Washing my hair." Or throwing darts at his article.

Greta's dimpled smile crimped into a scowl. "Mr. Kendrew has heard every excuse except the truth. Just tell the man you're not interested."

Adam. Not Cole. Her heart resumed its normal pace. "All right. I'll speak to him." And if he'd already hung up, she'd be polite and call him back. Elissa patted Greta's shoulder as she walked to the door. "You realize, Adam is only interested in me because of who my father is."

Greta snorted. "Miss Lissie, one day you're going to see how captivating you are. I pray it be before you turn up an old maid."

"There's nothing inferior about spinsterhood." Because she had vision and purpose. One day she'd be the owner of the *Review*, and she'd be able to hire qualified women, enabling them with opportunities to shine. "Did Adam say what he wanted?"

"Something about taking you out tonight for dinner since you wouldn't let him get you a birthday gift."

Because Adam Kendrew could go through money like she could go through typewriter ribbons. One would think the editor of the finance column would heed his own advice. Wait. Dinner? "Tonight?" She glanced at the clock, her knot of nerves unraveling for the first time since the courthouse fiasco. "That would be splendid."

She'd evade Cole and halt Adam's incessant pleas for dinner in one grand swoop. The perfect plan. Maybe this would be an endeavor she could succeed at. But then, why did her breath stagger in her chest?

CHAPTER 4

Of all the restaurants in Pittsburgh, Adam had chosen Ginobli's. While Elissa once had been mesmerized by the hand-painted murals of Venice decorating the walls and ceiling, her past memories caused this place to lose all appeal. She angled away from the table to her right, the one she'd occupied years ago with the man she purposefully avoided this evening. Fighting a scowl, she stabbed an asparagus tip.

Adam smiled, the skin around his hazel eyes crinkling. "How's everything?"

Awful. "Delightful." The urge to squirm in her chair snaked across her shoulder blades, but she stiffened against it. Not exactly a lie. The chef had seasoned her baked chicken to perfection, she'd managed not to drip her soup down the front of her caramel-colored dress, and she'd not caught anything on fire. Candles in the middle of a table was an atrocious idea. "Thank you for this evening."

Adam's chin dipped, and his mouth crept up on one side. "Glad you let me celebrate you."

He shoved a forkful of pork loin into his mouth, and Elissa tightened her grip on her water. Pork. The same meal being served by Greta to her parents and Cole—Benedict Arnold—Parker. The homey image plaguing her mind made her stomach lurch. He didn't belong in her house. Or with her family. Or with her, for that matter. The continued befuddlement of how her father simply welcomed—

"How are you coping with Cole back?"

The slightest pinch of enmity flavored his tone, and he struggled to keep from frowning. The only person not enthused to throw confetti at Cole's arrival at the *Review*, besides her, was Adam. Maybe they could build their relationship on the only thread they had in common—an extreme loathing for Cole.

"I'm fine. There's nothing between us anymore." She smoothed her napkin over her lap, ignoring Adam's pleased grin. "I believe we can work together as adults." And as soon as the urge to break her clipboard over Cole's handsome head vanished, she'd believe her diplomatic statement just as Adam had.

"Did I hear him call you 'Spunk' this morning?"

"No, 'Spark.'" That infernal name.

His eyes loaded with questions Elissa couldn't bear to answer. "Sounds like there's a story behind that."

An awful one. The sparklers had not only singed her hair, but also her confidence. Not like she'd ever blended in, but her shorn locks had catapulted her deeper in the misfit zone. "Let's just say Cole is teasing me for something that had happened ages ago." And she wouldn't trigger Adam's memory because it seemed as if he'd forgotten her awkward years. If only she could.

"Not very gentlemanly. Should I have a talk with him?"

His eager tone lit warning flares in her mind. Those two didn't need another reason to fight. "I appreciate the gesture, but I can handle the matter." The matter who had an attractive face, but a hollow heart.

"Of course." He lowered his fork and leaned forward. "Happy birthday, darling."

The asparagus lodged in her throat. And now she'd forgotten how to swallow. She lifted her drink to her lips, praying a good flush of water would force the rebellious vegetable to its proper spot. It did. "My birthday was three weeks ago."

His lips stretched to a full smile, displaying perfect teeth. "It wasn't my fault you've turned down my every invitation until tonight."

Guilt spoiled her last bite of meat, turning it sour in her mouth. Since when had she buckled in her resolve not to give in to Adam's persistent attention? Maybe since Cole stepped back into her life. No, not her life. Just Pittsburgh. And the *Review*. And currently her parents' dining room. But *not* her life. "Listen, Adam." She forced her attention from the flickering candle between them and met his gaze. "I don't want to encourage—"

"You always say that." He gave a slight shake of the head, but it didn't knock the sparkle from his eyes. "Believe me, I know you're the toughest gal around when it comes to protecting her heart." His expression softened. "But it's a heart worth waiting for."

Elissa observed him. Could Adam truly be in love with her? Her prevailing thought had always been he wanted her solely because of Father's status, that he might desire to marry her with hopes of running the *Review*. She was as protective over the newspaper as she was her own heart, but she'd allowed the latter to get broken. *Perhaps it's healed now.*

"Pardon?" A golden brow arched high on her date's face, revealing she'd spoken the last bit aloud.

"Forgive me, Adam. I was …" What was she doing? Reflecting? Dreaming? "I was hoping for something that might never happen."

A shadow flickered across his sharp features. Could've been from the candle, but the sag in his shoulders revealed her words had wounded him. Was there something unpleasant lurking beyond his genuine countenance, or was she the biggest fool who'd ever worn silk stockings? A handsome, reliable man had offered himself to her more times than she could number, and she'd been stubborn to a fault.

She stretched her hand across the table, and he clasped her fingers in his. "I really admire you, Adam, but I think I might need more time."

"I won't rush things, Elissa, but can we keep seeing each other?"

Tomorrow's leftovers weren't the only things on the table. There was also the small matter of his heart. She caged a sigh. If his admiration proved honest, maybe she could grow to feel more for him. Perhaps someday love him. Boy, that was a tall order and a lot of maybes, but miracles could happen. "I'm comfortable with that."

If only her gut hadn't clenched at her words.

The masses loved a good retribution day. Like in the Old West when the sheriff got the drop on the gang of bank robbers. Or on the silver screen when the gorgeous damsel hugged the neck of the prince after he conquered a boatload of pirates. Or in Pittsburgh when Franco Cartelli, a convicted murderer, was sentenced to the electric chair.

No matter how Cole looked at it, an article about an impending execution didn't make him feel all fuzzy inside. But ... society needed to be informed, and reporting was his job. He fed the paper into the typewriter's mouth and let his fingers talk for him.

About halfway into the piece, Elissa stepped into the newsroom. Her tubular dress couldn't hide her curvy frame. The pale pink color reminded him of soft rose petals, but the look she gave him? All thorns.

He was tempted to glare daggers himself after showing up at the Tillmans' last night only to find Elissa out on a date with Kendrew. Cole cut a quick glance at the fair-haired financial reporter five desks away. Jealousy knocked on the gates of his soul, but Cole couldn't answer. He couldn't even be angry with the guy. Not this time, at least. He had no grounds to punch Kendrew like he'd had in high school. Though the idea caused his fingers to curl into a fist. It wasn't the blamed man's fault Elissa had chosen to eat out with him rather than dine with Cole and her parents.

As for the meal, it would have been pleasant if Mrs. Tillman hadn't served cold stares with every course. First, at him. Next, at

Mr. Tillman. Then at Cole again. Between the two Tillman women, they could freeze the Allegheny River in mid-August.

"Mornin', Spark."

Only Elissa could make a scowl look striking. "Refrain from the pet names, Mr. Parker."

"Just being conversational." He cracked his knuckles and straightened in his chair. "But if you don't want to be friendly, Jane and I have work to do."

"Jane?" A dark blonde brow spiked then sunk in realization. "You call your typewriter Jane? Because of Jane Austen?"

Her favorite writer.

He patted the side of Jane's metal body. "Absolutely. Thought the name might give me inspiration. By the way, I was wondering if you could introduce me to Elliot Wentworth." He shouldn't have enjoyed the rounding of Elissa's beautiful blues or the inviting way her mouth parted.

"I—I can't. Mr. Wentworth only writes for the *Review* on special occasions."

Cole dipped his chin. "Well, if you see the mysterious fellow, please let him know his article on women's suffrage was the talk of the *Dispatch* newsroom for days. I found his expressions intriguing." He couldn't use the word 'enchanting,' because it'd give him away. He'd known from the moment he'd read the byline it was Elissa's moniker—the last name of the two main characters from *Persuasion*, Ann Elliot and Captain Wentworth. Her love of Austen novels had never been a secret, and Cole had been compared to Mr. Darcy on too many occasions. Which reminded him. "You kept the dog?" The little spaniel had been his companion for most of last evening.

She pulled out her seat and paused, her posture stiff like the wooden chair she clutched. "I did." Elissa's mouth opened but then snapped shut, her gaze darting to the visitor entering the newsroom. A delivery boy approached her, holding a vase filled with … white lilies.

Elissa's tight-lipped smile didn't fool Cole. She couldn't be more uncomfortable if porcupine quills lined her pretty dress. Why? He leaned forward in his chair. Who had sent the flowers? Whoever it was knew about her fondness for white lilies. Though now Cole would think she'd prefer yellow roses, given her daily corsage.

"Thank you." Eyes wary, she received the arrangement as if it would bite her.

The delivery boy waved a hand with a "Have a great day," but Elissa didn't shift her gaze from the flowers.

She withdrew the note and read it. Her shoulders relaxed, and a small smirk replaced the fixed frown. Her expression ... he wouldn't call it happy, but relieved.

His heart smacked against his ribcage. Had she thought he'd sent the flowers? Was that why she'd been tense and agitated? He needed to rethink his strategy. He didn't want Elissa anxious, but to be ... what did he want her to be? Happy and carefree, like when they were young. Before he'd dashed her spirits.

Setting the card on the table, she rounded her desk and walked down the aisle toward Kendrew. The couple exchanged smiles, tightening Cole's stomach. While Kendrew's grin sparkled bright enough to make any dentist proud, Elissa's hadn't crinkled her nose.

Maybe instead of aspiring to get her to throw herself into his arms, his goal should be to make her smile at him. A genuine one that traveled into her beautifully sculpted nose and then danced in her eyes.

He pushed his gaze to Jane's weathered keys, knowing full well he didn't deserve Elissa's smile. Or her. But if God gave him another chance, couldn't she?

"I need your help." Cole handed Elissa his submission.

As their fingers touched, the brief contact jolted her insides. Tomorrow she'd place a wire basket on the corner of her desk.

Anything to keep from exchanges like this one.

Her breathing evened, and she glanced at the headline.

Franco Cartelli Gets Death Penalty.

The words reached in and grabbed her gut, shivers coursing every which way. "What ... kind of help?" Surely, he wouldn't ask for advice concerning his article. Not a seasoned reporter like him.

"I need to put together a classified." He spread his palms on her desk, drawing her attention to his scarred knuckles, reminding her of the day their paths had first crossed. "I want to hire a helper for my mother." He bent lower and fixed his eyes on her.

She took in the angles and planes of his face, only two feet from hers. So familiar yet different. His chin still bore the slight cleft, but somewhere over the five-year span, it had shifted from boyish charm to manly attractiveness. Her fingertip tingled to trace his jawline as she'd done dozens of times in her youth.

She pushed back in her chair, increasing the distance between them. Wait. Had he said ... "A helper for your mother?"

His head tilted to one side, their gazes locking. "Yes."

Her tongue pasted to the roof of her mouth, and she forced her stare onto the coffee ring on her desk.

"Do you know anyone?"

She fidgeted with the pleats in her long-waisted dress, glancing up. "Go talk to Roy. He's head of that department." And the less she talked to Cole—or looked at him—the better off she'd be. This past week had been trying enough without him bumbling about, invading her space, spiking her heart rate. He didn't need to know her secret.

His onyx eyes dimmed. "I don't know how to list the qualifications. I need a female who can help Mom out with the harder tasks." He pushed off her desk and tugged his vest straight. "She needs to be responsible. Trustworthy. I'll be working so I won't be able to supervise. What if the person should steal or ..." He rounded her desk, sunk in his chair, and slashed a hand through his dark hair. "Maybe this isn't a good idea."

Elissa stared. In all the time she'd spent with the spirited Cole Parker, he'd never second-guessed himself. He'd always had a protective edge when it came to his mother, but then … he'd left her too. The sympathetic inclination, though small, dissipated. Any man who'd desert his own mother wasn't worth a speck of respect.

Her father's door opened, and he poked his head out. "Elissa. Please come here."

She gave a tight nod.

Cole dipped his head and raised a brow as if he'd expected a reply, but the only answer she could give him was a turn of her shoulder as she stepped into the office.

Her father pushed the door closed with his shoe. "I'm wondering how long you're going to ignore me."

She sat in the chair across from his desk and studied a fingernail.

"Lissie?"

Light streamed in from the open blinds, striping the floor. She glanced over at the man who'd raised her, provided for her, and most recently betrayed her. "Do you remember the Christmas when I wanted to buy Mother a brooch I'd seen in Shadley's front window?"

He scratched his cheek and regarded her with quizzical eyes. "No, can't recall that one."

Of course, he wouldn't. She puffed her cheeks with air and slowly exhaled. "I even brought you to the store to show it to you. I wanted to work for it. Remember I asked if I could help with anything here at the *Review* to earn money?"

Confusion veiled his face.

"You never answered me. So I worked after school babysitting for the Gershaws."

"I remember vaguely." He slid the chair back and sat across from her. "But I'm going to keep listening because this is the most you've said to me in the last four-and-a-half days."

"The week before Christmas came, and I still didn't have enough. So I picked up a few other jobs." She and Cole had shoveled sidewalks until her arms had burned. "I finally had the right amount, but when I went to buy it, the brooch was gone." The memory triggered her emotions, thickening her voice. She paused to collect composure. "Christmas morning came. I'd bought her a hat that ended up being too big, and you'd bought her ... the brooch."

"Oh, Lissie."

"I had no clue I'd been in competition with my own father." Her chest tightened, and she pushed her words around the lump in her throat. "Mother gushed with delight, and she grinned for five minutes. You told her how you just knew she'd love it. But ... I wanted to give it to her. I never understood how you could betray me."

His gray brows dipped, and he gave a small nod. "I'm ashamed to say, I hardly remember that." He tapped his pencil, fast at first, then slower. "I do know, I wouldn't intentionally hurt you. I must've passed the window on the way home from work, and the brooch stuck out to me. Probably because you'd showed it to me, but I must've forgotten."

Which hurt worse, forgotten or betrayed? The only men she'd ever loved had done both. She smoothed the wrinkles of her dress on her thighs, a million retorts tangling in her brain. The steady hum of the newsroom clogged the air more than the hefty odor of the aftershave Father religiously used.

"Why haven't you told me this before?"

"Because it changed nothing." Elissa swallowed around the frustration. "You did it again. Took what I wanted and gave it to someone else. Only this one hit harder."

"Lissie, I—"

"How many times have I pleaded with you to give me a chance?" She slid her eyes shut for a couple breaths to keep them from watering. "An opportunity to prove I can write more than an occasional editorial on how to set a proper table? Begged to use my name rather than a fake masculine one? Father, you of all people know how I feel about the injustice women face. You are in the perfect position to advocate for our rights, but you refuse again and again."

The seat of Father's chair could have been upholstered in cactus flesh for all the squirming he was doing.

"Instead of granting your only child an opportunity to accomplish her dream, who'd you give the biggest headline of the year to? The man who used your influence to get into Columbia then never returned to make good on his commitment to you." She'd been a fool to believe Cole would fulfill his end of the bargain—work at the paper after college. Though who was to say Cole would've been satisfied with the paltry editor job? Not when his name had been viewed by millions across the nation.

Father leaned back, his chin so low it appeared like it was glued to the knot of his crooked tie. "Let's not forget the commitment to you. A tender heart was broken."

"He didn't care about me. I was the pawn he used to gain your favor. So he could better himself." He'd climbed the journalism ladder, but for years Elissa had hoped he'd trip on one of the slippery rungs. "The only love he had was for himself." She glanced at her shaking hands and curled them into fists, her fingernails biting her palms. Cole shouldn't have any influence on her emotions. She'd spent her last tear over him and wasn't about to peel the scab from the wound.

"He loved you, Lissie."

A bitter laugh escaped. "If that's love, then it belongs in the funny papers."

"We need him." He leaned forward and slid a folder her direction, its corner catching on his sleeve.

"What's this?" She opened it, red numbers staring back. Large numbers. "Eight thousand dollars?"

The crease in his brow deepened. "That's the remainder of the amount I need to pay off."

"What?" The scripted letterhead announced the judgment.

"'Harper's Trust and Loan.' You took out a loan?" She'd known key advertisers had withdrawn their backing and sales had been down, but this?

Father bounced a thick knuckle against his chin. "We've been spending more than we've been bringing in. Things escalated quickly." He gathered the folder along with a few other papers and stood. "If we don't generate more sales, then … we'll have to sell."

Sell the Review.

Her heart forgot to beat, and a shiver stole through her. "No."

The paper was all she had left. What she'd poured her soul into. The selling of the *Review* meant the death of her dreams. Why couldn't she keep one thing she loved? Why must everything be ripped from her fingers?

"That's why we need Cole. As much as you hate to admit it, he's a big-time journalist. One who's not only been the *New York Dispatch*'s golden boy but also syndicated across the country. People will notice, and hopefully, sales will kick up. I already had an advertiser call and renew their contract after they saw Cole's name on a byline."

"But can't we do something else?" Desperation pierced her numbed senses. "Cancel the gala tonight." She stood as though her heels hitting the planked floor sealed her declaration.

He stared at her as if she'd asked him to use his own blood as ink for the press. But why pay for a lavish party when there was a threat to shut down for good?

"The few pennies saved by cancelling the celebration wouldn't accomplish much. We need steady inflow."

"But we ordered the ballroom downtown, decorators, an orchestra. What about the din—"

Her father raised a callused palm. "The gala is on for tonight. The employees look forward to it every year."

Her shoulders crumbled, and she placed a hand on his desk for support. "They'd understand." Most of them would, at least. The ones with families to feed and shelter.

He reached over and gently squeezed her elbow, pain surrounding his pale blue eyes. "Sorry, Lissie, but I won't do that to the staff. They work too hard. God will help. He's never left us hungry, and I don't think He'll start now. We have to trust."

A peace settled inside. God had always been faithful when humans hadn't.

"I'm sorry for not talking to you first about Cole. Do you forgive me?" The marked humility in his voice and traces of regret in his eyes made refusal impossible.

She'd never faced the pressure of running a newspaper that'd been distributed for over sixty years. There had to be a way to rescue it. She and her family had put too much of themselves into this operation to have it be sold. "Yes, all forgiven. But next time, please put Mr. Parker's desk in the janitorial closet."

"You still addressing Cole by his surname?" Her father chuckled. "I bet that grates him."

Which was exactly why she'd continue to do so.

"You know, since you're spreading forgiveness around, maybe Cole should be your next candidate."

The awkward silence answered for her. *Never.*

Her father shook his head. "Sketchy thing about resentment, the more you feed it to keep it alive, the more it devours you." He ran a hand along his desk until his fingers landed on the Bible he kept by the lamp. "I work with words every day, but in the end, only His Word matters." He smiled, looking younger than his fifty-eight years. "God delights in mercy."

So what was he saying? She should be merciful to Cole? Conviction skated on the slippery edge of her resolve. Offering forgiveness to Cole would mean opening up to him again, a dangerous feat. Her heart balked at the thought.

"Almost eleven, kiddo. Aren't you expected at your other work?"

She wrapped her fingers around the doorknob, uncertainty marking her movements. "Yes, but I don't think I'll be needed much longer." Though she'd embrace any reason to leave the newsroom and Cole's presence. She pressed a kiss to her father's weathered cheek. "See you tonight."

Elissa wasn't sure how much of her other work could be accomplished before having to leave to prepare for the gala, but one thing secured her resolve—she'd not be the one who broke a promise. Drawing in a calming breath, she set off to Mrs. Parker's.

CHAPTER 5

Amuffled *thwack* resounded from the backyard of Cole's mother's apartment complex, triggering his alertness. Was the intruder trying to break in again? He hurdled the picket fence, sprinting toward the noise. Several hall rugs were draped over the clothesline, and stocking-clad legs were visible below the tremoring foyer runner. His pulse slowed. Nothing out of place.

He wasn't keen on the idea of Mom being outside in the cold, especially when the low, gray skies threatened snow. He'd put the classified for a housekeeper in tomorrow's afternoon edition. No more stalling.

Cole unbuttoned his coat and tugged his tie knot, thankful he'd turned his article in early so he could help with whatever needed doing before the gala tonight.

Soft humming floated on the brisk air. Definitely not Helen Parker. Curiosity forced his feet into motion toward the mystery rug assaulter. A flash of blonde hair froze his steps.

Elissa.

Why was she here? And wielding an old broomstick like Max Carey at Forbes Field? A smile overtook his mouth. This was a picture he wanted branded into his memory. This image spoke of a girl he'd once known before sophistication had gobbled her up. Attired in a faded dress, petite Elissa swung away while humming "You Call Everyone Sweetheart."

Cole inched toward her, drawn by her carefree movements and

glowing complexion.

She took another shot at the rug, expelling a veil of dust.

He closed in. "I've only called you that."

She shrieked and turned, the broom handle whacking him in the side of the head, his hat falling to the ground. He doubled over, eyes stinging and vision blurring.

"Oh, goodness." Slender fingers clutched his shoulder. "Are you hurt?"

He sucked air through his teeth. "Nope. Just admiring the dead grass." And as soon as his ears stopped ringing, he'd lift his head.

"Let me see how bad it is." Her breath feathered against his temple, and the gentle pads of her fingertips stroked his hair. "You're not bleeding, but there's a raised, tender area. Right here." She skimmed the spot above his ear.

He pushed his palm against his eyes, hoping the pressure would alleviate the throbbing ache.

"I'm sorry, Cole. You frightened me."

He'd be beaten senseless any hour of the week to earn the compassion saturating her voice. The soft lull drew him to full height, his composure stabilizing with each passing second. Her radiant complexion, the natural pout of her lips, the pencil-thin brows that raised and dipped with her words swelled his interest. Yet what held his breath captive in his chest were her eyes, a deeper hue of blue lingering behind unshed tears. "Elissa. I'm okay." For the most part.

A heavy exhale lowered her shoulders. "I thought … you were at the office." If her bottom lip quivered anymore, he'd be obliged to soothe it with his.

Should he mention she'd referred to him by his given name? Better not. If he didn't draw attention to it, maybe she'd continue. After five days of enduring her stiff addresses, his fortitude could stand a break. He snatched his hat from the ground, brushed it clean, and carefully placed it on his head with a crooked smile, mindful of his injury. "You didn't have to."

"To what?" She talked to his collar.

"I wanted someone to assist my mother, but I didn't expect it to be you."

Her chin snapped up, her features tightening. "You think because you told me your mother needed help, I bowed to your request and scurried over here?"

He slacked his hip against the clothesline post and folded his arms. "Hey, if you want the job, I'd like to conduct a proper interview. How about dinner tomorrow?"

She shoved her hands on her hips, her eyes slits of ice. "I've never met a more infuriating man."

His grin stretched wider. "I didn't think you needed the money, but I'll pay you for what—" He held up a hand, and she batted it down. "Stop, Elissa. Every laborer is worthy of wages." Laughter rolled in his chest as he reached for his money.

"So you're going to pay me for five years' worth?"

His fingers fumbled his billfold. "Five?" Her words staggered into his heart and regained footing. "You've been coming here the entire time I was gone?"

"Yes." She stooped and picked the broom handle off the ground, chewing her bottom lip. Was she embarrassed he knew her secret or fuming at the reminder of his absence? Or both?

A biting breeze curled lazy snowflakes around them, but warmth flooded Cole. Even when he'd hurt her, abandoned her, she had looked after his mother. Could she be more endearing? But distrust glazed her eyes thicker than the ice patches on the sidewalk.

"I had no idea." He traced a seam on the rug hanging beside him. If he didn't keep his fingers busy, they'd most likely reach for her. And she wasn't open to that. Might never be. "Mom never said a word."

She shrugged. "I asked her not to." Her hand was shaking. Or was she shivering?

Shouldn't he have noticed the way she rubbed her hands over

the thin fabric of her soiled dress? Or the quick spurts of breath tugging her shoulders forward? Fine gentleman he was. "Where's your coat?" He asked even while shrugging off his own.

"Inside. I didn't want to get it dirty."

"So you'd rather get ill? Smart." He wrapped the wool coat around her slender shoulders, surprised she accepted the gesture.

A small smirk tipped her lips, but not enough to satisfy him in his pursuit of an all-out, nose-crinkling grin.

"I was only going to be out here for a couple minutes. But you distracted me."

"Now we're even." He latched his gaze on hers. "You've distracted me since the moment I saw you at the courthouse."

Her soft expression turned rigid. Swirling around, she pulled a smaller runner off the line and hung it over her arm. Golden tendrils of hair escaped from her scarf, falling across her jaw, reminding him of earlier days when her locks had been short, and he had coursed his hands through them. He'd favored that style on her. His Spark.

"I meant what I said right before you nailed me with the broomstick."

"Didn't catch it." With her free arm, she reached for another rug, but Cole stepped in front of her, catching her hand.

She jerked her fingers from his, disgust flooding her eyes as if she'd touched a snake.

"I said, I only called you that." The weight of the runner on her arm pulled the jacket collar off her shoulder. He adjusted it for her, catching the way her frame stiffened beneath his fingertips. "You were humming 'You Call Everyone Sweetheart.' Truth is, the only woman I ever called sweetheart … was you."

Elissa blinked, willing herself to harden against the words squeezing her chest. Yes, he'd called her sweetheart. Her ears almost tingled from the memory of the soothing timbre of his voice when he'd spoken it after their first kiss.

A snowflake landed on her cheek, the chilled prick shoving her back to reality. "You don't expect me to believe that."

Of course, he'd had sweethearts. What about the rumors of him and that silent-film glamour girl? She bit the inside of her cheek. How many times had she come close to knocking the cozy picture of him and Kathleen Stigert off his mother's wall with the feather duster? The woman had fame, fortune, and more curves than the Monongahela. Not to mention, a natural poise that poked Elissa's jealousy.

He exhaled, the vapor from his breath as hazy as the emotion in his eyes. Was he frustrated? Hurt? And why did she care?

"It's the truth, whether you believe it or not. I've never forgotten—"

"Don't." She tossed the rug back on the line with the others and jerked out of his finely cut overcoat. The earthy scent of vetiver and sandalwood charged the snow-ridden air. What did he do, wash his coat in his expensive—no doubt, foreign—cologne? "Spare me one of your signature speeches." She shoved the jacket into his hands. "I've scratched below the gilded surface of your words and found them cheap and flimsy. Spoken by a man with more ego than integrity."

She ducked under the clothesline and walked as fast as her frozen limbs would carry her. Forget the rugs. She'd come back later for them. If at all. Mrs. Parker would understand. The woman had her son back, and—

Her shoes were no match for the icy walk. With her feet sliding forward, the rest of her stumbled backward into … his arms.

"I got you." His breath pulsed in her ear.

She slid her eyes shut, collecting herself, ignoring the broad chest pressed to her back. *Trying* to ignore. With masculine delicacy, he set her onto her feet. The cold air burned her lungs. "Thank you." Polite, calm, and perhaps the greatest bit of acting she'd ever performed because her insides hummed with chaos, embarrassment, and a terrible thing called attraction.

He nodded, a tenderness dabbing his brown irises. "You okay?"

"Yes." She adjusted her sleeve and pulled together whatever was left of her composure. "I should be leaving now if I'm to look respectable for the gala tonight." One glance beyond Cole revealed he'd left his jacket on the muddy, white-dotted ground. A prick of guilt stitched through her. He must've rushed after her as soon as she'd set her feet in motion. "Please relay to your mother I've left."

"May I see you home?"

Her back molars ached from clenching her jaw, but she'd yank out her bicuspids before she'd let Cole see her teeth chattering. When she felt confident her lips weren't frozen together, she answered. "No. I'll take a shortcut through Wadsworth Avenue."

A deep groove set between his brows, and he dipped his head. "That's not a shortcut. It's the back way. Take the cable car, and you'll get home sooner."

Which she knew. But confessing would mean she'd have to admit she traveled the back streets to avoid anyone seeing her filthy and dressed shabbily. She studied the cracks in the mortar behind Cole's head. It was bad enough for him to see her this way. While he'd never call her that name she'd once been taunted with, he knew the pain involved with "Shadyside Slob." She cringed at the thought.

"What I want to know is how you do that."

She slid her gaze to him. "Do what?"

"That." He made a circular motion around her face. "You hold your head perfectly still. Don't you ever get a crick in your neck?"

She threw propriety aside for a costly second and rolled her eyes. "I need to leave."

"Wait." His massive palm cupped her shoulder, his expression turning serious. "What about tonight? Can I escort you to the gala?" Warmth seeped from his touch, his tone, threatening to melt her defenses.

She shrugged, but his hand remained bonded to her. "Adam is

taking me."

He brushed snow from her collar, a wry smile forming. "Do *you* call everyone sweetheart?"

"Cole, I ought to slap you." Her fingers itched with readiness, but she bunched them at her sides. "If you think you can march back into my life after being silent for years, you're delusional. Nothing you say or do will change my opinion of you."

All smugness fled, and he shoved his hands in his pockets. "I'm not the same man who left you at Union Station."

Her lungs iced over, her breaths shallow. That wretched day. "No, you're worse. Because then you trampled my heart, and now that it's whole again, you return and hassle me. Do you want to destroy it? Is that your intention?" Her breath puffed between them. "There's one thing you haven't considered. This time, I won't let you do it." She spun on the balls of her feet, conscious of the icy ruts in the walkway. He called her name twice, and for once, it was nice being the one who walked away.

Frost etched a web of crystal lace on Elissa's bedroom window. She ran her thumb along the inside of the glass, taking in the slight chill with a sigh. At least the rest of her was warm now. After her extended moments outside with Cole, she'd feared her marrow had frozen in her bones. She released a breath, fogging the pane before her. Cole's face when she'd confessed her service to his mother feathered her thoughts. His eyes had widened and then flooded with an emotion she couldn't quite decipher—something between shock and admiration. And why had her breath flitted in her chest at his appraisal? Traitorous.

"You're wearing that tonight, dear?" Elissa's mother stood in the bedroom doorway, a grin brightening her face.

Elissa pasted on a smile. "No, my dressing gown isn't what I'd call formal. But you, Mother, look stunning."

"Thank you." She entered the room, her burgundy gown flowing with her steps. It didn't matter if Grace Tillman donned velvet and diamonds or a potato sack, elegance kissed her mannerisms. "This came for you from Charlie's Greenhouse." She held out the familiar box housing a yellow rose. "I thought Adam was escorting you tonight."

"He is." She received the small package and set it on her vanity next to her formal hair combs.

"Shouldn't the man be the one who brings you a corsage?" Mother's eyes never held a challenge, but the faint upward tilt of her lips usually preceded a propriety lesson. Like Irene Castle mastered in dance, Grace Tillman mastered in etiquette.

"I purchased this in case he brings the wrong color." Her hands fell to her sides. "It sounds silly, doesn't it?" More like pathetic.

The delicate smirk disappeared. "Why would you say that?"

"Alice Paul toured the country and inspired so many. She drew attention with her hunger strikes in jail. Made a difference. What have I done?" She gestured toward the box. "Wore a yellow rose. But does that change anything? No. It's insignificant." Just like her.

"Ms. Paul did create quite the stir while incarcerated." Mother wrapped a comforting arm around her. "But you've never been one for a gray uniform." Mother rarely teased, but when she did, it softened Elissa's edges. "You're showing the world the movement's not over—that we're pressing forward."

Elissa stared into eyes as blue as hers, noting the passion in them. "I've never heard you speak like this." Hadn't her mother thought her ideals indecent? Hadn't she almost disowned her upon the discovery of Elissa wearing a golden sash and marching down Fifth Avenue with a thousand other suffragettes?

"Keep on voicing your stance. If it's gotten this old conventional mama listening, I'm certain it'll affect many more." Mother's smile was ready, warm, and somehow filling, like fresh-baked bread brushed with honey. "Just make sure you keep your shoulders back while speaking." She winked, and Elissa laughed.

But her biggest contribution to the movement could be

squelched. "Father told me about the loan."

"Ah. This is what has you upset." Her eyes softened with understanding. "Your father's been staying up late, looking over the books again and again. It's been hard on him."

As much as the worry niggled in Elissa's chest, it had to be a hundred times worse for him. The paper had belonged in the Tillman family for two generations. Unlike her, Father had never tasted failure. Yet a sliver of her soul wept at the thought of her own aspirations dying. The paper was all she had left.

"I've always imagined myself running the *Review* someday." A dream she'd been clutching from her youth drifted through her fingers like the breath of wind through the bare willow's limbs outside her window. She skimmed the bristles of her hairbrush with her fingertips, and her mother appeared behind her.

"I know your heart is set on it. But should the *Review* fail, God can give you new dreams."

Elissa wouldn't know where to begin with a different life goal. What could replace the rush of excitement that pulsed her veins when the presses fired up? Or match the sense of accomplishment when she held the warm edition she'd poured her heart into? No, it was the paper or nothing.

"I'm glad you're speaking with your father again. He didn't need a strained relationship on top of the pressure from the paper." She combed her fingers through Elissa's hair like she had years ago. "He didn't tell me Cole was coming for dinner until late yesterday." Her lashes lowered. "I didn't receive Cole properly. I'm ashamed of how I acted. He deserves my apology."

He deserved nothing but a swift kick in the trousers. So hard, it'd land the man right back in New York. "Mother, you did nothing wrong. If anyone, it should be him who apologizes." And why couldn't she keep the emotion from her voice?

Mother, always discerning, stroked her back the same as she had the multiple times Elissa had come home crying from being teased at school. "It was certainly a shock, wasn't it? How are you faring, my love?"

Elissa tight-lipped a smile. "It doesn't seem real to me. He has been removed from here"—and her—"for so long. He's changed, yet is much the same." His persistence being one of the qualities he'd retained over the years. "It's almost as if he expects things to be the way they were before he left for Columbia."

Mother's stiff curls dipped with her chin. She reached over Elissa's shoulder, retrieved the hairbrush, and worked it through Elissa's hair.

Elissa slid her eyes closed, letting the soothing, rhythmic motion act like a tonic to her nerves.

"Could it be Cole wants to make amends with you?"

Her lids popped open, and now the bristles seemed to score her scalp like tiny daggers. "I wouldn't allow it." He'd set fire to that bridge. The only remains were charred memories.

Mother lowered the brush, a tranquil expression blanketing her face despite Elissa's outburst. "It's quite possible he's sorry for the way he treated you."

She unconsciously snorted, and Mother raised a brow. "For Cole to be sorry, that'd require an apology. Which he's not offered." Had he expressed his regrets on the note she'd torn up? She scrunched her nose. Maybe she shouldn't have acted so rashly, but then ... the man'd had plenty of opportunities since then to ask for forgiveness.

Mother responded with a dainty shrug. "Does he need to *say* he's sorry for you to forgive him?"

This morning, her father had told her to be merciful. This afternoon, her mother was telling her to forgive. Their words scratched her resolve both times.

"Forgiveness would only open my heart. And it has to remain closed as far as he's concerned."

Her muscles screamed with fatigue. Cleaning day usually left her drained, but this sort of exhaustion had nothing to do with beating carpets. The *Review*'s unknown future, Cole's enigmatic behavior, and Adam's continued attentions were three excellent reasons to stay home and lose herself in an Austen novel. She twirled a lock of hair around her finger, frowning. "Do I have to attend tonight?"

Her mother kissed the top of her head. "Elissa, I've never known you to be a coward."

CHAPTER 6

The jammed cable car had let Cole off three blocks from the William Penn Ballroom, and walking the crowded streets in his tuxedo wasn't his idea of enjoyment. He attracted hand-over-mouth giggles from a band of schoolgirls and smirking appraisals from their mothers. Couldn't a man stroll down Forbes Avenue in peace?

The frigid wind, sodden with exhaust fumes, bit his face, and he ducked his chin into his starched collar. He turned the corner onto Cherry Way and came toe to toe with a millionaire.

"Mr. Shelby." Surprise edged his voice, and warmth flooded his chest as Cole stuck out his hand to the man who'd inspired a lot of his early articles, though none had been published. "How do you do, sir?"

The older man's mustache twitched until recognition struck his eyes like the gust of air that stole through Cole's overcoat. "Cole the menace." Grinning, Shelby withdrew his hand from his pocket, a handkerchief spilling out onto the sidewalk. "I thought you were terrorizing New York. You didn't come back to peek in my windows again, did you, boy?"

The fragrance of wildflowers assaulted Cole's nostrils. He drew in a breath and spun on his heel. No Elissa. Only a group of men huddled outside the barbershop, smoking. He palmed the back of his neck. Crazy. He was going crazy.

"Something the matter?" Shelby stuffed his handkerchief back into his pocket, eyeing Cole with a raised brow.

"I'm being haunted by a woman." All there was to it. When he'd remained three hundred miles away in New York, the tremors of emotion had been manageable, but with his desk now only three feet from hers … the fierce current pulled. Like standing a yard from a tornado. Being sucked in was inevitable.

"Females. They do that, don't they?" His focus traveled over Cole's shoulder, and his mouth flattened into a grim line. "Hard to understand too. Even after thirty-five years of marriage."

Flickers of sadness shone in his former mentor's gray eyes. The heavy scent which punched Cole's senses a moment ago deadened, intensifying his confusion. "And to answer your first question, no. I gave up snooping around kooky inventors' homes." He fixed a smile on his face. "Did I ever thank you for not ratting me out to Mr. Tillman?"

"Ah, that was forever ago when you were a nosy delivery boy. Now you're a nosy reporter." Shelby's throaty chuckle followed. He withdrew a cigarette case. "I read your column every day." He snagged a smoke stick and offered one to Cole. "Impressive stuff."

Cole raised a hand in refusal. "Thank you, sir, but not nearly as impressive as all those inventions you came up with during the war. The scaled-steel bulletproof vests? That was genius." The flow of pedestrians thickened, and Cole shifted to the edge of the sidewalk. "I never knew one man could sell so many patents to the government."

Shelby lit his cigarette and shook out the match, tossing it to the ground. "It's only money. Paper with ink on it. No different than your newspapers."

No different. Right. "Except one holds value, and the other holds articles."

Shelby released a puff of smoke and regarded him with an easy smile, his cheeks tinged pink from the crisp air. "But both hold a considerable amount of influence and power."

"Indeed."

He glanced over Cole's shoulder again and narrowed his eyes. "Best be going. I have a late meeting to attend."

From the deep scowl on his face, it appeared to be an unpleasant sort of meeting. If Shelby's office—which doubled as a workshop— was located north on Reed Street, why was the man traveling south? "Did you move operations?"

"No." He raised his chin, and an odd spark of what appeared to be determination tightened his features. "I've no plans of going to my place tonight. It's time to meet them at their headquarters." His voice sharpened on the word 'headquarters,' and the awkward shift in demeanor reminded Cole of past conversations with this inventor. The man would speak as if you were privy to his thoughts but leave you as blank as a fresh roll of newsprint paper.

"Who are 'them,' sir? Are you working with someone on a new project?"

"I can't say at present." The breeze gusted, smacking his coat collar against his neck, and he adjusted it. "Good seeing you, Cole the menace. Stop by sometime. You still got your key? I remember how tickled you were when I gave it to you."

"I've got it tucked away, Mr. Shelby." Tucked away in his wallet, but he wouldn't let the man know. It was one thing to be sentimental about an influential gent taking you under his wing like Tillman had, but another to be mushy about it.

"Remember when I tutored you for that science exam? That was a special time for me." He took a long drag on his cigarette. "I still have it, you know."

"The test?" At the time, Cole hadn't the money to buy anything for Shelby as a thank you, and so Cole'd gifted him the exam.

"It's on my desk."

Cole's brows edged higher. With Shelby attaining major success, it would seem that tutoring a poor newsie would've been easily forgotten. "I'm thankful you helped me, sir. If it wasn't for you, I'd still be in ninth grade."

"Well, well." Shelby rocked on his heels and nearly collided with an old woman shielding her face from the wind. "It was good times, as I mentioned."

"Be certain you tell Hank that I'll be stopping by the office to challenge him in another round of chess. I've improved since the last time we played."

"He moved to Kansas a few years back to be near family. I have a new lab assistant now. Matthew's not as experienced as old Hank, but he's astute. Just what I need."

"I'm looking forward to meeting him."

"Matthew is a private person. Likes to keep to himself. Oh, before I forget, there's a small matter of a motorcycle." He dipped his chin, peering at Cole from above the rims of his glasses. "I was under the impression I'd be holding it only a year."

Cole's jaw slackened. "You still have my Triumph? I was sure it'd been scrapped by now." That two-wheeled chariot had taken a lot of punishment during Cole's teenage years, but he'd gladly take it back, even in pieces.

Shelby's false annoyance faded into rich laughter. "No, I still have it. I may have tinkered with it here and there, replaced a couple parts. Honestly, you should be thankful Jeffrey hasn't demolished it yet."

"Say, how's Jeffrey these days?" Cole had met the only Shelby child a handful of times. Must be in his late twenties now.

"Like I said, Cole, stop by and we can go to lunch. I really must be on my way." He tipped his hat and strolled off.

"I'd like that. Good day." Cole called after a rapidly retreating Mr. Shelby.

The man acknowledged him with a raised hand but never looked back. Odd fellow, that one. Acted like he'd never heard Cole inquire after his son. But Cole wouldn't pass up an opportunity to dine with the famous Mr. Shelby. Eccentricities and all. Cole would even foot the bill, especially if it meant a chance to pick at the inventor's brain. It'd be well worth the two-dollar lamb chops at the Penn Hotel.

A car horn blasted from down the street, snapping Cole back to his original mission. The gala.

Cole entered the ballroom, and by doing so, stepped into tradition. Forty years of "Appreciation Galas," as Mrs. Tillman called them, though Cole had only been present for nine, counting this one.

Gold ribbons of light unfurled from the swollen globes gracing the ivory pillars. But the queen of the room was the chandelier, postured with grandeur and brilliance as if it upheld the ceiling rather than being suspended from it. The glossy oak floor boasted more layers of wax than all the heads of Cole's old bosses back in New York. He never put that glop in his hair, even for swanky parties such as this.

"Mr. Parker." A female voice bled into his musings. Irene Harper approached, clopping heels matching the pace of a frenzied racehorse. "I am so glad I ran into you."

"Good evening, Miss Harper." Cole dipped his chin. "It's been a while since we last met."

"Too long." Her lips slanted, and her heavily sequined dress dulled in comparison to the sparkle in her brown eyes. "Not since high school. But back then, we ran in different circles."

Circles as in social classes. In those days, Irene Harper wouldn't have been found dead chatting with the poor son of a nobody. Seems Cole's job at the *Dispatch* had elevated his status in her opinion.

"I came over to tell you"—she placed a gloved hand on his bicep—"that I loved your article. Adored it."

His brow spiked, and he stepped back, her fingers falling to her side. "You enjoyed the article about an execution?"

"Oh no." Her beaming grin dimmed, pink dusting her cheeks. "The one from yesterday. I had no clue the women's shelter was being foreclosed on."

"Ah, I see."

"How did you discover this before the broadcast of the radio bulletin?" A note of awe sprinkled her tone.

Luck. The spread of gossip rivaled the speed of light, especially in a cramped apartment complex. He hadn't expected any truth to the claim, but when he'd called the shelter, the manager had confirmed it. But leaking sources was bad form. "Right place at the right time, Miss Harper." Nothing like a journalist using an overdone cliché.

Her high-pitched laugh clashed with the music as she angled herself in a flattering way. "I told my father, and he's going to make a donation." The words themselves innocent, but the heavy batting of eyelashes spoke danger.

"That's kind of him." The Harpers not only possessed considerable wealth but also had been the prominent patrons of the *Review* for decades. "Please relay my thanks."

"With pleasure, Mr. Parker." She fingered a sequin on her neckline. "If you ever need inspiration for a story, there's always something going on at the medical center where I volunteer. I'd be happy to give you a personal tour."

"Thank you. I'll keep it in mind."

She smiled again, and her gaze drifted to the dance floor. "I always love the *Review* parties. I rarely get a chance to dance."

An aggravating ultimatum stretched before him—encourage the flirtatious millionaire by indulging her with a dance or receive a rebuke from Tillman for disappointing the darling of the family who supported the paper. "I believe, Miss Harper, that—"

"Cole." Mrs. Tillman appeared, stepping between him and Miss Harper. "I have an issue I must discuss with you." With poised grace, she shifted her attention to the younger girl, whose smile faltered then renewed. "Excuse us, please, Irene. It's a pressing matter."

"But of course." Miss Harper dipped her chin and retreated to corner another notable bachelor.

Cole couldn't celebrate the victory of escaping Miss Harper

because now he faced a worse scenario than an awkward dance with a shiny-eyed girl. After his last encounter with Mrs. Tillman, he'd decided it'd be best to avoid her this evening. He resisted the annoying urge to tug his collar. "What can I help you with, Mrs. Tillman?"

Her lips curved in a gentle way. "I want to apologize for the way I received you yesterday evening. I was surprised at your coming and didn't respond appropriately. Will you forgive me?"

The gift of words ran deep in him, from smoothing his way out of trouble to flattering his way into high society. But here, in front of Elissa's mother, talent deserted him. She asked *him* to forgive *her*? After all he'd done to the two people she loved so dear? She couldn't know the motivation behind his actions. No one knew except him and God.

She patted his arm, softness flooding her eyes as if she understood his struggle. "Please know, Cole, you're welcome in my home anytime."

"Glad to hear it, Mrs. Tillman." Arrogance flavored his speech, and he despised it. Why couldn't he sound thankful or genuine? Even as his stomach soured, her small mouth tipped into a soft smile before she joined her husband's side. Only ten feet beyond the parents stood the daughter. In another man's arms.

Cole's chest tightened at the sight of Elissa dancing with Kendrew. Her golden-hued gown accentuated her figure. Her hair, swept up with combs, revealed the graceful curve of her neck. A few curls framed her face, stealing his attention. Like the night Elissa had coaxed him to dance the Castle Walk with her despite Cole's busted thumb from a baseball injury that morning. They'd had an open field for a dance floor and crickets for an orchestra. He hadn't been able to peel his gaze from her then and couldn't now.

Kendrew's hold tightened on her waist, his mouth bending to her ear, whispering. Cole's heart iced over, reality freezing his veins. If Elissa had moved on, then he should too.

She spotted him, and her neck, so elegant a moment ago,

strained. He swallowed a groan and joined the handful of newsmen by the refreshment table.

"Here, Parker." Frank shoved a glass of sparkling juice into Cole's hand.

"It's been a while. Glad to have you back." Henry, the longtime copywriter, lifted his glass in cheers. "I never thought we'd see you again. The *New York Dispatch*." He let out a low whistle. "Why you'd leave there to come back to this place, I'll never understand."

"It was time for a change." Cole took a sip and smiled. "Besides, you riff-raff are more of my kind of company. You wouldn't believe this, Frank, but there wasn't a spittoon in sight."

Frank chuckled and smacked his rotund belly. "Ah, no wonder you came back. Them uppers don't know how to live."

Kendrew and Elissa joined their small group. Could the man grip her any closer to his side? You couldn't slide a typewriter ribbon between them. A growl stalked around Cole's chest. Dancing with Miss Harper seemed more pleasant than enduring Kendrew's calf eyes at Elissa.

"Evening, Cole." Kendrew nodded with a satisfied smirk.

He dipped his chin in response. What was Kendrew trying to communicate with that gesture? Cole's eyes strained from the challenge of keeping them from narrowing. Of all the delightful people in the world, why did Elissa pick the one who'd provoked Cole the most? He should've exposed the clown years ago.

Elissa flicked a glance at him then locked her stare on his boutonniere. A yellow rose. Just like the one adorning her gown. Her brow lowered and then hiked, blue eyes hazed as if contemplating Cole's motive. Their gazes connected, and she broke the moment, training her focus on the table beside them.

Conversation lulled among the group, awkwardness setting in.

Elissa's attention snagged on an older man with a thick mustache. "Bartek." She motioned for him to join their circle. "Did you bring the Graflex? I'd love a picture of the table centerpieces. Greta loves gardenias."

"Not tonight. The missus made me leave everything fun at home." Bartek nodded toward the opposite side of the room where his wife chatted with Mrs. Tillman. "Don't even have my tobacco."

"Too bad, Elissa." Adam patted her hand like she was a toddler. "That might have also been good for your little society column."

Little?

Fiery flecks lit Elissa's eyes, and Cole all but cringed. Growing up, there'd been many a night when Elissa had filled Cole's ears with her dreams of being a success in a man's world. No way could she be satisfied with a monthly editorial with a masculine byline. Because with Elissa it'd always been about something big. Getting the big article. Then having a big career. Kendrew couldn't have chosen a more condescending word.

Elissa nudged a warning to Adam and snuck a glance at Cole. Did she truly think Cole was oblivious to her writings? Elissa penning under the byline of Elliot Wentworth could be no more of a secret to Cole than Samuel Clemens for Mark Twain.

Frank leaned over, his vest buttons pulling taut, and lowered his voice. "My nephew is a bellhop here. Says there's a speakeasy under the lobby. Complete with a tunnel leading outside in case of a raid. Ironic, huh? A swanky place like this is also a juice hall. Want to go check it out?"

Speakeasy. Drink. The words pulsed in Cole's skull.

CHAPTER 7

Elissa mashed her lips together, hiding a frown. Cole shifted his weight from foot to foot as if physically balancing Frank's offer. He'd last worn that expression the tortuous moment they both wished to forget. As always, the urge to rescue him took prominence. "Cole, would you like to dance?" She blurted the question without consideration.

His gaze held hers with an intensity that squeezed her gut. "I'd be honored."

Frank shot her a mischievous wink, Henry elbowed Cole and mumbled in his ear, and Adam stiffened, withdrawing.

"Oh, please, boys. It's only a dance." But if it was only a dance, why had her palms moistened to an unfeminine degree? She'd made the impetuous mistake of speaking before her mind could rein in her mouth, and now she had the bothersome task of retaining some measure of composure. "There's no harm in two adults dancing." With that, she towed Cole to edge of the dance floor by his elbow.

"Hurry back, sweetheart." Adam's voice reached her from several feet away.

She winced, recalling the conversation earlier with Cole. *Do you call everyone sweetheart?* No, she didn't. Moreover, Adam's tone had sounded more possessive than endearing, scratching a nerve.

"I wasn't expecting you to ask me to dance, Spark, but I'm grateful."

As for Adam calling her article 'little,' she knew above anyone how paltry her editorial contribution to the *Review* was. Yet he had no right—

"Elissa, I would understand if you choose to ignore me, but could you at least loosen your grip?" Cole's mouth hitched in a smirk as his stare trained on her fingers wrapped—more like clamped—on his arm. "I already have a collection of scars from you."

She huffed and relaxed her hold, ignoring his toned muscle beneath her touch. "You weren't even bleeding today, and I doubt you have a scar. A bruise, probably." His hair covered the area, forbidding her from confirming her suspicion. And no, she would not run her fingers through his dark locks for a second time today. Too risky to her resolve to dislike him for the next several decades.

"I'm not talking about the beating you gave me earlier." He stopped, and they both waited for the orchestra to conclude the current song. "I'm referring to the time we fell off my bicycle because you put your hands over my eyes. Those trash cans we crashed into weren't kind to my torso."

Or her shoulder. As if Cole had read her mind, his gaze slipped from her eyes to the blemished area. Though paled with time, her own scar was clearly identifiable. She shifted under the weight of his stare, her breath hitching.

His lips twitched, and his perusal skimmed from her shoulder to her mouth.

She tugged the hem of her elbow-length glove, ignoring the heat sliding up her spine. "That was your fault for boasting you could ride to my house with your eyes closed." Reminiscing about their youth wasn't the best approach for keeping her emotions in check. She secured her stare on his lapel. "Why'd you wear that?" Curiosity had been gnawing her since she'd spied the flower, now straying crooked. "Are you making fun of me?"

"I thought we could match." He winked. "Adam came through for me and bought you the perfect corsage."

His jest ignited heat in her veins. Adam hadn't come through for Cole. Or for her. She would have been content with white, or even pink, but Adam arrived on her doorstep with a red corsage. Red! It'd taken him a half-hour to persuade her the slight had been unintentional, clinging to the excuse the color stood for ardent love and not anti-suffragism, but she remained unconvinced. Every soul in the nation was aware of Tennessee's War of Roses. She sighed. No man took her seriously. Not Father. Not Adam. And definitely not Cole, given the pert grin he wore now. "I wear this for principle's sake. Something you hardly understand."

He blinked at her words. The song had ended, and they, along with several eager couples, stepped onto the dance floor, waiting for the orchestra to play.

"Believe me. I comprehend conviction." The rasp of his tone deep and penetrating, Cole straightened his flower. "I haven't donned a red rose since the chaos in Nashville. The bosses sent me there to woo a national advertiser, but I got netted in the event. That was one heated day, and I don't mean the August weather."

"The Hermitage Hotel? You were there on voting day?"

"I was."

Her heart fluttered. Those both for and against the movement had rallied in the streets of the final state needed to pass the Nineteenth Amendment, and she'd longed to participate, to be part of history. But Father deemed it too dangerous. Yes, mobs had invaded, causing pandemonium at the revealing of the verdict, but a part of her felt she'd missed out. "It must have been an amazing experience." Oh, to have witnessed the capturing of a long-awaited dream. She'd heard the legislative members had shown their true colors on their lapels that day, most being against the cause. Thankfully, even the staunchest belief could be swayed toward good, and the deciding official, while wearing red, had voted yellow. "Tell me, what color did you wear?"

"Same as today."

The music commenced, but she was incapable of moving, her

arms heavy against her sides. Who was this man before her?

Cole noticed her hesitation and held out both hands, inviting her to join him. Dance with him.

She swallowed and stepped into his arms, moving slow to keep perfect poise, despite her trembling knees.

Her hand slid into his with alarming ease. The way he glided his thumb over her index finger was all too familiar, all too terrifying. Even with them both wearing gloves, the warmth spread between their palms. She'd created considerable distance so his hand couldn't curl around her back, only skim the side of her hip. She met his eyes, and for a strange second, it was like time had never passed— yet back then she'd positioned herself close enough to count his eyelashes and absorb his whispered promises. Her heart stiffened. She shuffled another step back.

Cole had the nerve to laugh.

"What's so humorous?" Even though she'd asked him to dance, she'd never agreed to enjoy it. And to be sure her eyes wouldn't betray her and do something preposterous, like gaze into his dark irises, she forced her stare on his black bowtie.

"Are you making room for Adam?" He regarded the gap she'd created. "I'm sure he'd fit comfortably between us."

"If you'd rather, we could invite Miss Harper. I hate to see her straining her poor eyes when she could admire you from a closer proximity." She kept her tone light and cool so Cole wouldn't suspect her of jealousy. But really, the woman couldn't have been more obvious about her intentions, with her tinkling laughter and sultry stances. Irene could snag any sorry soul she desired, but she'd set her sights on the most handsome man in the room. Adam was pleasing to look at but came up short compared to Cole's confident presence and irresistible features. And Cole in a tuxedo challenged Elissa's resistance ten times worse. Yet did it matter how attractive he was if she knew him to be capable of breaking her heart?

Nope.

Let him empty his charms on Irene, and she on him. Together

they could pump each other's heads full of airy nonsense and float away, leaving Elissa in peace.

"Didn't think you noticed her conversing with me." He ducked closer, breaking the invisible barrier she'd built. His focus bonded to her lips. Was his aim to kiss her? Smooch her right in the center of the dance floor? He angled at the last second and whispered, "As I recall, you were in the arms of your *sweetheart*."

She cringed at the word, then despised her show of emotion.

"Since we're on the subject of Kendrew, what exactly is the status of your relationship?" He straightened and nodded with a suave nonchalance at an older pair dancing beside them.

Elissa embraced the opportunity to breathe again. "I don't see how that's any of your concern." She tipped her chin in the graceful manner she'd practiced countless times in her mirror.

"It's not." He gave a low growl. "But I can't for the life of me understand what you find interesting about him. An obituary has more life than that man."

She stilled, remaining in their stance, garnering a few glances from the surrounding couples. "Just because there's bad blood between you two doesn't mean you should be insulting."

"Insulting?" He blew out a noisy breath. "I'm not the one who insulted you."

Her brows wrinkled. "I didn't say you offended me. I said—"

"I understood what you said." He didn't bother to control the volume of his tone, and Elissa was thankful the orchestra chose that moment for a crescendo. "Tell me, Spark, did Adam ever tell you why I socked him that day?"

She bit her lip and resumed their dance, keeping their steps to a simple sway, her mind unable to concentrate on graceful movements. "No." A ten-year-old skirmish in the schoolyard shouldn't possess the power to rouse aggressive emotions in Cole. However, his taut jaw and severe glare affirmed the occurrence still bothered him.

"Of course he didn't." He let out an unsettling laugh. "Maybe you should ask Kendrew when you get a chance."

"Or you could tell me."

His hardened eyes melted into something she didn't want to delve into. The others around them stopped moving. Were they creating a scene? She sheepishly glanced about. No. The song had ended. *What*? That was either incredibly short, or she'd been in a daze. Either way, her obligation had ended. She dropped Cole's hand, but the bothersome tenderness still lingered in his expression.

For sanity's sake, Elissa needed to get away. Far from Cole and his ability to impact her emotions. "Honestly, Cole, who are you to criticize Adam? As I remember, he wasn't the one who was reckless with my heart."

CHAPTER 8

Elissa rejoined Adam by the refreshment table and matched his scowl with one of her own. Whatever Cole had meant about the reason behind their decade-old fight, she was going to discover it.

"Nice that you and Cole are still friends." Adam's smile wobbled more than Frank after he had a few drinks in him.

"We're not friends."

For a handsome man dressed in a tuxedo, Adam appeared rather foolish with his mouth gaping open and eyebrows furrowed so low they made a straight line across his forehead. "Then why on earth did you dance with him?"

"I have my reasons." She glanced over her gown in search of any loose threads or sequins. She'd stashed her travel sewing kit in her silver clutch, but everything was holding together nicely—unlike her emotions. She lifted her gaze from the satin fabric only to be speared with Adam's glare. "What?"

"Is that all you're going to say? You have your reasons?"

She should've stayed home. Darcy's companionship ranked higher than the two gentlemen currently tarnishing her evening. At least with that dear creature, she didn't have to be concerned about sucking in her gut, keeping her shoulders back, or refraining from dumping her punch on certain people's heads.

Adam glowered.

She sighed. "It's personal." Though her temper fumed at Cole, her heart couldn't humiliate him by suggesting she'd asked him to dance because his expression had reminded her of the first day they'd met. When Cole'd begged her father for a job. When his own father had abandoned him and his mother.

Adam pulled her hand into his, selecting that moment to replace irritation with charm. "Elissa, if we're ever going to mean something to one another, then we need an honest relationship."

Bingo. Her lips stretched into a smile, and she placed her other hand over his. "You're absolutely right. No secrets between us." Her grin widened at his enthusiastic nod. "So how about I tell you why I danced with Cole, and you tell me why he punched you in tenth grade. Deal?"

"In tenth grade?" His laugh sounded more like a cough. "That was a long way back."

"Did you forget the reason?" Hard to believe since the man's face was as guilty as Franco Cartelli's during his murder trial.

His shoulders slumped. "I remember, but I think it will cast me in an unfavorable light."

Elissa had already formed speculations. Maybe he'd tripped Cole in front of the entire school. Or ridiculed Cole for having holes in his trousers.

"I invented the Shadyside Slob nickname."

But not that one.

Her throat welded shut, her breaths burning at the memories of those tormenting days. "How could you?" She pulled her hands from his arm, the idea of touching the man who'd blackened her years at Oakland High unbearable.

"It was a long time ago." His face heated ten shades past ruby. "I didn't know you like I do now. And really, Elissa, I couldn't understand how sloppily you dressed. Your family was wealthy."

Her toes begged permission to kick him in the shin. Adam had no idea how hard she'd struggled to look presentable, to avoid snagged stockings and stained clothes. But somehow her awkwardness had always overtaken her. Though Mother had never shown it, Elissa knew she'd been a disappointment. A humiliation. "You should be ashamed of yourself. Yes, my family has money, but I never fit in with anyone—"

"Except Cole." His scornful tone suggested she should be embarrassed by her one and only friend.

"Do you have any idea of the pain you caused me?" The tears she'd cried because of that awful nickname, which had spread throughout the entire school, ranging from loud taunts in the lunchroom to giggled whispers as she walked through the hall. Somebody had even carved it on her desk. She'd never understood why or how it originated. Until now. "You used your popularity to hurt others, Adam. You knew all you had to do was suggest it, and those feather-brained friends of yours would see that it caught on like wildfire." And with her being a year younger than Adam and Cole, the ribbing had continued after they'd been gone.

"I didn't realize it would catch on like it did." He adopted a pained look. "Honestly. I only mentioned it to a couple of people."

In Adam's feeble defense, most of her classmates had already looked down upon her. The nickname had only sealed the case against her.

"I'm sorry, Elissa." Regret shone in his amber eyes. "I should've apologized years ago. You're so different now than what you were then."

The ache in her heart stretched to her shaky fingertips. How could she put into words the effort she exerted every day to keep that clumsy little girl from showing up again? A retreat to the ladies' room was vital. Her skin flushed hot, and tears threatened to swell. "I accept your apology, but I need time."

"I'll wait." A sadness crept over his expression. "As long as it takes."

Elissa spared a nod in his direction and then pivoted toward the doors. Four steps to the exit. She could hold it together that long. Jay Lewis bounded in, blocking her retreat. Her father's press foreman reeked of cigarettes, a sure indication he'd spent the first part of the evening in the lounge.

"Did you hear the latest?" His brown brows squished together. A scowl usually ornamented Jay's face, but this moment, disbelief stretched across his sharp features. "The radio news bulletin?"

"No. What happened?"

"He's dead." Jay pulled a large hand over his face.

Cole stepped beside Elissa, his commanding presence somehow comforting. "Who's dead?"

Jay blinked. "Why, Daniel Shelby."

"Mr. Shelby." Cole's breathy whisper iced her blood.

She braved a glance at him. A muscle ticked in his jaw, but other than that—stoic.

A small crowd gathered, and Jay filled them in with the tragic news. "There was an explosion at the Halloway Building. The whole thing went up in flames. Poor guy was inside."

Confusion settled between Cole's brows. "That abandoned place on Bootlegger Alley?"

"Yeah. They're saying a still exploded." Jay's mouth pulled into a grim line. "That's the third explosion in six months."

Elissa worried her bottom lip. Why had Mr. Shelby gone to the Halloway Building? Everyone knew Bootlegger Alley—Garson Street and its surrounding area—was rumrunner and drug lord territory. Surely, the respectable inventor hadn't been caught up in crime. A chill slithered through her bones. "It's awful. His poor family."

Cole held up a hand. "If the building was in flames, how'd they know Shelby was inside?"

"The radio bulletin said the police got an anonymous tip." Jay shrugged. "Someone claimed they saw Shelby enter the place. Plus, they found a fancy walking stick with his initials on it among the rubble. The firemen are still working to get the flames under control, I think."

Cole blinked, and the befuddled daze cradling his eyes sparked into confidence. As he shifted to face her, her hand unintentionally skimmed his forearm, but he caught her fingers in his. "We gotta do an extra."

She choked on her own breath. "Did you say 'extra?'"

His gaze latched on hers for an excruciating second, trapping her rebuttal in her chest. He squeezed her hand, withdrew his touch, and scanned the crowd. Most likely looking for an ally. "Yes. We need to do an extra. Let's get your father." He turned on his heel, but Elissa clutched his elbow.

She expected the action to halt him, but the momentum jerked her forward.

He stroked her knuckles with his thumb, surprisingly tender for such an uncomfortable situation. "Again with the death grip on my joints?"

"Cole, we don't do extras. Not anymore." Surely, he knew this. Even if they pumped the article out in record time, it couldn't compete with the expediency of radio. But then, Cole always had a soft spot in his heart for Mr. Shelby. Maybe he wanted to do a memorial for him. "I'm sorry. I remember how fond you were of him." She slid her hand up his arm to rest on his shoulder.

His dark eyes flashed with an intensity that knocked her heart four notches past racing. Elissa clamped her mouth closed before a tiny gasp could escape. She'd forgotten how powerful his stare could be and the weakening effect it had on her.

"What's going on?" Her father's voice ripped into her thoughts, drawing her back to the present. "Lissie, you all right? Your cheeks are fiery red."

She dropped her hand from Cole's shoulder and placed a palm to her cheek. "We just found out Daniel Shelby has been killed."

"Sir, I suggest you call in the crew for an extra."

Her father's eyebrows spiked. "It's risky. One where money could be lost if it turns out unsuccessful." While his words agreed with Elissa's, the twinkle in his aged blue eyes said otherwise. Father's weakness for excitement mixed with Cole's power of persuasion equaled a whole lot of trouble.

She needed to intervene. "This will be considered old news. Nobody would buy a story they already know about."

Even Jay's shoulders curled forward in disappointment. What was wrong with everyone? The *Review* had no excess funds to throw around. Zero. To support this crazy impulse, they'd need to call in a quarter of the newsroom staff and fire up the presses. Then there were production costs. Paper and ink. And what newsie would want to give up a Saturday night to stand on a street corner? Only to come back with bundles of unsold extras?

A dull ache spread behind her eyes. No. Completely illogical. If the men needed a surge of something thrilling, they could go for rides on the massive dumbwaiter she'd spotted on the way in here. At least the men would be contained, and no money would be thrown away. "I'm just as competitive as any of you, but even I see the absurdity in this. There's nothing to be covered that isn't already broadcasting all over Pittsburgh."

"Something isn't adding up." Cole's fingers flexed at his side, his flinty stare aimed at her. "He was murdered."

The chatter hushed, and all eyes fixed on him.

The hair raised on her arms, sending a chill to her gloved fingertips. "It's most likely an accident. Anything could've happened."

"Shelby was murdered," he said, his deep rasp emphatic.

Her father yanked out his pocket watch and frowned. "It'd be a close call if we did an extra. How do you know all this, son?"

"A hunch."

"I can't run presses on a hunch."

Elissa exhaled the breath trapped in her chest. Father was on her side. No extra. No money squandered. She'd have to keep an eye on Cole. His lofty ideas could be the driving stake in the *Review*'s for-sale sign. She wasn't sure how they handled funds in New York, but around here—

"What about facts?" Determination flickered in Cole's eyes, his gaze slipping from Father to her. "How about an interview with one of the last people to see him alive?"

Elissa shivered. "Who would that be?"

"Me."

CHAPTER 9

Cole fed Jane a crisp paper and poised his fingers over her keys. Elissa stood beside him, wringing her now gloveless hands, nervous energy rolling off her, misting him with doubt. What if this endeavor turned out a failure?

When he'd confided in Tillman about those few moments on the street with Daniel Shelby, his boss approved the extra and assigned Elissa to be his copy editor. Cole's chest had swelled at the thought of spending the next hour with her, crafting an out-of-the-ordinary editorial. But witnessing her lowered lashes and uneven breaths jabbed his confidence. How would he get her to trust him if he failed? He rolled his shoulders, but his fitted jacket restricted his movements. He screeched back his chair.

Elissa jumped.

"Didn't mean to startle you." He attempted to shrug out of his coat, smacking his elbow on the armrest. A twinge of pain shot to his fingers, and Elissa stooped beside him. Dainty fingers tugged his sleeve, and he worked with her to slip his left arm free. Same with the right.

She relieved him of the jacket and draped it over the back of her chair.

"Thanks, Spark." He winked, but she scrutinized the floor as if counting the scores on the boards. She hadn't allowed him to call her Spark once since he'd returned. Where was his little spitfire? This wasn't working. He stood, the movement snapping Elissa's stare to his. "I think we need to pray first."

Her lips parted.

Cole swooped her hands into his before she could pull away. Head bowed, he prayed for God's help in writing with clarity and precision and also for His comfort to surround the Shelby family.

"Amen," Elissa whispered.

He squeezed her hands and released them. Her lashes lifted, a fringy veil drawn open to reveal the treasure of her gaze. If only he could memorize the placement of every lucid speck of gray amongst the blue depths in her eyes, but she turned and plucked a pencil from her desk drawer.

He flashed a smile. "Let's give Pittsburgh something to chatter about tonight."

A genuine look of hope swept across her face. He'd write a lifetime of articles if that's what it took to soften Elissa Tillman. Earlier, when she'd dismissed him on the dance floor, her spine had been stiff as if forged with iron, her mannerisms impeccably controlled. During their interactions over the past week, nothing had been out of place, from her sculpted hair to the straight-seamed stockings. Nothing to find fault with. She stood, sat, walked as primly as an etiquette handbook.

But just now, he'd glimpsed emotion behind the façade, an authenticity that bolstered his heart. He couldn't determine if her behavior had been a strange case of vanity or something deeper, but whatever it was, he'd uncover it.

But first, the extra.

The next fifteen minutes flew by in organized chaos, pulsing vigor through Elissa's veins. Cole would type a paragraph, and Elissa would pull the page to edit. He'd roll in another sheet, and the process would begin again. An intriguing fluidity until Elissa read the last paragraph Cole had added to the final draft.

"It's time to meet them at their headquarters," Shelby had said.

"One shrewd business deal deserves another." These words were spoken an hour before his death. Who was Shelby meeting? Was the headquarters in the abandoned Halloway Building? If not, why had Shelby gone there? The truth behind this story has yet to be discovered.

Her gut tightened. The paper shook in her trembling hand. No. She couldn't allow this.

Cole's fanatical typing paused. "What's wrong?" His eyes searched her face, the intense study causing all her nerves to gather in her chest.

"We can't print this." She choked the words out, realizing more than her hand shook. Her entire frame shivered. Even the pencil stuffed behind her ear wobbled.

His brow wrinkled. "Of course, we can."

"No, we can't." Alarm encroached her being, making the rise and fall of her chest as visible as the rhinestones dotting her neckline. Cole knowing Shelby had a meeting scheduled that close to his time of death was a vital piece of information. What if Cole was correct in his assumptions? What if the people Shelby met had killed him? "This needs to go to the police."

"And what, have the radio bulletin spill this news instead of the *Review*?" Cole scooted back his chair and stretched out his legs like a cat walking up from a nap. So casual. The fool. "You know full well the cops turn a blind eye to Bootlegger Alley. Saying a still exploded? I bet they hardly investigated it."

"Then take it to your cousin. He's on the level."

"Sure." He returned his gaze to the typewriter. "After we print it."

She slapped the paper onto his desk, ignoring the mild sting to her palm. "Don't you see? You're putting yourself in danger. If Mr. Shelby *was* murdered, the killer is still on the loose. And if they think you might know more, they might try to …" Emotion squeezed her throat. Wrapping her arms around her middle, she willed her composure to steady. She tried hard, so very hard, but the tears collecting in her eyes exposed her pretense of insensitivity. She sucked in a quick breath and turned from him and his penetrating gaze.

A chair screeched. She flinched. No doubt he stood, a droll smirk smothering his countenance. She couldn't face him. He'd tease her. Ridicule her because she'd admitted he might be right about it being foul play. Laugh at her sorry show of emotion. Elissa took two steps toward her desk, increasing the distance between them.

Maybe she should speak. At least give the appearance of strength. She ran a hand over her gown, smoothing invisible wrinkles, and lifted her chin. "I won't concede my opinion." The words came out bossy, but even that was better than weak. "Are you careless with your life, Cole Parker?"

He cleared his throat, his warm breath caressing her neck.

Cole was closer than she'd thought. Like reach-behind-her-and-touch-him close. Why hadn't she heard his footfalls? Sliding her eyes shut, she took precious seconds to prepare for a good dose of ribbing. That was Cole's way—making light of everything.

"Elissa." He placed a hand on her shoulder, and at once she wished the strap of her gown was thicker than a spaghetti noodle.

His warm touch sent shivers down the length of her arm to her fingertips. With a gentleness she never knew he possessed, he nudged her to face him. She complied because resisting his tender prodding would only validate any suspicions he might have regarding her crumbling veneer. But one sniffle, and she was sunk.

His onyx eyes sheened with compassion, causing her own to widen.

She worked her bottom lip, willing her pulse to steady. "I don't think—"

His hand slid down her arm and grasped her fingers. He flattened her hand on his chest. "Feel that?"

His tuxedo jacket remained draped over the chair, his stark white shirt the only barrier between her palm and his skin.

"Can you feel that, Elissa?"

How could she not? His heart pounded with fervor and rapidity, making her own rival its pace. "Yes." She should withdraw her hand. This interaction was too intimate for a couple of journalists in a newsroom, but she couldn't move. His eyes begged for her to understand. What, she didn't know, but as a courtesy to an old friend—not the lover who'd jilted her, but to the friend who'd once defended her name—maybe she should try. "What about it, Cole?"

"This heart almost stopped beating four months ago. I *was* reckless with my life. It was my own doing." His gaze dipped for an excruciating second, then fastened onto hers. "When I felt myself dying, I told God if he'd revive me, not just my heart, but me—the person I want to be—then I'd surrender to Him." He tugged her hand away from his chest and cradled it within his own. "He gave me a second chance to get things right."

Why did she get the feeling she was included in this somehow? She bit the inside of her cheek, dizziness swirling her mind. What almost killed him? Was that the reason he wasn't at the *Dispatch* anymore?

The door burst open, and Elissa yanked her hand from Cole's.

Jay Lewis appeared, eyes shining like a little boy's on Christmas. "Got that article for me yet?"

Elissa's gaze darted to Cole's desk and the semi-crinkled extra.

Before she could scramble to tear the blamed paper into bits, Cole swept it up and pushed it into Jay's hand. He clapped the press foreman on the shoulder with a crooked grin and arrogant lifting of his chin. So different from the tender way he'd interacted with her only a moment ago. "I'll walk with you downstairs. You can skim over it and ask me any questions."

Elissa took a hasty step forward but stopped when Cole glanced back.

He mouthed a quiet plea. "Trust me."

Heat pulsed through her. How could he say that? Yes, something had shifted between them over the past hour, but for him to request her trust? No. Too far. She narrowed her eyes, and he chuckled.

Their tangible, heady moment vanished. Cole returned to his nonchalant ways, and she acquired a giant headache.

Alone, she busied herself with cleaning out some folders and tidying her desk. She caught her reflection in the tiny mirror beside her pencil sharpener. The smooth up-do she'd styled this afternoon now frizzed, several wisps of hair escaping the pins. Black makeup smudged the skin beneath her lashes. A sigh escaped. She'd fussed and fussed, attempting to be pristine for this evening, but failed to preserve the perfection that exhausted her both mentally and physically.

The lilies Adam had gifted captured her jealousy. With the pad of her thumb, she stroked a veined petal. "Such effortless beauty."

"I disagree." Cole stood in the doorway, his shirtsleeves pushed past his elbows, his hair mussed like he'd fought the wind rather than assisted Jay with the press. Not fair. Dishevelment increased his attractiveness when it lessened hers. He strode across the room and joined her in admiring the delicate arrangement.

"Nothing about this is effortless. It had to break before it could grow." He stood so near his arm brushed hers. "Stretch beyond the shell and wrestle with dark surroundings. Yet … it persisted"—his gaze locked with hers—"and found the light."

Her heart threatened to wilt. Could he read her struggle? See *any* improvement from five years ago? Or did he view her as she did—the gangly girl who had to concentrate when she walked because of being pigeon toed, who approached simple tasks with a prayer for precision because of incessant clumsiness?

She swallowed a groan. This hadn't been her night. Cole had witnessed her iron façade weaken to mushy clay, and her mind become as jumbled as her appearance.

"Seems to me, Spark, you can't value the beauty until you understand the journey."

She coughed out a feeble laugh. "Since when did you become a philosopher?"

With his flawed knuckle, he pushed a wayward lock of hair

behind her ear, the smile lining his face treacherously soothing. "The moment I became broken."

Elissa willed her pulse to slow. She couldn't afford to plunge deeper into this conversation. No. Things needed to remain shallow. Her heart remained safer that way.

His husky voice tiptoed across her senses. "In my opinion, I've never seen anything more beautiful." His gaze wasn't on the lily but on her.

He smiled at her blush. Not a teasing smirk, but one of appreciation. One she could gaze at for an eternity, which was precisely why she needed to leave. Head to the nearest exit.

And she did.

CHAPTER 10

To Cole's relief, Sterling had been assigned to the Shelby case. The man was as honest as they came, which would ensure a quality investigation. What it hadn't provided was a strengthening of familial relations. Cole glanced at his cousin, who sat beside him on the church pew. All morning, Sterling's responses had alternated between grunts and growls. If that hadn't been enough, he'd stolen Cole's hymnal. Thankfully, the song leader selected hymns Cole already knew.

Cole sat forward, not wanting to miss a word this preacher said. He dug in his vest pocket and retrieved his notepad and pencil, jotting down the opening text and some statements, not caring if he attracted glances. Taking notes made him a better listener. He kept his gaze on the paper as the truth poured into his soul.

After the preacher closed with prayer, Sterling's petite fiancée, Sophie, leaned forward to speak around his brooding cousin. "You're welcome to join us for lunch, Cole."

Sterling grunted, and Sophie scowled at him. "Are you going to be like this all day?"

"Just until Cole promises not to interfere with a police investigation again." He spoke to his bride-to-be, but his heavy glare was channeled on Cole.

Cole tucked his Bible under his arm. "I called you right before the newsies hit the streets." The least he could do after Elissa's distress over the extra. She didn't want Cole murdered by lunatics.

That meant something, right?

Sterling shook his head. "Not good enough. I want to be alerted first. Show some respect next time."

"You do the same." Cole could play this game. In fact, he was rather good at it. "You call yourself a policeman, but you stole my hymnal. That's gotta be breaking some sort of code."

That pulled a wily grin from the grump. "Just be careful, Cole. Don't do anything else stupid."

"Fair enough. And I'll be happy to join you two for lunch."

"It's got to be close by." Sterling favored Sophie with a smile. The rascal. He could glare the hair off a cat and then charm it to purr in his ear. "I'm conducting interrogations at Shelby's place today."

Cole mashed his lips together. His hunch about Mr. Shelby being murdered had been correct. The authorities had confirmed it this morning, claiming they'd found traces of dynamite. "That could be interesting. Can I come?"

Sterling scowled. "No."

The man was too severe for his own good. "Remember to tell Sophie about the time I used your varsity jacket to wrap fish and hide it under the stadium bleachers. The hot summer sun helped everything smell real nice."

Sophie raised a brow, curiosity shining in her emerald eyes.

"After you explain what happened to provoke that stunt." He winked at his girl. "Let's just say it involved underpants and a flagpole."

"All right, you win." Cole chuckled as he made his way out of the pew. "Now let's eat before you tell her all my secrets."

"I don't have that much time." Sterling teased from behind him.

"There you are." Elissa's father tripped on the leg of the church pew and bounded into the aisle with as much grace as a mule in a parlor. "I was hoping to catch you before you left."

Cole had chosen to sit near the front so he wouldn't be distracted when Elissa arrived. She'd already occupied his thoughts half the night and most of the morning, but here, in church, that was God's time. "Good morning, boss. How did the extra fare?"

Tillman shifted his gaze to the left. "That's what I need to talk to you about."

A knot tightened in Cole's gut. Had he been mistaken? Maybe he shouldn't have pressed about the extra, even though it had felt so right at the time.

Elissa stood by the door, chatting with the preacher's wife, resembling an angel in her ivory dress and halo of golden hair. She wouldn't forgive him if he'd lost more money for the *Review*. He slid his gaze to his cousin. "Hey, I don't think I can join you today for lunch." He jerked his head toward his boss, and Sterling nodded.

"Maybe next week." Sterling tapped Cole's upper arm with his Bible and led his fiancée out the door Elissa stood next to.

Tillman fidgeted with the brim of his hat. "Since I just cost you a meal, how about you come over to our house? Then I can talk to you and Lissie at the same time."

Cole's heart jolted at the seriousness marking Tillman's expression. How much did they end up losing by firing up the press last night?

Elissa's appetite shrank from small to non existent. The last time she and Cole were in this house together was the day he'd made the promise.

I'll come back to you, Spark. You hold my heart.

Those words. She squeezed her fork with her thumb and index finger. When he'd only been gone a few weeks, she'd mentally rehearsed them, trying to picture the certainty in his eyes and the deep resonance of his voice, but then weeks turned to months, and months turned to years. The words she'd clung to had tormented her. Not to mention the words she'd whispered in his ear the second before he stepped onto the train.

"Something wrong with your lunch, dear?" Her mother's voice burst into her pathetic thoughts. "Are you feeling okay?"

Elissa cleared her throat and hoped the face she made resembled a smile. "I'm well, Mother." To make the torture complete, Cole sat across from her at the table, throwing curious glances her way. She set her feet as far under her chair as she could. They'd bumped toes twice already, and her heart couldn't take another accidental touch.

Her father set his fork onto his plate and leaned forward, his reputation for being the first to clear his plate intact. Really, he shouldn't ingest his food so fast. Maybe that was causing the heartburn he'd complained about last week. She fingered the edges of her napkin and squelched a sigh. Most likely, the stress from his increased attempts to save the paper had caused his unease.

"Now, young man." Her father lifted his chin and used his boss tone. "About the extra."

Cole's mouth flattened into a line as he met her father's stare. His shoulders straightened as if preparing to carry the news about to be thrown on him.

Elissa's pulse kicked up. She'd asked Father before church if the extra profited them or proved to be a flop, but he wouldn't answer, just encouraged her to pay attention to the sermon. Oh, she'd tried to pay attention, but her eyes kept finding Cole. She didn't miss the reverent way he bowed his head during prayer, and she almost fell out her pew when he retrieved his press pad and scribbled notes. Cole had accompanied her to church several times while they dated, but back then, he'd seemed disinterested, apathetic.

"How'd it fare, sir?" Cole flicked a glance at her, and she quickly focused on her barely eaten lasagna.

Her father cleared his throat. "Well, I believe I have to let you out of your contract."

Elissa's heart tumbled into her gut. "Why?" As much as Cole's presence had sent her life off-kilter, she couldn't let her father be cruel to him. "He was trying to help the paper. Please, reconsider."

"Lissie." A slow smile spread across Father's face. "The extra was a success. So much so, I insist on letting Cole out of his initial agreement and paying him for it."

Cole shifted in his seat. "With all due respect, Mr. Tillman, can we talk about this privately? I would—"

"Wait." Realization hit. "Are you saying Cole hasn't been getting paid?"

Mother stood, her chair creaking with the movement. "I'll go help Greta with dessert and coffee." She disappeared from sight.

"It wasn't my idea," Father said. "When Cole called me wanting a job, I told him I couldn't pay him the salary he deserved. He persuaded me to allow him back on staff if, and only if, I withdrew his name from the payroll."

She couldn't believe it. Why had he put in the hours, work, if he hadn't earned a dime? She stared at him until he glanced over. "Cole Parker, why did you come back?"

"Mr. Tillman, we had a deal, and I expect the terms to be kept private."

Cole's boss grinned like he'd just been told the president of the United States wanted to give the *Review* an exclusive.

Elissa's demeanor shifted from confusion to something Cole couldn't identify, but he liked it. "Spark, I told you last night. I believe God gave me a second chance to get things right."

At that moment he knew she'd understood his meaning. Because it happened. She smiled ... and her nose crinkled.

A wave of triumph swept through him so hard he wanted to let out a whoop. He desired to freeze time and count the crinkles her grin chased up the bridge of her nose. Soak in her glowing complexion kissed by the sun. Maybe run his thumb along her bottom lip.

"Yes. Well." Tillman interrupted the moment, but Cole allowed himself a little greediness and let his gaze linger until his boss said,

"As for the second reason I asked you to come here …"

The edge in his tone warned Cole. He'd heard it many times before—the first time he took Elissa on an official date, the summer evening when he'd kept her out past her curfew, and the day he'd left for Columbia. His throat went dry. He grabbed his water and took a sip. The swell of conquest he'd experienced a moment ago deflated. But he needed to know. "What's that, sir?"

Elissa set her fork down. She'd hardly eaten anything. Mostly shoved the lasagna around her plate.

"I've been thinking." Tillman plucked his napkin from his lap and tossed it beside his plate. "I haven't been fair to my daughter."

His breath collapsed in his chest. This could be bad. Very bad. Was Tillman going to order him to leave? But why be upset now about the way Cole had treated Elissa? The man could've simply said no when Cole had called that anguished day from the hospital. Well, he wouldn't be a coward in front of Elissa. He'd take whatever Tillman wanted to dish out. Cole deserved it.

"She needs an opportunity to prove herself." The father smiled at the daughter, and Cole deduced that maybe this could turn out all right. "She's been dedicated to the paper for so long, learning every aspect of the business. I think she could run it better than I."

Elissa furrowed her brow. "Oh, Father, please. I would—"

He raised his hand. "Let me finish, Lissie." Clearing his throat, he went on. "She's a brilliant journalist, and I think she needs a shot at an article worth her talent."

Cole nodded. "I agree."

Her jaw went slack in such an unfeminine manner, it tempted Cole to lift his glass in a hearty "cheers." She caught herself and pressed her mouth shut, even patting her lips with her napkin as if to cover it up.

"But Cole, I want to be fair to you as well. Therefore, I've decided to have a friendly competition."

Cole's spirits sank at the word 'competition,' but the woman across from him straightened in her seat and glued her attention on her father.

"You both have two weeks to compose a masterpiece of an article. The Shelby case should give you plenty of good material. Both articles must be on my desk by nine sharp on the morning of the seventeenth. I'll review them and select the best one." He gave a firm nod, and Cole's heart seeped into his stomach. "And just to be fair, no names on the articles. Deal?"

"No." Elissa countered. "I can't agree to this."

Her father leaned over the table, his elbow missing the butter by an inch. "What? I thought this was what you wanted. Your work published."

"That's right. My work. Not Elliot Wentworth's." She cut a quick glance to Cole, and he gave a tight nod, accepting her confession. Something flickered in her eyes, but she snapped her attention back to her father. "If I'm to do this, I want my name on the byline."

"Agreed."

Elissa's scowl wavered, the right corner of her mouth lifting until the rest of her lips followed suit.

Cole felt like slamming his head onto the table, while Elissa all but bounced in her seat like a four-year-old being told she could play with the big kids. She sprung from her chair and pecked a kiss on her father's cheek. Then she slid her gaze to Cole. Whatever had been blossoming between them shriveled in the heat of her stare. For she now considered him her rival.

Cole pushed away from the table, the chair scraping against the oak floor. "Thank you for lunch." He pushed out the words with a quick nod. "I better be on my way. Sorry I can't stay for coffee. Please relay my apologies and thanks to Mrs. Tillman." He even impressed himself with his politeness. Quite an effort considering every nerve in his body pulled taut.

"I appreciate your changing your plans for me, Cole." Tillman stretched out his hand for his signature handshake, followed by his slap on the back. "I hope your cousin won't be cross with you for bailing on him."

He shrugged. "Sterling couldn't take much time for lunch, anyway. Has investigations over at Shelby's building."

"Is he still there?" If the eagerness in Elissa's voice wasn't a dead giveaway, the shining eyes were.

Like giving steak to a hungry Doberman, he'd just fed Elissa her first scoop without even trying. A fist tightened in his stomach. This could get dangerous. Elissa herself had said it last night. *The killer is still on the loose.* What was her father thinking? "Don't know. But what I do know is that if I don't go pay my dear mother a visit, it'll be my obituary you'll be writing."

"Please pardon the interruption." Greta stepped into the dining room. "Elissa, Mr. Kendrew is on the line."

Elissa slouched for only a second, but the brief action lifted Cole's chin. Was it possible Elissa didn't want to speak to Mr. Sweetheart? "Thanks, Greta. I'll … um … be there in a moment."

"Greta." Tillman chimed in. "Hold the dessert and coffee."

The older woman gave a polite nod and regarded Elissa with a raised brow.

Elissa stood and pushed her chair in. "Glad your extra worked out, Cole. Good luck with the competition." She stuck out her hand, a mischievous smile slanting her lips.

Cole was either smart or foolish because he matched the smirk with his own and reached for her hand, holding onto it longer than a typical handshake.

Elissa's smile wobbled, but she held her posture well, considering he caressed her pinky with his thumb. "I better go see what Adam wants." And she ducked out the door with the same speed as last night.

"Can you come with me to my study for a quick minute, Cole? It's important." Tillman. How could he have forgotten his boss's presence?

He cleared his throat. "Certainly."

Down the hall and two steps into the room, Cole spoke up. "Sir, I don't mean to challenge your judgment, but do you think this competition is wise? Elissa's more competitive than anyone I knew in New York, meaning she might end up in some dangerous situations."

These killers had detonated a dynamite bomb, forcing Shelby to an awful fate, his remains charred beyond recognition. Who was to say what else these madmen were capable of.

Tillman sighed and pulled out a file from a drawer in his desk. "See this?" He withdrew a stack of papers, dropped it on the desktop. "This is what I found in Elissa's work desk. I need to return them tomorrow before she notices. But look. There're articles. Notes. Even some interviews."

Good thing Cole only kept his Bible and office supplies in his drawers at work. He'd never known Tillman to be one to pry. "What's wrong with that, sir? She writes occasional society editorials. I figure she'd have notes and such."

"These." He pointed to the papers. "These are all about the Cartelli case. The troubling part is that most of the interviews and notes are dated prior to the trial. Meaning she was—"

"Snooping around behind your back." A sudden coldness hit his core. "If her prying was risky in the Cartelli case, it could be just as—if not more—dangerous in this murder investigation."

"Precisely." Tillman's grimace matched the seriousness in his eyes. "And no doubt she will do it again. That's why I had to take matters into my own hands. This is where you come in, my boy."

"Me? You just set her against me."

"No. This gives the perfect outlet for you to keep an eye on her."

Cole scratched his cheek. "So the contest isn't legit?"

"It's on the up-and-up as far as the articles are concerned, but if Elissa is going to tread in places of danger anyway, she needs to have someone protect her."

And her father had chosen him. Cole's chest swelled, his lungs expanding to their fullest. Tillman trusted Cole with his daughter.

"I'll keep an eye on her." Now this contest had increased in interest, giving him a bigger prize than a featured spread.

CHAPTER 11

Cole stared at the office where one of his childhood heroes had once worked. Icicles hung from the entrance like jagged fingernails, ready to rend his heart and bleed his memories. He blew out a breath, fogging the crisp air. Daniel Shelby had been a good man. Eccentric, yes, but still good. The itch to discover the identity of his killer, or killers, niggled under Cole's skin. Not because of the story he could land, but because of the man he'd honor.

He stepped onto the entryway. A lanky officer greeted him with folded arms and lifted chin. Poor execution, if the man intended the stance to be intimidating. "You need to take lessons from my cousin."

He blinked. "Pardon?"

Cole set a hand on his shoulder, and the man shirked away. "Sorry, officer. Came to see Sergeant Monroe. He's my cousin."

The man assessed him with a wary eye. "Wait here." After one more scrutinizing glare, he stalked into the building. Cole should've flashed his press badge and derived amusement from watching the officer snarl in disgust. The joys of being a newshound.

Cole pulled his hat lower against the chill. Nothing like being left out in the cold. If not for the intention of retrieving his motorcycle, he'd be at home inhaling Mom's chocolate pie. Hopefully, that rusty motorized mechanism still ran. Shelby had said he'd tinkered with it, but Cole had left the thing in sorry shape.

"Parker." Sterling's low voice held an edge sharp enough to slice the icicles overhead. "I told you not to interfere." He stepped outside, his massive build blocking the door as if Cole would endeavor to sneak past him.

"I called your captain about an hour ago. He said I was cleared to pick up my bike. It's in the garage." He flicked a glance that direction. "I think." Shelby's main office was located in the front of the building with the addition of a small workshop in the back. The garage stood off the alley behind the place.

"Yeah, it's there." Sterling's stern brow relaxed into an almost normal expression.

"Good." At least it hadn't been tossed into the rubbish pile. Maybe he could get it looking decent, make it a project to keep his head clear of nose-crinkling females. "Why are you conducting interviews here instead of across town at your quaint headquarters?"

"Captain's orders." Sterling shrugged. "You know, for a second, I assumed you were going to pester me for information like your old flame tried to earlier." His mouth twitched to one side, the equivalent of a belly laugh for any other person.

"Elissa was here?" Of course she had been. That girl would compete against her own grandma if it meant nabbing the coveted editorial real estate.

"Do you have any other old flames?" The teasing reached his eyes, and he gave Cole an easy shove.

"You know I don't. Please tell me you had the decency to invite her inside." Temps dipped below freezing this afternoon, and Cole's bones registered every drop in degree.

"Only because she had to visit the powder room. Other than that, she got no further than you—"

The door swung open, revealing a petite brunette. Her sad eyes turned to Sterling. "I—I think I'm ... is it possible to retrieve my belongings another time, Sergeant?"

"I can help if your things are too heavy for you, Miss Kerns." Ah, his cousin had better watch out, his sensitive side was showing.

She hesitated. After a quick glance toward the door, she shook her head. "Thank you, officer, but I think I should be on my way. I don't want to interrupt … anything." After a quick dip of her lashes, she hastened past. This kind of cold wasn't for women who looked like they would snap in a stiff wind.

Then it hit him.

Recognition rolled through Cole, energizing his mental processes like so many times in the past. Dread's whispers pricked his conscience. He shoved his chilled fingers into his jacket pocket and contemplated his next move.

"Cole." Sterling nudged him with his shoulder. "Didn't you hear me?"

"Huh?" He blinked. "No, what'd you say?"

"Nothing of consequence." He quirked a brow. "I'm more curious what you're about to say."

"I can't." No. He'd come to help honor, not dishonor. "I need to go." He'd return for his bike another time. Propping up his coat collar, he readied for the walk home. "See you later, Sterling."

Iron fingers clamped his shoulder. "You're withholding information, I can see it. Whatever it is you're hiding better not be glowing on tomorrow's news."

"Trust me. It won't." Because he'd never write it. But with this competition, he had to come up with something. He'd have to discover a different angle.

"Let's make a truce." Sterling's smile duplicated the one when he'd outplayed Cole in marbles when he was eleven, promising a truce *after* one last game. Cole had lost his best shooter in the match.

"Your truces never work out for me."

Sterling actually laughed, probably remembering the same incident. "No, this one will benefit us both. You tell me what made you cringe a moment ago, and yeah, I saw that. Then I'll return the favor and answer any questions about the case."

"That's mighty generous, cousin." But then. "What's the

catch?"

"All I ask is for you to treat classified information like it is, classified. Meaning don't print anything without my approval. This little agreement is also an insurance factor for me, knowing you won't be issuing any more extras behind my back."

A risky bargain. He scratched at his chin's late-day stubble. Was gaining access to the closed vaults of this case worth being restricted on what he could print? The information he'd receive from Sterling would help keep Elissa safe. Her welfare trumped all. "Deal."

"Good. Now out with it."

"Shelby had a relationship with that woman. What'd you say her name was? Miss Kerns?" Cole pointed to the street where she'd retreated.

Sterling blew out a breath. "You sure? What makes you certain?"

"Perfume."

"Explain." Sterling made a circular gesture with his hand.

"When I spoke to Mr. Shelby the other day, he reached out to shake my hand. His handkerchief spilled onto the ground. It was then it struck me. Perfume." Perfume he'd only recognized because Elissa wore the same fragrance. "And then that woman walked past, and the same wildflowers hit like a sock to the nose. The same."

"I need more evidence. You know how many women in this city wear that identical perfume or a variation of it? And his reeking of her perfume doesn't mean he'd had a full-blown affair." Sterling stood silent for a handful of seconds. "But I can't dismiss it, either. This morning, Miss Kerns was impatient to attain clearance to retrieve her belongings. Arrived seconds before you, but when she saw Mrs. Shelby, she skittered like a scared kitten. You saw how she raced out of here."

"Plus, Shelby talked sadly about his marriage in that short conversation. I can't remember his exact words, but it made an impression on me." Cole rolled his shoulders twice against the chill. "You know, this entire case seems off."

"How so?"

Cole shook his head. "I can't pinpoint it. But when I first heard the news about Shelby, something bothered me. I'll keep thinking on it." He had to. That silly contest required it. "Question is, what are you going to do?"

Sterling's brow lowered as he set a hand on the door handle. "Let's have us a little chat with Mrs. Shelby."

"I thought you were questioning Mrs. Shelby." Cole stood a healthy distance from the open office door and whispered to his cousin. "Who's the tall man with the gaudy tie?" Poor guy's swing necktie, with its bright orange leaves appearing more like flames, begged for someone to throw a bucket of water on it.

"That's Mr. MacAfferty. He's her lawyer." Sterling nodded toward the gentleman with a beaked nose and shoulders like a linebacker seated next to the prim Mrs. Anna Shelby.

"I didn't know she was a suspect."

"Everyone's a suspect."

Sterling had a habit of repeating lines from dime novels. As much as Cole could tease him, now wasn't the time.

"I think MacAfferty came to show support. He's a longtime family friend."

"Ah."

"Let's see what I can dig up. Remember, you're a fly on the wall."

"Such a way with words, cousin."

Sterling walked into the room, his expression shifting from sly smirk to taut and serious. Cole kept to the side of the room like a good little journalist but made sure he selected a spot where he could hear everything without straining. Thankfully, Mrs. Shelby had only met him once or twice in his youth, so the likelihood of her becoming unhinged at the sight of a newspaperman was slim.

Cole had always been amazed at the size of Shelby's office.

While most would prefer a closed, private space, Shelby had been the opposite, choosing a large, open area that almost rivaled the newsroom in size.

He spotted Shelby's desk and on it, Cole's science test. Shelby had kept his humble science exam all these years. A stitch of sadness panged his heart. Cole hadn't even aced the test, yet Shelby had been proud enough to bust a vest button. The man had given Cole a key to come and go, tutored him every day after Cole completed his paper route, and always had a stocked supply of peppermints, Cole's favorite. Yes, that test would go home with him today along with his bike.

Sterling pulled a chair across the floor, its legs skidding against the wood. He joined the MacAfferty fellow and Mrs. Shelby at a small table at the far side of the room—the area Shelby would jokingly call his employee lounge because it boasted a small sink and ice box. "I know this is a difficult time for you." He flipped a notepad open. "But I need you to answer a few questions. Where were you Friday evening?"

She dabbed her eyes with her handkerchief, then lowered her hand. "Home." Her voice came out willowy. "I was home all evening."

Sterling scribbled on his notepad and then looked up. "Did you have any visitors? Any phone calls? Someone who could vouch for you being where you say you were?"

Pointy shoulders stiffened. "No. Not a one. The maid was off, and I was all by myself." She darted a glance to MacAfferty, who nodded with a glum smile.

Again, Sterling jotted something down. Wonder if he'd let Cole look at his notes? Sterling leaned forward in his chair, elbows leaning in his knees. "Have you met Matthew Young?"

Cole lowered his brow. Why would he mention Shelby's lab assistant?

"No. I mean, I've seen him from a distance, but Dan never made a habit of inviting him or any *other* employee to our house."

The last phrase had an icy spin to it. "What does Mr. Young have to do with anything? We need to find the person who killed Dan." She bit her bottom lip, eyes filling with fresh tears.

"No one has seen Mr. Young since yesterday afternoon. He may have skipped town."

Cole itched to yank out his pad and scrawl this info down. Shelby's lab assistant nowhere to be found the day of the murder? He leaned against the wall and crossed his arms.

Sterling relaxed in his chair. "What about Jeffrey?"

Mrs. Shelby sucked in a quick breath. "What do you mean?"

"We haven't been able to contact your son." Sterling lowered his pencil, peering at the older woman. "He hasn't been at his house in Point Breeze. Do you know where he is?"

She shook her head. "I spoke with him on the phone late last evening. He was having a difficult time. If it hadn't been for ..." Her lips pinched tight.

"For what?" Sterling prodded.

"Nothing. It's nothing. Dan and Jeffrey exchanged a few words that day."

"Exchanged? As in, they fought?"

She gave a small nod. "But they always have. Both had different views on life."

Interesting. The lab assistant and Jeffrey were missing. And Jeffrey had a row with his father the day of his death?

Sterling tapped his pencil against his notepad. "Okay, Mrs. Shelby, let's discuss the Halloway Building. That place has been vacant for years, and yet your husband went there. Do you know why?"

She shook her head. "I have no idea."

"There was evidence of old stills and other moonshining equipment in there. Was he involved with the production of alcohol in any way?"

"No." Her tone was strangely adamant compared to her previously frail responses. "Dan never drank."

Sterling gave a tight nod. "This last question is a delicate one."

She dipped her chin in compliance.

"Was Mr. Shelby unfaithful to you?"

"Of course not!" She raised her hands, thrashing the stale air, her handkerchief waving a blur of white. "How dare you say such a thing?" Her red-rimmed eyes narrowed.

MacAfferty slid an arm around her but directed his glower at Sterling. "Sergeant, was that necessary? The woman just lost her husband."

Sterling didn't blink. He held the man's stare and tightened his jaw. "It was. I have to know if he had an affair, namely with Miss Kerns."

The handkerchief fell.

Silence crept over the room like the afternoon's chill.

"Remember, Mrs. Shelby." Sterling was the first to speak. "You may be asked this in court. It's best you answer honestly now and not perjure yourself later."

MacAfferty leapt to his feet. "Listen, I won't let you intimidate her. Bullying her to confess something that wasn't—"

"It's okay, Paul." She lightly tugged on his hand, her eyes sad. "We can't cover this up."

MacAfferty blew out a noisy breath Sterling didn't pay any regard to and sat back down with a growl.

Cole pushed off the wall, remaining silent but taking in everything. Everything from the way MacAfferty was protective over Mrs. Shelby to the way she darted glances with several blinks at the man as if she were speaking in code. No doubt Sterling observed it.

Finally, Mrs. Shelby shifted her attention to his cousin. "He was in love with Miss Kerns. They were to be married after the divorce finalized."

Cole's heart smacked into his heels.

To Sterling's credit, his demeanor remained calm, almost expressionless. "When did you become aware of all this?"

"A few months after Miss Kerns was hired, Dan started working longer hours. He'd been withdrawn too. Never mean, but almost as if his thoughts were elsewhere." She fidgeted with the beading on her sleeve. "He's never been one to show affection or say 'I love you,' but he'd do little things, such as work on crosswords with me while we listened to records. Dan always loved music."

Cole felt sorry for her. She probably didn't know she rambled on, but maybe she needed to release the agony her heart held captive.

"At first, I only had hints about the infidelity. Like the perfume. He'd come home nearly doused in it. A woman's fragrance doesn't get on a man unless she's been cozying up to him, but he wouldn't be open with me. Paul confirmed my suspicion."

With a heavy nod, the lawyer slunk in his seat.

Sterling's brows creased. "Go ahead. Mr. MacAfferty, please relay your part in this."

"I'm Dan's best friend. He'd come to me a couple weeks ago inquiring about divorce settlements, legal proceedings, and everything involved." MacAfferty gave a somber smile, his stare distant, unfocused. "I asked him point blank what was going on. He confided in me that he was in love with his secretary and wanted to marry her. He asked me to draw up divorce papers." The man pulled a hand across his face, and Mrs. Shelby drew in a ragged breath. "I was torn. I felt Anna should be told, but not only was I Dan's best friend, I was also his lawyer, and there are confidentiality laws. But—"

"It wasn't your fault for telling me." Mrs. Shelby brushed a tear from her face and shifted in her chair toward MacAfferty. "I needed to hear what Dan wasn't man enough to tell me." Her shuttered breathing made her collar quiver. "Paul advised me not to fight it. That'd I'd get a bigger settlement if I gave him a quick divorce. He was dead before I ever received any papers."

Sterling's gaze toggled between Mrs. Shelby and MacAfferty. "How come Miss Kerns never mentioned any of this when I spoke to her?"

Mrs. Shelby's gaze lowered. "I pleaded with her not to tell. She swore to me she'd let his memory be honorable." Her head snapped up almost wildly. "The woman had the audacity to tell me she loved Dan enough to keep his name from being smeared in the mud."

MacAfferty reached over and covered her hand with his.

"He stabbed me in the back, Paul." She pulled her hand away and hugged herself, swaying as if the motion comforted her. Though the rage in her eyes revealed it hadn't. "Thirty-five years of marriage meant nothing."

"That will be all for now, Mrs. Shelby." Sterling's voice was authoritative yet calm. "If I think of any other questions, I'll phone you. If that'd be permissible?"

She gave a gentle nod, slowly rose from her seat, and turned to MacAfferty. The man retrieved her coat from the back of the chair and helped her into it. He held out his arm, but she shook her head. "I need to use the powder room first. I must look horrid."

MacAfferty stepped back and allowed her past him. When the door clicked shut, MacAfferty faced Sterling. "Sergeant, I need to say one more thing."

Sterling exchanged a look with Cole and then stepped closer to the lawyer. "Go ahead."

"Anna never mentioned the will. But I think it may be important."

"What about it?" Sterling raised a brow.

"Dan told Anna the day before his death that he was going to revise it." MacAfferty sighed.

"Was he changing the will to allow Miss Kerns a share?"

The lawyer nodded. "Miss Kerns was to be the sole beneficiary of the entire estate."

"What's strange is, Mr. Shelby told her about changing his will but *not* about the affair." Sterling scratched the back of his neck. "I would think the two go hand-in-hand. Wouldn't the changes to the will prompt Mrs. Shelby to ask questions about an affair?"

MacAfferty shrugged. "He told her he was revising it but didn't disclose what the changes were." He flicked his gaze to the ceiling and huffed. "He wanted me to do all that. Just like in business, I'm the middle man."

"What time are you available, counselor? I'd like to see this will."

His chin dipped, revealing a thinning hairline. "It's missing."

CHAPTER 12

Cole knocked on the Tillman front door for the second time that day. He hadn't a reason other than to see Elissa. The bizarre and disturbing time at Shelby's workplace had his mind lingering in a state of bewilderment. With no appetite for dinner, he'd spent time in his room praying. As much as that had helped calm his restlessness, Cole Couldn't shake the need to confer his theories with Elissa, to gain her perspective on the situation. She might balk, might cling to her view of him being the competition, but he had to try. Because Elissa could hold her own in investigative journalism like no one else he'd ever known.

The lock clicked, and the door yawned open. Mrs. Tillman appeared fresh and elegant as if at any moment she might be drawn away to town.

"Evening, Mrs. Tillman." He removed his hat. "I was hoping to speak to Elissa if she's available."

Hesitancy shone in her eyes, then traveled to her mouth, lips squishing together.

Had she changed her mind about welcoming him? He fidgeted with the hat's brim.

She blinked as if remembering her manners. "No, Cole. She's not here."

"I see."

"Strangest thing. She dashed past me in her cleaning attire, so I assumed she was going to your mother's."

"That's where I came from, ma'am. She wasn't there. Nor did I pass her on the way." He shoved a hand in his coat pocket. "Does she volunteer anywhere else?"

"No." She tapped the doorknob. "I caught her mumbling about you and Mrs. Henry." Her brow furrowed and head tilted. "Wasn't she your tenth-grade teacher?"

Understanding struck him like a bundle of wet newspapers. She wouldn't. Not sophisticated Elissa.

"Can you make sense of it?"

"Yes. Unfortunately, I can."

Her eyes widened. "She's not in trouble, is she?"

"Of course not." Not if he could find her first. "She'll be fine, Mrs. Tillman. No need to worry. I'll bring her home."

A soft chuckle poured from the gentlewoman. "If I didn't know any better, I'd suspect you two were up to something. Like way back then."

"Those were good times, ma'am." The best. With his favorite girl … before he let the world taint him.

He offered one more kind salutation and then jogged down the walkway to the street. He threw his leg over his Triumph and kick-started the shiny machine. Shelby had done more than tinker. Cole had left behind a rusty, sputtering scrambler, and today he'd been met with a restored-to-almost-new motorcycle. Sad he'd never get the chance to thank Shelby. He squelched a sigh and revved the engine. Regret had long been his sparring partner, but he hadn't the time to enter the ring now. No, he needed to catch Elissa before she wound up in jail.

The sting in Elissa's right pointer finger didn't compare to the pang of disappointment swelling in her gut. Earlier, she'd unlocked the powder room window in Shelby's office building—the only room she'd been able to gain access to, due to Cole's strict cousin—but she hadn't devised a different plan when she'd found said window frozen shut. The vigorous jostling of paint-chipped wood accomplished nothing but slicing her finger with a fresh splinter.

Careful to keep her balance on the piled wooden boxes, she flicked a glance at the alley behind her. All quiet. The darkness gained mastery over the fleeting daylight. Soon her visibility would be nothing.

She sighed.

Shouldn't she be thrilled about this contest? Happy about finally securing the opportunity? Yet following Father's announcement today, she couldn't get past wondering *why*. After years of her pleading, why now? Considering the *Review's* current financial state, she'd think Father would take no chances. The showcase of her name could anger current and potential advertisers. Could she risk damaging the *Review* for ambition's sake? Her short-term dream could abolish her long-term one.

What if Father thought he was playing it safe? Not expecting her to win against Cole? Her confidence wavered a degree. Uncertainty had a steely grip, but she wouldn't side with it today.

She glared at the stubborn window.

One more time.

Forget the numbing chill. And her frozen extremities. She shook her arms, a futile attempt to get the blood circulating, and planted both hands on the sill. "You're going to move this time. You got it?"

"Employing my old techniques?"

"Wha—" She whipped her head in the direction of the familiar voice and lost her footing on the stack of wooden boxes. Limbs flailing, she fell back and landed in Cole's arms for the second time in two days.

Shadows danced across his features, but the amusement in his eyes shone brighter than noonday.

He tipped his head toward the blasted window. "Wouldn't budge, huh?"

And neither could her speech. Their breathy vapors tangled in the air, alerting her to the closeness of his face. The fragrance of vetiver mingling with aftershave swirled her senses. The length of her arm pressed against his expansive chest, and the awareness of his sculpted biceps beneath her shoulder blade ignited a surge of warmth. For Pete's sake, even her earlobes burned. She avoided his stare and fused her gaze on the dip in his chin. Which probably wasn't the best course of action, considering his freshly shaved cleft.

Oh, brother. The jolt must've rattled her brain. Harboring attraction to Cole was about as safe as guzzling cyanide.

His smirk deepened to a scowl. "You're not hurt, are you?"

"You frightened me." Her words sounded a bit rusty, but she could blame the cold and not the headiness coursing through her. "And could you kindly put me down?" His palm stretched across her back, no doubt taking in the heavy pounding of her heart.

His mouth tipped up in a delicious—no, not delicious, irksome—smile. "That's two now, Spark. On the third one, I'm going to start charging. Rescuing beautiful women could be a nice profession change for me."

Her brain hiccupped over the word *beautiful*, and she barely recollected being set onto her feet. "I—I don't need your rescues. Thank you very much." She rigorously brushed her clothes as if she'd fallen in the dirt instead of the safety of his arms.

He perused her attire, gaze snagging on her frayed trousers.

Once again, her attire demonstrated a failure of propriety, but what else could she have done? Climbing through a window had required this particular clothing. She met his suave smile with a hardened glare. "And if you'd like to switch professions, you have my blessing." She peered again at her trousers to be sure the buttons were closed, but thankfully, her overcoat extended past her waist, securing her modesty.

"I can always count on you for encouragement. And—" He tapped her lowered nose.

She snapped her gaze from her drab clothes to his dazzling eyes.

"Unlocking windows? I'm not sure I like you using my old break-in tricks to commit felonies."

She crossed her arms and raised her chin. "You broke into the school to get back your baseball glove after Mrs. Henry confiscated it." If she hadn't witnessed Cole unlock the window after everyone had left algebra, she'd never have had the idea. That day seemed like yesterday and a million years ago simultaneously.

"I was a juvenile, you're an adult. An adorable adult, but still an adult."

Her mouth slackened, but she caught it before it proved embarrassing. She didn't know how many more compliments her composure could stand. Was he being serious? More than likely, he was mocking her. "How'd you know I was here?" She stooped to collect her purse she'd deposited earlier on the ground.

"I paid you a visit, and your mom said she overheard you talking about me and Mrs. Henry." His lifted brows disappeared under his hat. "Sterling said you came here this afternoon. I put two and two together."

She nodded, wisps of hair tickling her right ear. A mess. She must be an atrocious sight—from her faded cleaning clothes to the hairpin now coming loose.

"Ah, she's back." Cole put his hands on her shoulders.

"Who?" She mouthed because her vocal cords had frozen under his intense stare.

"My Spark." He tugged that troublesome hairpin, and it fell to the concrete with a ping. His fingertips trailed down the tender spot behind her ear, sloping her jaw, stopping beneath her chin.

Despite the biting air, a warmth spread through her and somehow found its way to the drafty corners of her heart. Was she developing feelings for him … or had they never left? Terror hooked her by the spine. Yesterday, she'd run when dormant feelings had surfaced, but today she'd be brave. "I can never be your Spark again." She'd stripped any bitterness from her tone and left only raw truth. "I can't return to that girl." Because *that* girl had been awkwardly flawed and too easily wounded. She swallowed. Too easily left behind.

He nodded, a frown appearing for only a second, and then he withdrew his touch.

Relief and disappointment battled for prominence, intensifying her shiver.

"I need to get you sheltered from this cold." The protective edge in his deep voice did funny things to her already flipping stomach.

Be strong, Lis. "You can go home, but I'm going inside." She needed this scoop more than he did.

"That's still breaking and entering. Still illegal." He tipped his head to the side, the waning light giving his perfect cleft ample exposure. "Besides, I was in there earlier. I didn't see anything of great importance."

"Your cousin let you peruse the place?" She stiffened, thinning her gaze on the cheater. "This whole competition is biased. I'm not going to beat you if you're getting exclusive information."

His crooked smiled serrated her nerves.

"You don't think I can win against you, Mr. Parker? I may not be a front-page journalist, but I have just as much *gumption* as you."

He dipped to her height, his breath feathering her neck. "I know that better than anyone, Miss Tillman," he whispered and then straightened.

Would he stop doing that? Her thoughts scattered more than the wind-driven snowflakes.

His gaze scanned the alley before settling on her. "How come the majority of our conversations are out of doors? Come on, Spark. Let's go inside. At least we won't draw attention in there." He jangled a key.

"How did you ... did Sterling give you that?"

He tugged her elbow, leading her around the building. "You kiddin' me? Sterling wouldn't do such a treacherous thing. No, Mr.

Shelby gave me a key back when he tutored me."

She huffed. "It won't work now. Probably been changed several times since then."

Cole adjusted his hat and winked. "But this isn't for the front door. It's for the secret one."

Despite her untamed pulse, she kept her facial expression nonchalant and followed Cole to the intriguing secret door. "All I see is a bush."

"The entrance is behind it. Hug the wall. So the twigs won't rip your clothes." Cole's tone revealed he'd had plenty of experience. He smoothed the way, snapping branches, batting cobwebs.

Her Oxfords sunk into the soil with each step. A twig hooked a lock of her hair, and she worked it loose. She groaned.

By the time she reached his side, the door was unlocked and cracked open. She moved to slip past him, but he wrapped his fingers on her shoulder.

His pensive eyes reminded her of his cop cousin, but the crinkles at the edges spoke all of Cole. "Any information I have is yours. If you're curious about what I have so far, here." His hand remained on her shoulder while the other retrieved his notepad. "It's yours."

As if she couldn't see past this. "You're only doing this so I'll give you anything I find."

He scowled. "Did I ask that of you?"

"No. But it's either that or …" She matched his scowl with one of her own. "You have the same look on your face."

"What look?" He sighed and dropped his notebook back into his pocket.

"Badminton." She shoved her chin into the air. "At Kennywood. You let me win because you believed it wasn't a fair contest. Because a man could always outmaneuver a woman. Well, not in this competition."

"Man alive, Elissa." He yanked off his hat and raked a hand through his hair. "Badminton had nothing to do with your gender. I let you win because you were an awful loser. I couldn't have you angry at me. You were my dance partner that evening. Remember?"

A wave of warmth slid up her neck. Those dances. One in particular when he'd kissed her at the end. Had Cole recalled that too? Because he cleared his throat and focused on the branches behind her head. Shoving all memories aside, the truth became evident. "So I'm right. You think I'm going to lose and then I'll be *cross*."

"Woman." He snagged her wrist and, despite his tone, gently tugged her into the Shelby building. "I can't win with you."

"For the first time, I agree with you."

While keeping steady eye contact, Cole reached past her, brushing her side, and pulled the door tight behind them. Darkness shrouded her.

"I'm hoping you packed a flashlight." His voice was more distant, revealing he'd angled away. "Since this little escapade was all your idea."

"Of course I brought a light." She fished around her bag, locating the tubular Eveready. She clicked it on. "I came prepared."

"Right."

Elissa angled the light toward her face in hopes he'd catch her eye roll. "Remember, I never asked you to come." Any hesitancy she'd possessed had dissolved the moment she had realized Cole thought her writing insufficient. She could overcome him and his journalistic prowess.

"And what exactly did you come here for?"

A breakthrough. "Something newsworthy."

Cole chuckled. But it was deeper than she remembered from years before. Like life had settled into him and pulled his fervor down a notch. He'd been quick to smile over these past days, but even that seemed different. Matured and a bit toughened. He'd told her he almost died. A mystery that had been sidelined by the Shelby case and zero alone time with Cole. Until now. Should she ask? Curiosity battled with her defenses. Delving into Cole's past could revive her deadened emotions. Compassion had been her weakness. That and the man who at the moment regarded her with a piercing stare.

"If you want something newsworthy, you should've asked." He stuck out his hand. "Give over the flashlight. You're waving it around like a madwoman. It's making me dizzy."

She surrendered the light with a sigh. His hand lingered on hers longer than necessary, but what terrified her more than the dark was the comfort of his touch.

Oh, she'd better win this contest, without losing her heart.

CHAPTER 13

For all Cole knew, the police could be staking out the Shelby building. There'd been nothing abnormal in the back alley, but who was to say they weren't in the front? While his nerves operated on high alert, Elissa hummed as if they weren't invading a dead man's office.

"Shine the light here." Elissa pointed to Shelby's desk.

"I forgot how bossy you are."

Her cheeky smile throttled the air from his chest. "Only when necessary."

It was necessary for him to peel his focus from the brilliancy of her eyes because he was seconds from wrapping his arms around her. No matter what her declaration may have been, she had been acting like herself again. Her stunning, carefree self.

Elissa opened a drawer, removing a small glass bottle. "Cayenne pepper." She scrunched her nose and returned the spice bottle. "Who would dare?"

"My aunt would pour it on her food. But only because—"

"Look. This might be something." Elissa thumbed through a journal. "It's an appointment book." Her gaze steadied on the opened page.

A wayward ringlet fell across her cheek, but she didn't tuck it back in place. She studied the book, her posture slouching like it did in random moments at the newsroom. When Elissa immersed herself into her work, her stiff refinement disappeared, but in every other situation, she'd be as pristine as a fashion plate. As if she'd concealed her genuine nature from all the universe, only being herself around the comforts of her passion—journalism. No wonder she'd clung to the paper, it'd been her security, her world. It wouldn't leave her, hurt her.

A taut band stretched across his chest.

She needed to win the blamed contest. He wouldn't steal this opportunity from her. But would she value the triumph if Cole hadn't shown effort? If she discerned any charity on Cole's part, it'd deepen her misery. Her distrust.

"Cole. Come here."

He stepped closer, and the lemon scent of her hair tousled his senses. "What'd you find?"

Unaware of his nearness, she eased back, bumping into his chest. A faint blush fanned across her cheeks then vanished. "Look at his meeting for today. I wonder what this means." She tapped the page with a manicured fingernail.

His eyes went to the scribbled words. "Today's Sunday. Why would he have an appointment on a weekend?" The initials "A. G. P." were scrawled, followed by the time, nine p.m.

"Maybe he didn't want anyone to be here. Maybe he had a secret rendezvous." Her rich tone dripped with curiosity.

"But her initials are 'A. K.'"

Her brow scrunched. "Who is *her*?"

"Shelby's secretary and mistress."

Elissa's mouth hung open, incredulity glazing her eyes. "How do you know?"

"Found out today when I came to pick up my Triumph."

"Does Mrs. Shelby know? I mean, I would be … wait. Your motorcycle? It still works?"

Ah, a hint of excitement replaced her disbelief, and hope surged through him. "Yes, it works. In fact, Shelby pretty much replaced all the old parts with new ones. It's ready for my favorite blonde. I can give you a lift home. Not like you aren't dressed for riding."

He pointed to her trousers, a smile skimming his lips. Never had pants looked so good than on the woman two feet away. He would whistle if there weren't a risk of getting slapped in the face.

Pulling her lower lip under her teeth, she fought against a smile. She'd loved that bike as much as he. Together, they'd blazed many adventures. But nothing had compared to having Elissa's arms snug around him, depending on him for safety. If he won her precious trust again, he'd never mishandle it.

She blinked, and the mask of sophistication took hold. "Well, I'm still shocked Mr. Shelby would be unfaithful. What will the community say when they read this tomorrow?"

"Whoa there." Cole took the appointment book with his free hand and set it back on the desk. "We're not printing that. At least not until I get clearance, and even then, I'm still not sure."

"What do you mean, 'clearance'? Have you talked with Father?"

"No. Sterling. He asked me not to publish anything of that nature for now."

Disapproval splashed in her eyes, waving ripples on her forehead.

"I know it's a great scoop. The gossip-hungry city-folk will feed on it like vultures, but unless it pertains to the case, I don't see how tarnishing his reputation will help anything." Once a reputation had been soiled, the cleansing of it proved impossible. Thankfully, the *New York Dispatch* had been discreet with Cole's termination, but if this information about Shelby was leaked, the dead man would be forever associated with scandal, and with no chance to redeem himself.

Skepticism threaded Elissa's movements, from the way she tipped her head to the side, to her narrowed eyes. "How did you survive in New York? I'd say the cutthroat journalists there wouldn't bat an eye to spread vulgar details."

"No, they wouldn't. But believe it or not, I have a heart." He tapped his chest and drew Elissa's stare. Was she thinking of yesterday when he'd pulled her hand over his heart? Or a time from earlier days when she'd rest her cheek on his chest in an embrace? If only he had the freedom of pulling her into his arms now. He tightened his grip on the flashlight and pushed the thought aside. They needed out of this place. Not only was being alone with her far too tempting, the danger of being caught inflated with each passing moment. "I know I still have to write a story for tomorrow's spread, but I think I'll do a memorial editorial. Maybe call a few of his charities and build his character up before, well ... you know." Hadn't Shelby donated to Dr. Sheffield's charity, funding the new medical center? Cole would check on that first thing in the morning.

"But shouldn't he be exposed? Infidelity is beyond wrong. His poor wife, how she must be hurting."

"She is." Mrs. Shelby's pain-pinched expression had tormented him all day. She'd lost the man she'd loved in several ways, and there was no quick remedy for that kind of anguish. "She needs our prayers."

"But why protect the guilty?" The adamancy in Elissa's tone reflected the fervor in her eyes. "Why shield his integrity when he had no regard for anyone but himself?"

The implication of her words penetrated his confidence. Did she group Cole in the same pile as Shelby? Someone with no scrap of decency. Cole hadn't lost the woman he loved to another man. No, he'd been dead to Elissa the moment he'd wronged her. Labeled unforgiveable. "There's something to be said for mercy."

Her eyes widened at the last word.

"Besides, Mrs. Shelby wishes for the indiscretion to remain hushed. I'm sure the news will get out somehow, but it won't be from me." Everything in him stood against the sin of adultery, but would exposing Shelby benefit anyone? Wouldn't it create more grief? Maybe Cole wasn't the best authority on this matter. "Don't you think it'd be hypocritical of me to point the finger at someone else when I've made major mistakes as well? Ruined opportunities. Hurt those I love."

Her gaze lowered to the floor.

"Now, let's get you home."

"What?" Her chin whipped up. "I still haven't found anything useful for—"

"If I have to pick you up and carry you, I will." He tried to give her a no-nonsense look, but she crinkled her nose at him. Not a nice crinkle.

"Oh no you won't." She reached over and snatched the flashlight from his hand. "Not if you can't see me." With a quiet snicker, she clicked it off.

The windows were at the front of the building, so where they stood, no moonlight flooded in. She was being playful, and it lightened the tension in his shoulders. He heard a shuffle of feet and reached, briefly touching her hand. "I better not trip and tear this place up. Sterling would have my neck."

"Then I insist you do."

Cole's smile widened. "Ah, I know where you are now." In front of him, and to the left. He soft-footed forward.

The light smack of her soles signified her retreat, but he caught her by the waist. Her soft laughter riddled the air, and he eased her close. A sharp intake of air replaced her merriment, but she didn't jerk from his touch, only leaned closer.

Mercy.

With her warm body against his, the rapid rise and fall of her chest triggered a longing for the only woman he'd ever held in his arms.

"Cole?" She said his name on a sigh.

He slid his eyes shut, inhaling the citrus scent from her hair. "Hmm?"

A doorknob rattled.

She stiffened in his embrace. "Who's that?"

"Not sure." He kept his tone low. "We need to get out of here."

It rattled again, this time with muffled masculine voices.

"Don't turn the flashlight on." He grabbed her hand. "Stay

with me." His lips brushed her ear, and he hardened himself against the shiver quaking her frame. He needed to stay agile, alert. Guiding her to the closet, he prayed it wasn't locked. It opened with a soft click, the hinges whispering in the dark. Elissa needed no prompting, for she all but threw herself into the narrow space. He followed her inside, and with a steady hand, closed the door. Perhaps it was Sterling or other policemen making rounds, but Cole couldn't chance—no, wouldn't chance—Elissa's life.

Elissa struggled to remain silent while an umbrella cane stabbed her side. Whatever hung behind her—a raincoat maybe—made a swooshing sound if she moved. Cole stood in front of her, a shield between her and whoever was on the other side. She placed her palms on his back, steadying herself. His heavy breathing pulsed against her fingertips. If she'd known earlier she'd be hiding with him in a coat closet the size of a matchbox, she would've stayed home. Safe.

A stripe of pale gold shone beneath the door. Whoever it was had turned on the lights.

"It's here somewhere." A gravelly foreign voice became louder with each word.

Was he standing right in front of the door? Was this man Shelby's killer? Would these people set fire to this place too? She sucked in a quick breath, and Cole shifted.

"Search everywhere, but no desk. Boss searched there already." That voice again. But what accent was it? Russian? German? "Old screwball hid it somewhere tricky."

Someone grunted in response.

She tried to count the number of men by the heavy footsteps. Two? Three? A whole army could be out there for all the noise they made. Cabinets opened. File drawers slammed. Papers rustled. What would happen when their search led them to the closet? *Oh Lord, help us.*

"We're taking too much time." A new voice sounded. "I don't want to be here if the cops swing by."

"I need to look behind cabinet. Help me move then search closet."

Alarm trembled through her. What could they do?

Cole angled toward her and grabbed the umbrella cane. "We have to make a break for it," he whispered. "I'll distract them, and you run. Go through the door we entered. Can you find it?"

She trembled. "I'm not leaving you."

His hand slid up her arm to her shoulder and finally cupped her face. "You must."

And with that, he burst open the door.

With nothing but a lousy umbrella for a weapon, Cole lunged from the closet ready to swing at anything within range.

Two men with their backs bent forward as they held onto a pine cabinet gaped at him. The cabinet landed with a thud, and they both bounded toward Cole. He expected a couple of muscle-clad men like Sterling, but they were more like Uncle Wooly and Cousin Clarence. One chubby. One wiry.

"Who are you?" The stout man with an accent as thick as his neck shouted his demand.

Cole crossed the room, turning the men's backs on the closet, giving Elissa more space for her getaway.

Chubby grabbed Cole's shoulder, and Wiry threw a punch. Cole jerked his head, missing the fist, and elbowed Chubby in the gut. He doubled over, blocking Wiry from taking another blow at Cole's face. In his peripheral vision, he caught a glimpse of Elissa, crawling on her hands and knees.

Cole swung the umbrella, diverting attention from her, but he smacked it on the desk, breaking the handle in two.

Super.

Both men stood yards away, and Wiry held a knife.

"Now." Knife-wielder's lips twitched in a wicked smirk. "We're going to try this again, and this time you'll answer. What's your name?"

Cole backpedaled until he hit the wall. On one side was the desk. Opposite that was the cabinet the two clowns had abandoned. His blood pulsed in his skull. They wouldn't take him down without a fight. He clenched his hands and primed to attack.

"Drop your knife." Elissa popped up from behind the desk pointing a ... oh, she wouldn't. "Or I'm going to start target practice."

Cole would have bent over laughing if the situation weren't so severe. Both men looked at each other with puzzled expressions.

Chubby took a step toward her. "Now little miss, put that gun down."

"No." Her thumb pulled back the hammer with a finesse that made Cole cringe.

Cole stared at her, trying to communicate with his eyes what his mouth couldn't say. *Don't pull the trigger, Spark.*

The knife clattered to the planked floor.

"Okay, boys." Cole kicked the knife toward Elissa and rounded the desk to her. "You have exactly ten seconds to scamper out of here before I call the authorities."

Elissa's tiny gasp revealed her surprise, but she didn't know the danger hadn't subsided. The two men didn't waste time. They sprinted out. Cole shut and locked the door behind them and returned to a perplexed Elissa.

Her lifted brows plunged, and her mouth frowned. "Why'd you let them go? They could be Shelby's killers."

"Indeed. They could." His gaze traveled over her, checking for signs of injury. She shivered, but there were no marks of any kind. Another shiver, but this time he wrapped an arm around her. "Spark, you saved the day." He forced his tone to sound light, but his heartbeat would probably remain spiked clear into the next decade.

She was either too shocked to realize his arm circled her waist, or she didn't mind. He prayed it was the latter.

"But you let them go." She stared at the door out of which they'd fled.

"I had to."

She stepped out from under his touch. "Why?"

"Tell me, gorgeous, where'd you get this … pistol?" He pointed to the desktop where she'd placed it. "And while you're gabbing, would you please tell me why you ignored my instructions to leave?" His wry smile slid into a frown. "Really, Elissa, you could have been hurt."

Her lashes lowered. "I said I couldn't leave you."

Man, if only he could kiss her until her perfectly placed lipstick disappeared. He held out his hand, and to his delight, she took it. "You found this gun in Shelby's desk, didn't you?"

She smiled. "I was looking for anything useful. At first, I would've settled for a paperweight I could launch, but I landed a gold mine instead."

"Mmm-hmm. Watch. It'll explain why I had to let those bozos go." He picked up her weapon of choice and pointed it at the filing cabinet.

Elissa shrieked, "Cole, what are you—"

He pulled the trigger and smiled when a small flame flickered out the barrel.

Elissa slapped a hand over her heart, eyes wild. "You mean, I held up those two men with a cigarette lighter?"

"Sure did. One of Shelby's creations he used to let me fiddle with."

"I didn't—" The words dissolved into laughter. Her shoulders shook, and the lock of hair he'd loosened earlier danced along.

The melody of her merriment absorbed into Cole's soul. Her eyes shone brighter than the blue flame from the lighter, and it was just as hot. Hotter.

He moved closer. Drawn by an invisible pull.

The laughter faded, but a grin stretched across her face. Beautiful.

Cole spoke first, unable to shift his gaze from her. "I've missed that."

"So have I." She didn't draw back at his nearness, but inched closer, angling her face toward him.

If he dipped his chin four, maybe five inches, his lips could claim hers. Should he? Would this be considered impulsive, even though he'd been longing for this moment since the day he'd recognized his mistake? Before any more contemplation, she lifted on her toes and kissed him.

CHAPTER 14

Her first thought? That she shouldn't be doing this. Her second? That he was still a really good kisser.

Cole wrapped his arms around her waist, drawing her close. She slid her eyes shut and slipped into the tender, remembered rhythm. The way he tilted his head to the right so she didn't have to strain on her tiptoes. The way he broadened his chest so she could lean against him when her breath turned shaky and her knees threatened to cave. All familiarities from past kisses, yet something struck her as different.

She couldn't tug the words from the sensation, but she could feel his desperation. He tightened his grip as if he never intended to let go. The pounding of his heart beat a thunderous cadence against her palms. She sighed against his lips, and the feeble attempt to regain her emotional control vanished as his fingertips trailed up her spine and threaded into her hair.

The force of attraction hadn't become stale in five years but had only intensified, with a fierceness quivering every cell. A dizziness waved through her. She shuffled her foot to regain balance and stepped on Cole's toes. She gasped and reeled back, her elbow knocking a glass frame off the desk, onto the floor.

Shattered.

Evidence of her faults ridiculed her in the image of fragmented remains across the planks.

"Elissa?" He stared at her, his husky voice reminding her of the kiss she'd started and the embarrassment flooding through her.

"I can't do this." Her voice shook. Away. She needed away from this place. From him.

Cole reached for her, but she took another step back. Her sanity depended on not letting him close. She glanced at the broken glass, picturing her heart amongst the rubble. She couldn't allow him to break it again. "I can't …"

"Sweetheart, it's okay." Cole stooped and lowered his head, his hat obscuring the view of his face. "This was mine." He brushed away specks of glass from the rim of the picture and fastened his gaze on her.

She cringed, unsure if her response was due to the truth that Cole could've cut himself or because his eyes pierced hers. And her heart.

"See?" He held up what remained of the frame. "Mr. Shelby kept my test all these years. I was going to take it home today, but when the whole ordeal with Mrs. Shelby happened, I forgot." He shrugged and then smiled. "No harm done."

Oh, there was plenty harm done. This was why she couldn't be near Cole. It'd taken years to confine the clumsy, awkward Elissa—the foolish girl whom Cole had obviously despised. She'd determined she wouldn't go back again. Cole had been the only one who'd seen her for who she really was, and he'd abandoned her for it. She hadn't been good enough. Never could be. "One week. How pathetic."

He picked some larger shards of glass off the floor and tossed them into the wastebasket. "What is?"

"I've resisted Adam's advances for years. Then I'm with you, no, not with you, but around you for one week. Not even a week, six days, and I find myself …"

Cole straightened.

She couldn't finish for the sake of drawing attention to their heated moment. "Let me say that if you intend on—why are you smiling?" Because no humor could be found in this. But then again, he had a record of taking the matters of her heart lightly.

"Why wouldn't I smile?" His grin spread infuriatingly wider. "You just told me you're not attracted to Adam, but you are to me."

She gasped. "I did not."

He chuckled. "Yes, you did. And in case you haven't noticed, I'm attracted to you." His expression turned serious, and she couldn't breathe. "Very much so."

Her mind flicked back to earlier, when he'd been more heroic than anything she'd seen on the silver screen. Jumping into the arms of danger, creating a distraction, all so she could escape. To keep her safe. The man didn't make sense. Though right now, she didn't either because she found herself wanting to draw near him again. Fixing her stare on the rubble of glass pooled between them, she could laugh, or bawl, at the significance—the major thing that separated them was brokenness. "I'm a fool."

He stepped over the mess, only a touch away. "It was an accident."

"No. It was a reminder." Proof that she couldn't open up to Cole Parker without slipping back into the girl he'd left. All those years since had been a lost endeavor. A front. She hadn't changed at all. Turning toward the door, she fought against a rising sob. "I'm ready to go home."

Cole barred his arms over his chest and met his cousin's glare. "Do you want the jail-free version or the truth?"

"There's a difference?" Sterling lifted his brows.

Cole sank onto Sterling's sofa, his hand brushing something way too frilly to be in a man's apartment. "Is this lace?" He flicked the edge of a pillow.

Sterling groaned. "Sophie insisted. Said I needed to get accustomed to living in a place that holds a feminine touch."

For a war hero who'd gunned down the enemy, Sterling

surrendered far too easily to his red-headed charmer. Cole grimaced. He'd never gotten an opportunity to be a hero of any kind. The draft board had dismissed him due to his arch-less feet, and tonight, Elissa had rejected him for a reason he'd yet to discover.

Surprise and exhilaration had collided, exploding in Cole's chest when her soft lips had met his. Five years had been far too long away from her searing touch. She'd fit perfectly in his arms. He couldn't say it was like old times. It wasn't. They'd both matured since their teenage years. Tonight's embrace hadn't been flippant or rebellious, like sneaking a kiss behind the bleachers during the last football game of his senior year. No, it'd brimmed with reciprocated attraction and depths of emotion.

"Okay, out with it." Sterling sat in the adjacent chair, holding his coffee mug. The rascal didn't offer Cole any, but what did Cole expect? He'd knocked on his cousin's door, rousing him from sleep. The man was one of those early to sleep, early to rise sort of guys.

Cole removed his hat and slapped it on his knee. "I caught Elissa breaking into the Shelby building."

Sterling spewed his coffee. "What?"

Cole sighed and handed him his handkerchief. "You're worse than a child."

Sterling's eyes narrowed, and he grabbed the cloth from Cole's hand, wiping his mouth. "Breaking and entering is a serious offense."

"Yeah. And you were her accomplice."

Sterling scoffed. "I only allowed the girl to use the powder room." He stiffened. "She unlocked the window."

"You got it. But she didn't succeed. It was frozen shut." He could still picture the frustration pouting her lips. Lips that tasted like peppermint and enticement.

"I underestimated Miss Tillman."

"I know the feeling. She was determined. So I let her in." He held up a hand. "And before you launch into a boring monologue of code violations, let me say Shelby gave me a key." Cole dug it from his pocket as proof. "And permission the last time I saw him."

Sterling shook his head. "It's still considered part of the investigation. Which is off-limits to the public."

"Then to be fair, you need to relay that information to the two knuckleheads who came in while we were there."

Sterling shot forward. "What?"

"We hid in the coat closet while two men searched Shelby's office."

"For what?" Sterling scratched his jaw, fire lighting his eyes. "Shelby didn't hold valuables at his office, but a common crook wouldn't know. But what if they were there for a purpose?"

"Like the will?" Cole leaned back and kicked out his heels.

"I did a thorough search of that place after our interrogation with Mrs. Shelby. I found nothing."

"Neither did they." Cole shrugged. "Except discovering they shouldn't trifle with a blonde aiming a loaded cigarette lighter."

"The one in Shelby's desk." Sterling cocked a brow.

"She didn't know it wasn't a real gun."

His cousin took a slow swig of his coffee, but there was no hiding the humor in his expression. "So tell me, what's it like to have a woman defend your sorry hide?"

"Feels good." His pride could stand a nice wallop. And as long as Elissa was safe, he was happy. It wasn't as if he hadn't tried to protect her. If she only knew how much he'd sacrifice to keep her safe. Problem was, she didn't. Not now. Not five years ago. She had no understanding that the reason he hadn't returned was to protect her. From him.

"How bad was the place destroyed?" Sterling lifted his pocket watch from a side table and scowled. "I need to head over there and investigate."

"The office isn't bad. Papers are scattered, and furniture's been moved." Cole had cleaned up the glass and tucked the broken frame and his test in the small storage compartment on his bike along with … "The knife. One of the men had a penknife. It's in the Triumph."

Sterling nodded. "Could you identify them?"

"No doubt."

"Come with me to Shelby's. Then we'll swing by the station and look at some photos." Sterling moved to the adjacent kitchenette and rinsed his mug. "By the way, do you want some coffee?"

Funny man. "Does Sophie know the kind of cad she's marrying in a few days?"

He flashed a grin. "She's smitten by my charm."

"Smitten? That word's about as masculine as this pillow." Cole launched it at his head, and Sterling batted the thing down with a chuckle. "It's a good thing she's—"

The phone rang.

Sterling answered. His rapt attention on the rotary dial and the way he cemented the receiver to his ear marked an interesting conversation.

"I'll be right there." Eagerness flavored his tone. He hung up and glanced at Cole. "Jeffrey Shelby's been located."

"Half-witted. Harebrained."

Elissa's penance had been insulting herself, alphabetically, with every pluck of a pin from her hair. Not only had she realized she possessed an expansive vocabulary, but Cole's wandering fingers had loosened several pins as if he'd been intentional about ruffling her appearance as well as her composure. Yet she couldn't be angry with him because *she* was the one who'd kissed him. And then ruined everything.

Last two pins. "Idiotic. Imbecilic."

Hair unbound and cascading over her shoulders, she glared at her reflection in the vanity mirror. Pale blue circles taunted her from under weary eyes. Only twenty-four, yet losing her bloom. Could she blame fatigue? Had her efforts in becoming the perfect lady, the perfect journalist, the perfect … everything, drained the life from her?

A pair of scissors lay on the vanity, inches from her fingertips. It wouldn't take much. Four, maybe five slices, cutting her tresses, severing herself from the prison of propriety, freeing herself from the haunts of the past.

Could she do it? Bob her hair? Again?

Hecklings and sneers echoed loud in her ears, the same as they had eight years ago. It'd been an accident, but society had frowned all the same. Now, there were a select few, such as silent film stars and dancers, who proudly displayed the style, but the Pittsburgh community hadn't fully embraced it. Just like it'd never welcomed her.

Maybe it was time to declare her independence from perfection's bondage.

Her fingers curled around the metal shears. Hand trembling, she grabbed a chunk of hair at the nape of her neck and slid her eyes shut.

No.

She'd sworn never to return. That lifestyle had left her reviled and abandoned. She'd carved a new path, and fatigue or no, she'd walk it. The shaking didn't subside. She shoved the scissors into a drawer, took another glimpse of herself, and wept.

CHAPTER 15

"I told him the next time he came in here, I'd shoot him." The stocky man motioned with the rifle he'd been clutching since the moment Sterling and Cole had stepped into Gibson's Drug & Retail.

His cousin clapped Mr. Gibson on the shoulder. "Don't shorten your life by ending his." Both Sterling and the proprietor glared at Mr. Shelby's son, Jeffrey, in a drunken stupor, collapsed on a bench, arm dangling over the side.

Cole surveyed the damage again. Busted storefront windows. Rubble splayed across the floor. Fragmented glass. A groan settled in his chest. This scene closely resembled the one he'd left hours ago at Shelby's office.

"I'm sure young Shelby here will pay for his offenses. But you're welcome to press charges." Sterling reminded the enraged man for the third time over the past fifteen minutes.

Gibson snorted. "He'll be lucky if I don't drag his pampered carcass to court. Given what 'e's done." His seething glare snapped to the two bricks Jeffrey had launched through the windows, lying beside a tilted magazine rack.

Jeffrey's head lolled, facing them. "Lousy service."

The owner's broad chest expanded, lips pulling, revealing crooked teeth.

Sterling stepped between the two. "Next time, Mr. Shelby, visit the place during business hours to purchase tobacco." He muttered something under his breath and then peered at Cole. "Come on, help me get him to the car."

"There will be no '*next* time' for that fool." The man spat. "He'd better pay, or I'll hunt him down at his fancy house."

Sterling gave an exasperated grunt and crouched beside Jeffrey. Cole positioned himself opposite. The pungent odor of bile and liquor accosted Cole's nostrils, his stomach clenching tighter than the grip he had on the drunken man's arm.

Propping each side, they hoisted Jeffrey up, his limp weight pulling. They dragged him out of the building, the tops of his shoes skidding against the cement walk.

The next several minutes consisted of stuffing Jeffrey's thick body into the back of Sterling's car and cranking the starter despite the cold temperature.

Cole warned his cousin a few blocks into the drive. "Maybe you should drive at a slower pace." The brick-paved roads caused the springs to rattle and Jeffrey to moan.

"Where have you been, Shelby?" Sterling ignored the caution and adopted a stern tone. "You've delayed our investigation by your absence, and now to be arrested for drunken and disorderly conduct."

Jeffrey belched.

"You need to slow down, pal." Thirty-five miles per hour was ideal for a Sunday drive, but not at night with an intoxicated man.

Sterling grunted. "I know what I'm doing. Come on, Shelby, tell me where you've been for the past day and a half. Did you go into hiding?"

Jeffrey muttered something. "Forgot the tobacco." Another groan and then he retched.

Sterling slammed the brakes, and Jeffrey's knees hit the floor. "He's vomiting." His mouth twisted in disgust. "In my car."

"I can see that." Cole's throat thickened. Not only because of the sour air but because he'd known this way of life. Known the devastation that emerged. Was this a common episode for Jeffrey, or a one-time ordeal? Was this the reaction from the news about his father? Cole scratched his chin. Or did this travel deeper? Murderously deeper?

Elissa pressed her palm to the door of the *Review* building and took a steadying breath. She'd never been a fan of Mondays, but this particular one hit hard. Her eyes ached from last night's sobbing, but at least her resolve had been strengthened—she'd remained true to her purpose.

I can do this.

Pretending was a skill she'd mastered. She projected elegance to such a degree that no one would ever know she calculated her every step. If she could fake poise, she could fake indifference toward Cole. Her heart began to protest, but she silenced it with three words. *See you soon.* The exact phrase Cole had said after she had spoken three words of her own, pouring out her soul, raw and exposed.

The situation at Mr. Shelby's office had proved painful—feeling Cole's touch again, his embrace—but she would suffer a thousand heartbreaks when he'd leave her again. And he would. Yes, he likely enjoyed her carefree spirit, but it was linked to a gracelessness he could never love, could never commit to.

Cole seemed to appreciate women like Kathleen Stigert. The actress, whose picture adorned his mother's wall, was the epitome of poise and beauty. Cole'd said he hadn't dated other women, but what had really happened between those two? Had Cole crushed her hopes as he had Elissa's? Or had the famous beauty become wise to Cole's charm and split with her heart intact?

"Are you going in, or are you going to stand there looking pretty?"

Her shoulders tensed. "Good morning, Adam." She forced a smile, but it was nowhere near as chipper as his.

He tipped his hat to her and then reached for the door. "Allow me."

"Thanks." She slipped inside, hoping he wouldn't pursue a conversation. Coffee and more coffee was needed before she could begin thinking of anything coherent to say. After tossing and turning most of last night, she'd overslept and missed breakfast. Which was probably better. Her mother would have launched more questions than her constitution could handle.

Adam followed her into the cloakroom. She made quick work of hanging her scarf and jacket while he chatted about the New York Stock Exchange. Due to the blustery day, her hat was secured with too many pins to remove without making a mess of her hair. Making tweezers of her fingers, she eased the one near her temple, but Adam knocked her elbow while blabbing about his most recent investments, unsettling her once-smooth style. She huffed. Oh, she'd just leave the blasted thing on since the black felt matched the trim on her red dress.

"So what do you think?" Adam fingered the brim of his homburg.

"Sounds great." If you enjoyed rambling about shareholders and such.

His grin widened. "Perfect. I'll pick you up at eight."

Her stomach bottomed out. What on earth had she committed to? She couldn't go on a date with Adam, not while her lips still tingled from the residue of Cole's kiss. There had to be a way of escape, but her brain remained in a fog. Oh, this was going to be a pip of a day.

Coffee.

Adam walked alongside her and tucked her hand into the crook of his arm as if he were escorting her into the court of England instead of a noise-ridden newsroom. She attempted to pull away, but he held her fingers pinned between his elbow and his side. At least Cole wouldn't be here for another half-hour, eight-thirty being his staple time of arrival.

Her stomach sank at the sight of Cole at his desk, his jacket already shed, his tie knot loosened, and his sleeves pushed past his elbows. His eyes met hers, and something unreadable spread across his face when his gaze traveled to Adam.

Adam smirked as if he'd won the prize of the day. She withdrew her hand and braved her way to her desk, nodding at Frank's greeting.

Cole resumed typing, not sparing her a glance when she reached her desk. A muscle ticked in his jaw. This was a good thing, right? She had planned on pretending indifference. If Cole was upset with her, then she should be happy. But the gnawing ache in her chest didn't agree.

To unsettle her more, Adam approached her with a smile Stretching longer than the Liberty Tunnels.

"I forgot to tell you." Adam spoke louder than his casual tone. "I secured our usual table at The Star before the show. So you might want to wear something more formal."

"Usual table?" She planted a hand on her hip. "We were there once and with a group of people." Jay's fiftieth birthday dinner.

His smile didn't dim in the least.

She sighed. "Adam, come speak with me a moment." Standing, she motioned to her father's office, empty now because her father had an off-site meeting with a potential investor.

Adam walked by Cole, whose gaze was welded to his typing, and he followed her into the office. He took the only seat in front of the desk, leaving her father's chair. She decided to stand.

"I'm glad you asked me in here." He drummed his fingers on the armrest.

The glint in his eyes caused a million questions to pop in her mind. She bit the inside of her cheek, steeling herself to take control. "Listen, about tonight—"

"I know why Cole's not at the *Dispatch*." His annoying tapping stopped, and he leaned forward. "He didn't quit. He was fired."

The word burned a hole in her heart. Fired. Why? She both wanted and didn't want to know the reason. "How'd you find out?" And why had he gone to the trouble?

"I've an old college friend who recently got hired there." Adam stood and rounded the desk, squaring himself in front of her. "Cole's a drunk."

Her throat closed, the information settling in her gut as if she'd swallowed a handful of rocks.

"Seems our golden boy had been so hooked on the stuff that he'd started skipping work. He'd leave during the busiest part of the day. At first, they assumed he was out chasing a story, but when he began missing the deadlines, the bosses knew the truth—he was pursuing the bottom of a bottle. Or he'd be so hung over he missed the day entirely." His smile nauseated her. "Last straw was when he didn't show up for an entire week. Didn't notify the *Dispatch*. His coworkers thought he'd dropped off the face of the earth."

"Maybe he was injured." Her voice trembled. Hadn't Cole said he almost died? "People usually assume the worst."

"I don't know all the details except this ... when they found Cole, they told him not to come back." Adam put his hand on her shoulder as one would a toddler. "You needed to know this."

She shrugged off his touch. "I don't know why you think I need to hear regurgitated gossip." Cole's pained looked at the gala—when Frank had mentioned the underground speakeasy—flashed in her mind. Since that time, Elissa had wondered at her spontaneous dancing invitation to Cole, but perhaps he really had needed her rescue.

"I'm not addled, Elissa." Adam shirked his right cuff down. "I see the way the man looks at you."

It took all her willpower not to suck in a heavy breath. She'd never seen a difference. Cole had always peered at her that way. As if his gaze could stretch into the depths of her, sifting out the phony from the genuine. The main reason why she couldn't be around him. He knew her. He could *see* the true her. It proved disastrous the first time. And she wouldn't let there be a second, but still, to throw shadows on Cole's character was beneath her. Adam should be ashamed of himself. "It doesn't matter, Adam.

As you can see, I'm a grown woman capable of forming my own judgments."

His stare turned a degree colder. "I know this. But I also know you and Cole have a history. He may try to turn his charms on you. What if you surrender and then he leaves you again? Alcoholics are unstable. He may beat you. Or worse."

Her hand flew to her heart. "Adam Kendrew, that's the biggest bunch of—"

"Elissa, if you're not going to take any regard for yourself, then consider the future of this paper."

What nerve. "No one loves the *Review* more than I do."

The hard lines framing his eyes softened. "Then it's clear your father should be told. I'm going to warn him in case Cole repeats his usual habits."

"I think my father knows." Where that confession came from, she didn't know. But it made sense. Father had not only mentioned Cole had called him but also hinted about Cole being changed by the harshness of life. Could Cole have tricked her father, or had he called her father for help? She needed to find Cole before Adam did. "I'm not going out with you tonight."

Adam's brow lowered, and he took a step back. "Why?"

"There's no point in toying with the inevitable. We're not right for each other."

Adam blew out a breath and shoved his hands in his pockets. "Is this because of the Shadyside Slob thing? That was years ago."

"As much as it pained me to relive those memories, I've forgiven you. I hold nothing against you. But this." She motioned between them. "Can never happen. My heart knows this now."

He jerked a thumb behind him. "Because of Cole?"

"No." And it was the truth. Cole's presence only helped her see what had been plain the entire time—she had no affection for Adam. She pretended in so many areas, but she couldn't falsify this. "Cole has nothing to do with this decision. It's solely mine."

Adam flicked the cord of the blinds, and silence fell on them.

Elissa had to remain firm. She couldn't accommodate his feelings without violating her own. "It's for the best, Adam. You deserve a woman who will give you her love. And I can't."

Sadness flooded his hazel eyes, and he exited the office, shutting her in. She collapsed into her father's chair. Adam would get over her. He would. She wasn't particularly sure his affections went beyond admiration, given the cold stares he'd been donning lately.

She inhaled a ragged breath. The past twenty-four hours had been an unpredictable whirlwind. Could she endure any more emotional storms?

Her arms fell limp to her sides.

The world was against her today. How would she be able to focus on her work? Not only did she have her daily tasks to complete, but how was she going to craft a jaw-dropping article? And where in the world was the coffee?

After one more calming breath, she emerged from her father's office. Cole's chair was ... vacant.

She blinked.

No, her mind wasn't playing tricks. The man was gone. Her gaze scanned the room. Adam sulked at his desk. Frank spoke on the phone, chewing the end of his pencil. Henry typed frantically away on his typewriter. A few other newsmen gathered in the aisle, gabbing. No Cole.

Her heart launched into her throat. What if ...

Something on her desk caught her attention. His pen. Pulse skittering, she walked over, sat down, and scooped up the fountain pen. What if he'd left? Truly left? Cole's hardened expression when she'd walked with Adam into the newsroom seared her mind. There was no denying he had been upset. Hurt. Cole hadn't even acknowledged her. Her hands shook as she unscrewed the barrel. What if he'd left in search of a drink?

"Busy?" Her father's voice made her jump.

"Yes ... I mean no." She pressed her free hand to her chest, her thunderous heart doing nothing to calm her. "I'm not sure." Of anything.

"I see." Father's gaze shifted to the pen in her palm. "Come see me when you're finished." His cheek puckered with his smile, and then he strolled away.

Now was not the time to be embarrassed that her father was wise to her juvenile antics with Cole and fountain pens. But heat radiated through her, along with a disturbing sense of urgency. She unwound the paper and trained her blurred vision on his words.

Spark, I need a break.

The scrap of paper slipped from her fingers.

CHAPTER 16

Elissa's breath came in gasps. She scurried down side streets, searching the bustling sidewalks for Cole's tall frame and mesmerizing gait. Nothing.

Brakes squealed. She shivered.

The hair not imprisoned under her hat succumbed to the wind's fury, whipping against her cheek. She'd forgotten her overcoat, her thin, trendy dress a weak defense against Mother Nature. Hustling, her shoes scuffed against each other. Blamed pigeon-toed feet. She ignored the shame and set her sights on the first target.

Flannigan's.

County officials should be ashamed of their continual blinded eye toward speakeasies, but today she was mildly thankful. The odds of a Prohibition agent raiding Flannigan's was about as high as her respect for a bootlegger. Zero.

Her fingers wrapped around the tarnished door handle, and she squeezed her eyes shut, praying for bravery. After one more inhale of frigid air, she straightened her shoulders and strode in. A wall of cigarette smoke assaulted her. She blinked, clearing her vision. Her mouth parted at the sorry lack of lighting and an even sorrier lot of men with their heads drooped over beer mugs. It was only nine o'clock in the morning, for goodness' sake.

"Pardon, miss." The bartender called from behind the bar. "Only escorted females are allowed here."

Ha! A speakeasy with a touch of propriety. What irony.

"I can be her escort." A fellow cackled and slapped his palm on the counter.

"I'm ... uh ... looking for my ..." What? Childhood hero? Teenage heartthrob? Adult nemesis? "Friend." Her gaze darted around the dingy room. A few pool tables. Several mismatched chairs. No Cole. "He's not here." She turned on her heel and marched out.

The cold blasted her flushed face with an unrelenting vengeance. This could be a lost hope. There were over five hundred speakeasies in this alcohol-obsessed city. Could she visit all of them? Something kicked in her pulse, and her jaw clenched. She'd give her best effort.

Adam's vehement declaration of Cole's past had only endeared the man more to her. He had faults. Just like her. She wasn't influenced by alcohol, but she was controlled by perfectionism. It had swayed her decisions until she hardly recognized herself. Last night, her will sided with pretense, but at this moment, she wasn't sure. The line hazed daily, her emotions a constant tug-of-war.

She grimaced and plopped a hand on her hat, the pins which had given her fits earlier now losing the battle against the elements. Which gin joint should she storm into next? The establishment on Rose Street, The Steel Fountain, served the upper class. Would Cole go for that one? Or would he find a place more obscure, tucked away? She changed her direction toward The Thirsty Hound, picking up the pace and weaving between strangers. If Frank hadn't openly raved about it years ago when the prohibition began, she never would've known it lurked behind Great Allegheny Medical office.

She ducked under a drugstore awning, collecting her thoughts before venturing behind the popular healthcare building. The trolley bounded past, screeching along on the brown ribbon of rails, but a million streetcars couldn't deflect her attention from the handsome man opposite her.

Cole.

He stood on the diagonal corner, his gaze on the traffic, no doubt waiting for a break. Even from this distance, his face appeared hardened. She squinted. Was his hand in a fist? Her breath froze in her chest, and it wasn't due to the biting chill.

She'd provoked him. Led him on. Practically had thrown herself at him last evening and then walked in this morning on another man's arm. The shame enflaming her chest burned right to her stinging eyes. She had to get to him. Traffic slowed, and Cole jogged across the street and into The Thirsty Hound.

The padded stool creaked as Cole sat at the counter. He nodded at the elderly man four seats down and then checked his watch. Nine-fifteen. He could slip this in, and no one would notice. That was, if he—

The bell jingled above the door, and a familiar blonde stood, cheeks flushed and hat tipping to one side. He leaned over, getting a better glimpse. Yes, it was her.

Elissa caught sight of him and ran over. Since he'd returned, he'd hardly seen her scurry, let alone dash. His pulse throbbed. Thoughts pummeled his brain as to why she was here and why she was in such a state. None of them good.

He stood, and she almost collapsed into him. He cupped her elbows, steadying her, and took in her heavy breathing and panicked expression. "Elissa. What's wrong?"

Her pale fingers strangled the lapel of his jacket. "I'm here, Cole. I'll help you through." Desperation saturated her shaky voice, and pale circles rimmed her pleading eyes. Had she not slept any either?

His fingers skimmed up and down her arms. "Where's your coat?" He increased the pressure in his touch to chase away the chill rolling off her.

"I had to find you." Elissa's intense stare remained fixed on him. Grant it, he loved her attention, but not the edginess choking her voice.

"Spark, let's get you a drink to warm you up." He nodded toward the man at the counter. "Two, please. And make it strong."

Elissa gasped and jumped back, her hat flopping. "Cole Parker, I will *not* have a drink with you." Her bottom lip pouted.

Was she fighting tears?

"I came to help. That's why I searched for you. I barged into Flannigan's, but you weren't there. And then—"

"Elissa." He stepped toward her and peered into her face. "What are you talking about? Did you say you went into a speakeasy?"

Her face reddened, and she stared at his collar. "Yes."

The realization hit stronger than the aroma of the place. He gripped both of her trembling hands. "Close your eyes, sweetheart, and take a deep breath." He could've instructed her to simply look around, but this way might calm her more.

To his surprise, she listened. Thick lashes lowered, concealing those beautiful blues. Her chest rose, and then her eyes popped open. "Coffee?" Her gaze darted about, taking in several customers sipping from their mugs and gawking at the scene Elissa and he created. "I thought this was a ..." She tugged her hands away and placed them on her cheeks. "When I read your note, I believed you were ... well, I didn't know for sure, but I didn't want you to ... um ... falter."

His heart sank.

Of all the people in the world to discover his failure, why her? The one whose opinion mattered as much to him as the air in his lungs? It hurt, imagining how much she had knowledge of. He shoved his fists into his pockets and took his own advice, breathing in. "This used to be a gin joint, but now it's a café." It'd required agents on a state level to make this establishment dry because the city ones were too enamored with padding their pockets with hush money. "Come sit." He glanced at the clock on the wall. He still had ten minutes. "We need to talk."

The coffee cups were already on the counter behind them.

She took the seat to his right. Her flushed coloring waned to soft pink, dusting her cheeks and nose. He braced himself for the loaded questions about his past, but she didn't speak, only fussed with her appearance, tugging the hem of her sleeves, centering her belt, and cutting a quick glance to her stockings. Her gaze landed on the women's lounge door, and he saw the struggle in her eyes.

"You look gorgeous. Trust me."

"Don't lie to me. I know I'm a mess." She huffed a hair from her forehead. "But … this isn't about me."

This, meaning Cole and his problems. More like, past problems which shadowed his present and now threatened his future. "What you imagine a mess, I consider breathtaking."

Her face pinched.

He fought against a wince. His truth, she'd mistaken as arrogant charm.

A shiver rocked her body.

"You need to get warm. Here." He handed her the coffee. "And to show you how much I like you, I'll give you all the cream."

Her brows lifted in obvious surprise, and her mouth curved into a fragile smile. "I wouldn't think you'd remember."

"What? That you're a creamer hog?" He chuckled and handed her the small, ceramic pitcher. A few drops spilled in the process. They reached for the napkin dispenser at the same time, his hand stilling on hers. "So you know, I remember a lot. An awful lot."

Horror flashed across her face, and she pulled her hand away, the spilled cream forgotten.

Had he said something wrong? "I meant that as a compliment."

"Oh." She stiffened, her back poker-straight. With her lips mashed tight, she poured sugar into her mug, stirred for a second, and then poured some more. She glanced up and scowled. "Don't judge me."

He lifted both hands. "If you want to turn your coffee into liquid candy, far be it from me to judge."

She sighed, and her shoulders sagged. "I need this after the morning I had."

Morning, right. The image of Elissa hanging on Kendrew's arm burned through his thoughts. How could she have kissed Cole with a raw passion rendering him senseless and then a handful of hours later cozy up to another man? "Would you like to compare mornings? Because I'm confident mine was rougher." And would probably turn even more so, considering the way she'd dashed into the coffee shop. How much did she know? Who had leaked the humiliating details? She obviously hadn't been aware of them last night. So it was some time this morning. Her father had given his word not to disclose Cole's past. "Kendrew? Did he tell you about New York?"

She swallowed and gazed at a spot on the counter. "Yes. In Father's office."

His jaw tightened. The clinking of mugs and indistinct chatter from other patrons filled the silence between them. Knowing Kendrew would be sitting at his orderly desk, smirking like the devil when Cole returned, didn't help cool his broiling temper. What was his agenda? Make Cole look like a drunken beast and Kendrew the noble-hearted hero? And how had he even known about Cole's life at the *Dispatch*? He squeezed the handle of his mug and couldn't care less if it crumbled into ceramic dust beneath his grip.

"Are you angry with me?" Her voice was quiet. So much, Cole had almost missed it.

However jerky Kendrew had acted, it wasn't Elissa's fault. She had come to *rescue* Cole to the point of invading speakeasies. Despite the dark mood brewing, a smile tipped his mouth. "No, Spark. You're not to blame."

The fault sat heavily on Cole's shoulders. He'd been the one who couldn't control the cravings, who'd sunk deeper and deeper into its clutches. But then ... he'd found mercy. Found a Savior who'd carried a cross on His shoulders in order to remove the burden from Cole's.

Her gentle hand rested on his forearm, and he met her eyes

with a courage not his own.

"Is it true, Cole? You were fired from the *Dispatch* because of alcohol?"

"Yes."

"I'm sorry." Her gaze held concern, but no judgment. How he loved those eyes.

"I imagined I could control it, but it was the other way around." He forced himself to take a swig of coffee even if it turned to acid in his stomach. "I'd black out for hours. And the last time, I almost didn't wake up. Some cable car driver on his way home from work found me in a dank alley, hypothermic and fading fast."

She pressed her palm to her mouth.

He conjured up a smile. "It's not pretty. But I discovered redemption on the hospital bed. Brokenness, remember?"

Tears glossed her eyes. For him. His heart both ached and swelled. Did she care more than she let on? He'd reasoned her kiss last night had been a response to all the heavy emotion, but maybe it'd meant something more. It sure had for him.

"I can't say it's been easy, but I've been dry for four months. You can report that to Kendrew if you'd like." He offered his handkerchief.

She shook her head. "Adam won't be too enthused to hear anything from me."

"Why's that?"

She traced a coffee ring with her fingernail, avoiding eye contact. "I told him we aren't right for each other."

Hope. That elusive word had taunted him for the past week but now rose in his chest with a touch of confidence. No other woman had ever been *right* for Cole besides her. Not like he hadn't had opportunities, but he'd been raised with enough morals not to toy with females' hearts. Though he'd bet money that Elissa would disagree.

He rubbed his brow, lessening the strain. He glanced over and caught Elissa staring, confusion swimming in her eyes. "Sorry,

Spark. The past twenty-four hours are catching up to me. I haven't slept much." Sterling had commandeered most of Cole's night, from dealing with Jeffrey to another inspection of Shelby's office, and then a visit to police headquarters.

She lowered her gaze to her lap. "I didn't sleep either."

"But you weren't all over Pittsburgh with your save-the-world cousin." Cole muttered into his mug before downing the last drops. At least he hoped she hadn't been all over Pittsburgh. After the charade she'd pulled yesterday, he couldn't be certain.

Her mug clinked on the saucer, and she gaped at him. "Did you tell Sterling what happened last night?"

"Not all of it." He winked.

But she didn't laugh. Or frown. Her features froze, and her knuckles were as white as the napkin she strangled. "Am I in trouble?"

He eyed her coffee. She hadn't taken a sip yet. "From Sterling? No. But I had to tell him about us being in the Shelby building. And also about the men you scared off." Men who remained unknown. At headquarters, Cole had strained his eyes over hundreds of mug shots. No luck.

Her shoulders lowered with an exhale. "Thank you."

"I should be thanking you. By the way, I'm getting you a gun lighter in case you need to save my life again."

Her gentle smile warmed him more than a thousand cups of coffee. "Cole, I know what you were trying to do. Jumping out first so I could escape. It was heroic."

The admiration in her eyes caused him to fall for her harder. "Was it almost as chivalrous as the Fourth of July at Glenwood Park?"

She whipped her mug from her lips, eyes rounding.

"What's the matter? Too hot?"

She shook her head and fingered a lock of hair. "I'd rather not talk about that day."

"Suits me." He flashed a smile. "Only remember, you'd be bald if it weren't for my resourcefulness."

"You dumped your punch on me." She snapped.

"Because you caught your hair on fire." He laughed. "I solemnly swear to be your rescuer every time you twirl a sparkler like a baton."

Her eyes dulled, and the corners of her mouth pulled into a grimace. "I don't view it with the same humor as you."

The hurt in her tone bruised him. "Elissa, it was an accident. Don't be so hard on yourself."

She scoffed. "You have no idea."

He leaned close, his shoulder brushing hers. "Then tell me."

"You were there, Cole." Her eyes blazed layers of fire. "My hair had to be cut. Everyone made fun of me. Shadyside Slob all over again. And you added to the shame by giving me a nickname forever reminding me of my infernal clumsiness."

"Spark?"

She nodded.

His chest caved. He'd hurt her. "How come you're just now telling me?"

"Because."

So many unknowns hinged from that one word. Her closed-in posture and averted stare announced she wouldn't give any more clues to the mystery.

But she should know ... "The name Spark wasn't from then."

His words snapped her stiff, the napkin she held falling to her lap. "Of course it was. You hadn't called me that until after the incident."

"Only because it gave me the freedom to do so. I admit I allowed you to believe the nickname stemmed from that, and I'm sorry for the deception. My pride was too thick back then. But the reality was, I'd been calling you that for years ... in here." He tapped his temple. "Since the moment at Howe Springs, you were my spark of hope. Still are."

The full force of her gaze penetrated his, stretching into his heart and wafting the embers of longing into a blaze. He had to convince this girl he was in it for the long run. And maybe he should start with the words she needed most to hear. "Elissa, the day when I left—"

"Excuse me, Mr. Parker?" A reedy feminine voice floated over his shoulder.

He twisted on his seat.

Irene Harper stood an arm's length away, complete with a burgeoning smile. "I believe you were expecting me."

Elissa bristled beside him, and the sizzling moment between them extinguished.

CHAPTER 17

Irene's gleeful grin narrowed to a sardonic smirk. Elissa cut a glance to the napkin dispenser, catching her warbled reflection in the shiny metal. Pitiful. Messy. Why hadn't she escaped to the powder room when she had the chance? She frowned. Because her heart had had its way. She had wanted to show support for Cole, while all along the man had been waiting for Irene.

Played for a fool once again.

"Miss Harper, how are you this morning?" Cole nodded, and Irene acknowledged his words with a flutter of her long lashes. "Forgive my confusion, but I was supposed to be—"

"Elissa, something about you today reminds me of when we were in high school." Irene eyed her hat, her words so syrupy-sweet Elissa was surprised she didn't choke on them. "I can't quite put my finger on it."

"Allow me." Cole perused Elissa, his eyes hitching for a second on her mouth. "It's the radiance. She has this youthful glow, making it hard for me to peel my eyes from her."

Elissa stood, her foot smacking the stool's side. "Are you mocking me?"

The smirk fell from his face. "Never."

Thoughts scattered like a thousand puzzle pieces in her mind. Cole'd protected her against Kendrew when they'd been younger, but chose to have a coffee date with Irene now? Surging heat replaced the stinging chill that had overwhelmed her moments ago. Adam might have devised the Shadyside Slob title, but Irene had broadcasted it more than anyone, making Elissa dread walking to school. Hadn't Cole known that as well? Had Elissa not cried on his shoulder? Again and again.

"I need to get back." To real life. To guarding her heart. "To the office. One of us should probably work today." She aimed a cold stare at Cole, and his forehead rippled. Why the man was confused, she had no clue. And at this point, she didn't care.

"Nice seeing you." Irene didn't have the courtesy to glance at Elissa, but slipped between her and Cole, claiming the stool Elissa had vacated.

"Good day, Irene." With a smile as painted as Irene's eyebrows, she spun toward the exit. A large hand caught her wrist. "Do you need something, Mr. Parker?"

"You."

A muffled gasp sounded from Irene's direction.

"I need you to stay." Cole released Elissa and stood, giving her his seat. "I believe Miss Harper was about to tell me why she is here and *not* Dr. Sheffield."

Dr. Sheffield? The man whose charity Mr. Shelby had donated to? Was this for the memorial article Cole had mentioned last night? Air crept back into her lungs as the pieces came together. Cole had come for information and not a rendezvous with Miss Sultry.

Irene angled toward Cole, excluding Elissa. "He had a last-minute emergency and charged me to deliver this." She pulled an envelope from her plum overcoat. "He said it has all the details you need."

"Much obliged." Cole tucked the envelope into the inside pocket of his jacket. "Now if you'll excuse us, we have to return to work." He ignored Irene's jaw-dropping expression and clasped Elissa's hand, helping her to her feet. "Nice seeing you." He threw Irene's parting words to Elissa right back at her and kept his glare on the door without even a peek her way. Oh, she could kiss Cole for that. He squeezed her hand, and out they went.

Cole shed his jacket and draped it over his chair's back. Elissa paced the small span of floor behind their stations, her fingers clutching Dr. Sheffield's correspondence, her face pinched as if in deep concentration.

"During his final meeting with me, Dan announced that he'd withdrawn his charity funding on the grounds that his interests had changed." She rolled her eyes and tossed the letter onto his desk.

"I don't know why you keep reading it." Cole plucked the pencil from behind his ear and pointed it at her. "This one's yours." He'd made a habit of stealing her pencils, paper, and hopefully her heart soon. Though he didn't really want to steal that—he'd rather her freely offer it.

"Seriously, Cole." She snatched the pencil from his hand. "Dr. Sheffield all but spelled it out, didn't he? Mr. Shelby withdrew his funding because of a new interest. In other words, a new flame?"

"Think Miss Kerns had something to do with it?"

She let out an exaggerated sigh. "Of course. That's what gold diggers do."

"Gold digger, huh?" Cole steepled his fingertips under his chin, concealing his smirk. "Isn't the term a bit judgmental?" Though Shelby's former secretary wasn't high on the morality list, she was low on the suspect one. No motive. Why kill the man who wanted to share his millions with her?

"Cole, think. Mr. Shelby is in his late fifties. How old did Miss Kerns look?"

"Mid-twenties."

"There you have it. What would a woman want with a man thirty years older than her?" She strutted over to her chair and sat down as if resting her case.

The newsroom had grown quiet since the editorials were downstairs being inked by the monster. He glanced at Kendrew's empty chair. The man had rushed through his work and left early.

Smart move, considering Cole had some choice words begging to be released.

He fought against a scowl and forced his attention back on the task at hand. Cole had gained enough information from Dr. Sheffield's letter to craft a nice piece about Shelby. The man had contributed thousands to charity over the years. Supported the construction of the medical center which now serviced the community. Maybe the news would pad his character for when the facts about his affair leaked. Which hopefully, they wouldn't. "You know what all this means, don't you?"

Elissa raised a brow. "What? That men shouldn't be allowed to have pretty secretaries?"

"Nice theory, but no." He smirked. "It means not only do Mrs. Shelby and her son have a motive against Shelby, but so does Dr. Sheffield. Shelby stopped the money flow. It's rumored the doc had plans to add another wing onto the center." Which meant Cole should probably inform Sterling. Later. "How about we break for lunch?"

"Hmm?" Elissa's pencil went limp in her hand. "Now?"

"Can't get a Drake's sandwich past three, sweetheart. And it's"—he checked his watch— "five until two. I remember how much you loved their creamed chicken sandwich." Cole's stomach begged for a *yes*. "Maybe after that, a quick detour to the incline."

"On the Duquesne?"

"I have to remedy a past regret. Remember? You wanted to go up on Coal's Hill, and I said it was a silly idea." Those words had been born from hurt, which at the time, Elissa couldn't have understood. If he was going to be a permanent fixture in Pittsburgh, he needed to face his demons. The major one being traveling in the cable car which scaled Mount Washington.

Her brows squished together. "I can't recall. But you were right. It's silly to go up there without a specific reason."

"Then I should word it this way. I have a *specific reason* why I want to take you there. What do you say?" He almost threw a

Spark in there but refrained. He'd tread carefully with that name. "We had our lives threatened last night, so I think today we can enjoy a break."

Her lashes lowered. "I haven't started my article yet." Frustration lined her tone. "Maybe this isn't a good idea. You're not trying to distract me, are you?"

"Don't be so cynical." He pushed off her desk. "I haven't started mine either. Don't even have a lead." Because he didn't care if he won. Securing the headline once had been his ambition, but he'd discovered how empty it left him. Success had been a fickle comrade.

Her lips twisted. "I shouldn't."

"You wouldn't reduce me to begging, would you?"

"I might."

"Yesterday you put a dent in my ego by saving my life—for which, by the way, I endured a torrential ribbing from Sterling—and today you make me grovel?"

Her fingertips pressed against a growing smirk.

"Believe me, I'll do it." He stepped behind her chair. "Grab your coat and let's go."

"I—I don't think ..." The panic returned, tightening her mouth and bunching the skin at the corner of her eyes. "Now's not a good time. I really need to start this article. Maybe tomorrow?"

"Please?" He reached over, skimming her arm, and snagged his pen which he'd left on her desk earlier. His gaze roamed the graceful curve of her neck. How easy it would be to press a kiss there. He swallowed and straightened. "A sandwich, the incline, and my undivided attention. What's your hesitation?"

Her gaze hooked his, and a smile lit her eyes. "Well, since you put it that way."

If the floor disintegrated beneath his feet, he'd never know. He floated on the hope of her words.

CHAPTER 18

Elissa clutched the world's messiest sandwich. As if the huge helping of creamed chicken, cheese, tomato, and onions weren't enough, the short-order cook had shoved French-fried potatoes in the mix. The sides of her mouth ached at the notion of fitting that thing in for a bite, but her stomach rumbled in anticipation.

"Hey there, Miss Tillman." Howard Drake waved from behind the soda fountain. "Sammy told me you were here." He jerked the draft arm, filled a glass with cola, and handed the drink to a waiting customer. "Not your usual company." Smiling, he nodded toward Cole.

Cole's brow raised slightly, and he bit off a hunk of his sandwich.

"No, not today." She captured the tomato before it slid out of the sandwich and shoved it back with her pinky. "But the event with that group happens again a week from tomorrow." And hopefully, she could rally more people to come. Attendance had been pretty low.

"Sounds great. Enjoy your lunch." He shot another grin and returned to the kitchen.

"Thank you." She raised her sandwich to her mouth, ready to conquer it.

"'Usual company'?" Cole popped a potato in his mouth and reached for his Coke. "How do I get an invitation to that party?"

"You become female."

He choked on his drink, and Elissa's suppressed chortles ripped free.

"If it's all the same to you, I'll sit that one out." Cole wiped the side of his smiling mouth with a napkin. "I take it you come here for women's meetings?"

"I'm the chapter leader for Allegheny County." Laughter erupted from a group of factory workers at a table across the room. Her mother would frown at the display, but Elissa smiled. "We support each other. Discuss our hardships. The goal is to make the city aware of its injustice toward women."

"You amaze me." The deep resonance of his tone made her insides hum.

She stirred her drink with her straw. "Those women are amazing. Some work at the hospital. Others in factories. They work identical jobs as men but are paid reduced wages. I'm thankful for my position at the *Review* because at least Father respects me enough to pay me competitively." But for how long? Father hadn't mentioned the loans recently. Did that signify finances were improving? Or was he delaying the inevitable?

"I can see your influence." He eyed the single yellow rose in the small glass vase in front of the napkin dispenser.

Smiling, she glanced around the quaint area. Every booth had been decorated with a flower. "That would be Mrs. Drake's doing. She's the owner's wife and a dear friend of mine." She inclined her head to his plate. "How's it taste?" She took a nice-sized bite of her sandwich.

"They don't make food like this in New York."

Her jaw stilled mid-chew.

He leaned on his elbows. "Don't believe me?" The normal rasp of his voice softened. "I've missed a lot of things about Pittsburgh. I couldn't forget it. No matter how hard I tried."

"Pittsburgh couldn't forget you either." She bit the inside of her cheek, hoping with all hopes she didn't make a complete fool of herself. "But it's a little cautious, having you back within its borders."

His Adam's apple bobbed. "I can understand that." He shoved

the salt and pepper shakers aside and reached across the table, his hand beckoning hers. "I only want to know if I'm welcome, or if I should remain outside its perimeters. The heart of the city is important to me."

Her toes curled inside her shoes, and she wiped her hands with a napkin. Could she? The vault of her heart had been locked, and Cole seemed to be the only one with the combination. He knew which way to turn her feelings and push the pressures of her soul. Last time, he'd stripped that vault bare and ran off with the spoils. Could she trust him again? She stared at his hand, awaiting hers. Pressing her palms to her thighs, she inhaled a stabilizing breath. "I can't answer you now." The truth peeled from the swell of emotions. "But know I'm not as opposed as when you first arrived."

"Making progress. That's all a guy can expect." He flexed his fingers, reached for a fried potato, and grinned as he tossed it in his mouth.

Elissa relaxed against the wooden seat. "I'm not sure I can eat anything else." She'd made a meager dent in her meal, but she couldn't tempt her fluttering stomach.

"Ready to head to the incline?" Cole finished off his Angus beef sandwich and wiped his fingers with his napkin.

She nodded but remained uncertain why this meant so much to him. To every other local, the incline offered only a safe means for those who lived on Mount Washington to get to downtown. One more sip of her Dr. Pepper and she was set. Cole offered his arm with a charming smirk, and she tucked her hand in the crook of his overcoat.

"I'm glad you agreed to ride the incline." He paused at the door and held her stare. "I have something to tell you. Words I've never spoken to anyone."

He'd said it.

Cole's chest ached as if intending to explode, but he'd told

Elissa he had a confession to share, and now he had to stick with his promise and spill all. His breath puffed before him in foggy clouds.

God, I need your help.

As they walked up the grated steps to the incline entrance, Elissa's gaze scanned the bleak surroundings. Maybe this was a bad idea. A soot-crusted building at the base of a barren hill wasn't the most ideal place to impress a lady. He curled his hand around the scuffed doorknob to the incline station and held the door for Elissa to enter. The modest passenger waiting area possessed a few wooden benches and a yellowed sign listing the operating hours.

With a pat to Elissa's hand, still nestled in the crook of his arm, they approached the counter.

"Afternoon, folks." The attendant gave a hearty smile and adjusted his cap. "Round trip is five cents, sir."

Cole fished his pocket for a dime. "I'm paying for the lady as well." He turned and acknowledged Elissa with a smile, but she didn't notice, so preoccupied was she with digging around her purse. "Elissa, I got this. I asked you on this date, remember?"

She blushed and gave a small nod.

He handed the coin to the middle-aged man behind the counter.

"Taking the lady on the incline as a date, huh?" His thick-rimmed spectacles didn't conceal the laughter in his eyes. "I have to say this is a first." He dropped the change into the metal register.

"When the woman is tough to please, you have to think outside the box, my friend." Cole tapped the side of his temple.

"I think a dime fare is letting you off easy, Mr. Parker." Playfulness traced Elissa's smirk. "Next time should be at The Regent."

The most expensive restaurant this side of the Ohio River. Cole laughed, and his heart warmed at the delight in her eyes. "Since you just agreed to a second date, I'd be happy to foot the bill." He slid his arm around her. "Do you think your pops can give me a raise?"

Her shoulders rose with silent laughter. Probably because they both knew Cole wasn't collecting a salary. Thank God for the stock market and the benefits of having his desk beside the finance manager at the *Dispatch*. He'd squirreled away substantial savings from his former job, and the dividends from his stocks were an added bonus.

"All right, you love birds." The worker rounded the counter and motioned them to follow. "Watch your step, and don't move about in the car. This is an eight-hundred-foot long track, so make yourselves cozy." He held the door open with a grin wider than Mount Washington. "It's probably a good thing you have this car to yourselves." He winked, and Elissa's mouth parted.

Cole chuckled. He needed this dash of humor to keep his spirits light. The motorized box remained exactly how Cole had remembered, the yellowed woodwork, the stiff benches carved with people's names, smudges on the windows.

Elissa stepped through first and selected a seat. She chose the front—the exact spot he'd chosen sixteen years ago. He gritted his teeth. *One foot in front of the other, Parker.*

The man closed the door behind Cole, trapping him with his memories.

"It's a shame the river is so polluted, and the buildings are so ugly. The view could be remarkable." She closed her eyes as if envisioning an immaculate skyline, free from the ashy marks of factories.

This area bore the soiled fingerprint of the massive steel industry, and with it came the weighty recovery from The Great War. Yet its heart pulsed to the beat of resilience. Like Cole's. "My grandfather was on the team of engineers under Samuel Diescher." The designer and master builder had been sort of a hero to the locals, saving them from trekking the mountainous stretch on foot.

She scooted closer, her side brushing his, her nearness bringing much-needed warmth. "You never told me."

He shrugged. "Because I hated this place. Hated everything about it."

Elissa's mouth twisted, her eyes searching his face.

"I was ten when I last saw this view. My dad brought me." Heat poured off his words, and Cole could almost taste the fiery bitterness. "He raved on and on about his own father and about this incline. Its fortified steel structure. The steam engine. The cast-iron drum and air brakes." Amazing how much he remembered. Why hadn't the words abandoned him like the man who'd spoken them?

"Your father was an engineer, right? So I guess he followed in your grandfather's footsteps?"

With a slight hitch, the car began its slow climb. The squealing of wire cables and the clicking of iron track charged the air.

"Yeah. One of his jobs. According to Mom, he had several. None of which he kept long." Cole blew out a breath. If voicing this brought healing, the flaming pain slicing his chest would be worth it. "This was the best memory I had with my dad. I remember wanting to make him proud, even more than Granddad had." What a joke Cole's life had been. The only one he'd made proud was the bootlegger he'd kept in business. "Later, when he left, I despised this thing. And for a long while, despised him."

Her fingers wrapped around his arm. "You were young and forced to grow up quickly."

Cole glanced at his scored knuckles—the evidence of his work as a breaker boy in the mines. The foreman's cursing shouts, the chunks of skin amongst other impurities soiling the conveyor belt, the bleeding palms from hand-picking the sharp slate from the pile of prized coal, all left haunting effects on a twelve-year-old boy earning money to aid a depressed mother. "I'm thankful for that afternoon at Howe Springs."

Her eyes glistened with unshed tears. "That fountain was a refuge for both of us."

His routine stop between the mines and home, the place of

washing his wounds in the crisp, spring water, became the cleansing place of his soul. "I'm thankful for that pig-tailed girl who glanced up from her book and dragged me by the elbow to her father." Determination had marked Elissa's steps that day, and admiration had stamped Cole's heart. "If it wasn't for you, I may not be here."

Her sad smile matched her somber tone. "No child should be forced to work in those death pits."

Cole ran the flawed knuckle down her cheek. "You've always stood against injustice." His gaze traveled from her eyes to the yellow rose. "Never forget the impact you have, Elissa. It changes lives."

Biting her lower lip, she peered out the window. "A lot of men needed work back then. Father rejected dozens each day. I honestly don't know how I convinced him to hire you on."

"Because you pour your heart into your persuasions." He curled an arm around her, and she snuggled into his chest. "And who could say no to your heart?"

She stiffened but didn't break from his touch.

"Thank you for believing in me, Spark." He wished this trek lasted more than five minutes because he could hold her forever.

She angled her face toward his. "But if you hate this incline so much, why bring me today?"

"I can't run from the past anymore." His mind might insist he was that scruffy child his father abandoned, but his heart impressed him with an image of the true Father. The One who accepted him. Loved him. "I wanted to create a new memory with someone I care about."

"Cole?" Her voice rumbled against his chest.

"Hmm."

"Why didn't you come back?"

He tugged her closer. "I was scared."

She shifted in his arms. "Of what? Being stuck with me?"

He pulled back, clasping her shoulders, peering into her face. "Never." His chest tightened at the hurt marring her eyes. "It's just

… you looked exactly like her."

"What?" She jerked free from his hold. "Who is *her*?"

"My mom."

Her brows sank. "I don't understand. What's your mother have to do with you not returning?"

He flicked a glance back. Halfway to the summit. "Remember what you told me the second before I stepped onto the train?"

"Yes," she said, voice brittle, gaze lowered.

I love you. Words he'd hoped to evoke since the moment he'd recognized his love for her. Words that had seized his heart with a whisper of the future, but his past had screamed of nights of torment. Hearing his mother weeping when she'd thought he'd been asleep. Staring at his dad's empty chair at dinnertime. Each birthday, every holiday a misery because of an absent father. "When you spoke those words, you looked identical to my mother … the day my father left. She'd said 'I love you' with so much admiration in her eyes." He shook his head. "Mom didn't know he wasn't returning. Believed it was another business trip."

She'd gotten served the divorce papers five months later.

"You did the exact same thing. Left. You didn't even write to let me know you'd changed your mind about us."

"Because I never changed my mind."

Her fingers fanned against her breastbone, wariness returning to her eyes.

"I couldn't let go of you, but I didn't want to hurt you." This wasn't going as he'd hoped. Words lodged in his throat, and all his thoughts seemed to tumble down the barren hill beneath them. "Mom explained away Dad's abandonment by saying he had an adventurous spirit—that he couldn't stay in one place too long. The words she spoke to describe him, people used about me. Carefree, impulsive." And soon, failure.

The hard angles of her face softened. "You are not like him. Look how you stepped up to help your mom with the bills. You were twelve, Cole. Twelve. When most boys were cutting up in the alleys, you were in the mine, getting your hands mangled. Then delivering papers on your bike. Washing windows, shoveling walks. You never missed an opportunity to help your mom. I respected you as much as I loved you." She shifted in her seat as if she realized the weight of her words. But instead of looking mortified as he expected, she stared at him head on, with squared shoulders. "And if we would've married, then you would have been the same. A great provider, an excellent husband."

The car approached the summit, but he couldn't leave this unsaid. He grabbed both of her hands and peered into her face. "I'm sorry, Elissa. If you only knew the time I've spent thinking of you. Wondering what you were doing. Trying to get copies of the *Review* so I could read your society page."

She blinked at his words.

"I've known you were Elliot Wentworth. I'd know your work anywhere." He traced her jawline with his thumb, settling it under her lowered chin, gently lifting until her gaze met his. "You pour portions of your soul into your articles. Reading them, I felt close to you." He smiled. "I also know how to set a table for a formal dinner now."

She laughed even as tears escaped from her eyes.

He brushed them away. "I now know that I'm not the sort of man I once feared becoming, but it took years of pain to discover it. I'm sorry for ruining our future together."

She gripped both of his hands. "Maybe the future is only beginning."

He dipped his head and pressed his mouth against her waiting lips as if sealing the promise of a fresh start. Everything in him hummed with adoration for her. He slid his arms around her back and gathered her close. The roots of this relationship dug deeper than physical attraction. He could feel her love for him, from the delicate pressure of her lips to her tender fingers cupping his face. He couldn't defend himself against the surge of protectiveness waving over him. The contest. The murder case. He needed to keep this woman safe. She needed to stay in his arms for a lifetime.

The car stopped, but neither of them moved. Their lips, hearts, touching each other in the most magnetizing way.

Someone cleared their throat, and Elissa jumped back. A woman in her sixties, hands loaded with grocer's bags and eyes heavy with disapproval, stepped past them and sat down with a huff. Elissa's shoulders shook with suppressed laughter, but Cole didn't bother to hide his. He adjusted his hat, which had gotten bumped by Elissa's forehead during their smooching session, and he sent a wink toward the disgruntled lady.

She mumbled a "Well, I never," while they made their exit, hand-in-hand.

With a base lined with smoke-belching factories and the face of the hillside pocked with exhausted mines, Coal's Hill had been reduced to an industrialized wasteland.

"It's not promising." Elissa assessed the view with a crinkled nose.

"Everything has potential for beauty." Cole stroked her forefinger with his thumb. "Besides, I have the most breathtaking view around." He trained his focus on her and watched a tender smile bloom. "I kind of feel sorry for this place." They strolled down the narrow walk. "It was once a big shot. A flourishing mine, but greed plundered its depths, leaving it to decay."

"I know a man who bears the same name, who was also a big shot." She leaned in, pressing her cheek to his shoulder. "And though he may have been left to rot, God had a different plan."

"He did indeed." He kissed her forehead. "But this isn't a nice location for a date. I apologize for that. I'll make it up to you."

"How so?" Her smile curved sideways.

"You'll get your fill from The Regent, and after that, would you accompany me to my cousin's wedding this Wednesday?"

"Sterling and Sophie?" The sun broke from behind the prison-gray clouds, but the delight in Elissa's eyes shone brighter. "I really like her. We've had some great conversations. She's the only person

I know who can make that man smile."

"How do you know ..." Ah, Elissa would know his cousin's fiancée, considering she'd been helping with his mom's apartments for years. "Thank you, Spark."

"For what?"

"For being you." He tugged her closer. "Are you ready to head back down?

"Only if we can pick up where we left off." Her teasing smile ignited every nerve in him to burn with expectation. "I'd be delighted to be your date this week."

And hopefully, forever.

CHAPTER 19

Cole climbed the stairs leading to his apartment and loosened his tie knot, smiling. Having been weighted by unspoken words and punctured by regret, his heart hadn't been this light and whole in years. As for Elissa? She might have walked into work this morning on Kendrew's arm, but for most of the day, she'd been on his. And it would remain that way if he had anything to do with it.

His Spark.

Whispering a prayer of thanks, he unlocked his apartment door, shouldering it open. Movement stirred in the early evening shadows.

A man.

The guy's back was to Cole, hunched over the desk that sat under the window.

"Hey!" Cole dashed after him.

The intruder scrambled over the desk for the open window, papers scattering, the piece of furniture rocking from the movement and falling over. Cole hurtled the coffee table, side-stepping the desk, and reached the window. The man bounded down the last of the fire escape and leapt to the alley.

Cole sprinted out of his apartment and pounded on his cousin's door across the hall. "Sterling! Get out here!" He didn't wait to see if his cousin was in but rushed down the steps, jumping the bottom six.

"What's going on?" Sterling called from upstairs.

"Come on." Cole charged out the front door, off the porch, smacking the concrete. The wind threw its airy blast in his face, but he knew these streets with his eyes closed. He dashed in the direction the man had retreated. It led to Fifth Avenue, where the intruder could easily slip away. Cole glared down the busy thoroughfare. A man on a bicycle zipped by. Several men puffed cigars outside the hat shop. The postman jaywalked across the street, but—

A hand clapped his shoulder. Cole spun with his fist clenched and ready.

Sterling.

He blew out a ragged breath.

"Forget about me so quickly?" Amusement lit his cousin's eyes, even while his mouth held a firm scowl.

"A man broke into my apartment." His chest burned, though he wasn't sure if it was because of the biting air in his lungs or the sorry fact the blasted guy had escaped.

Sterling's gaze swept the area. "No luck finding him now."

Businesses he could have ducked into lined the avenue. And most likely he'd snuck out the back door of one of them. Confound it.

"Did you catch a glimpse of him?" A bead of water trickled down Sterling's temple. His hair was flattened to his head. Wet. He must've just gotten out of the shower when he'd heard Cole's pounding.

"Not really. He had a lean build. Black clothes, with the jacket collar flipped up and hat pulled low. I think his hair was dark. Nothing substantial." He kicked a piece of garbage out of the way. "Let's get back inside. If you catch a cold two days before your wedding, Sophie will murder me." He scanned the road again. Was this the same man who'd broken into Mom's kitchen last week? The one on the hunt for alcohol?

"What about Jeffrey Shelby? Think it could've been him?" Sterling's suspicious tone threw Cole's train of thought off its rails.

"Why would Jeffrey break into my room?" Cole tugged open

the front door to the complex and allowed Sterling to enter first. "Think he's the vengeful sort and mistook my room for yours? Wanting to vandalize it as he did Gibson's Drug Store?"

Sterling rubbed the turn of his jaw. "That's possible. He refused to answer any questions without his lawyer present." He smacked the railing as they trudged up the steps. "The only information he told me was that his father's death shocked him, and he turned to the bottle for comfort. Not those exact words, mind you." He rolled his eyes. "Let's check your room and see if the intruder left anything."

"The man who broke in was lean. That rules out Jeffrey. No way that stocky man could lose that much poundage in a day." Cole turned the light on, assessing the living room and adjacent kitchenette. Hopefully, the intruder had been careless. He grimaced. "It's probably the same guy who stole the case of wood ethanol. On the hunt again." Cole crouched by the overturned desk, inspecting the scattered papers for something foreign. Nope. All his.

Sterling leaned out the window with incredible skill for a man of his stature. "Nothing on the fire escape." He shrank through the opened space, standing to full height. "My gut is telling me this has something to do with the new will that's gone missing."

"Why would anyone think I have it?" Cole scowled and righted the desk.

"Because you were in Shelby's office last night." He eased the window shut, drawing closed the curtains. "Those two brutes saw you. We don't know who they're working for."

"But how'd they know it was me? Where I live?" Realization struck like a punch to the gut. "Someone's trailing me."

"Most likely."

Dread clawed Cole's chest. If he was being followed, then Elissa could be too. She could be in the sights of the killer. "Can you set up a patrol at the Tillman residence?" If not, Cole would camp outside her front door.

Sterling gave a tight nod. "Consider it done. Did one of those men at Shelby's office match the guy you just saw?"

"No. One was porky, and the other looked malnourished." But neither height nor build mattered when carrying a weapon. Cole'd be sure to stick close to Elissa. "Dr. Sheffield's stature seems the same. Think he could be angry because he wasn't getting any more charity checks? Did Shelby's old will designate funds to Sheffield?"

"The doc's not even mentioned. He'd have no reason to hunt for the new one." Sterling grunted. "Plus, I questioned him right after you told me about your suspicion. He had seven hundred alibis for the night of Shelby's murder. He was speaking at a convention in Erie."

"That excludes him." Cole palmed the back of his neck.

"You say the intruder had dark hair. Be more specific, brown or black?"

"Black."

Sterling gave a tight nod. "I'm thinking you've just met the elusive lab assistant. Matthew Young."

The wind subsided, but a howling chill echoed in the hollow of Elissa's gut as her heels clicked on the charred sidewalk lining Garson Street. She squinted against the noonday sun at the skeletal remains of the Halloway Building.

Why had Mr. Shelby come here that tragic night? Was the Halloway Building the mysterious headquarters he'd spoken to Cole about? She only had her lunch hour to discover all she could. After that, Father might become concerned. Elissa tugged her collar higher, deflecting the slight breeze.

The city had ordered the building's demolition to begin next week, due to the hazardous conditions the fire had wrought. This was her only chance to find a clue, a lead for her article.

She slipped on leather gloves as she skimmed the area. Except for some charred wood scraps, most of the debris from the explosion had been cleared. Stepping over a sooty plank, she made her way to the door Mr. Shelby would have gone through the last day he was alive. She tested the knob. Locked.

She could scour the grounds in hopes he'd dropped something the police hadn't found, but if Sterling was anything like Cole on a pursuit, she was out of luck.

Her heart quickened at the thought of Cole. She wasn't sure how to label their relationship. Holding hands and kissing had pushed them past the boundary of friendship, but the idea of being a couple again tested her courage. She blew out a noisy breath. The man was proving, even in his absence, to be a distraction.

She had to find her story. She had the same alphabet to work with that Cole did, right? This was her opportunity to prove she could piece together the puzzle of letters to fashion a masterpiece worthy of attention.

Elissa walked methodical lines around the building, her gaze pinned to the scarred pavement. After thirty minutes of straining her eyes, she decided her idea was a flop. Besides the soot swirling the air every time the breeze kicked up, she had noticed nothing.

A muffled cough yanked her attention from the blackened building to the adjacent corner. A man huddled in a weather-beaten doorway. His bleak clothing almost blended into his ashen face. His pack, torn and threadbare, lay to his side.

A hobo.

He coughed again, tightening his gray-whiskered jaw, and succumbed to a vicious bout of wheezing. The man needed water or something to coat his throat. She reached for the lozenges in her purse and froze. What if the man was dangerous? What if this was an act to bait her to give him aid, only to assault her? She shook her head. After proofreading scores of articles about Pittsburgh's crime-life, she'd allowed her reasoning to become darkened with fear. It was one thing to be cautious and another to be callous to the needs of others.

The stranger held his ribs with another fit of coughs, and Elissa walked toward him, fishing in her purse for the throat drops. She calculated her distance and stopped a good ten feet from the man, who was now hunched over.

Her fingers squeezed the circular tablets, while her brain suggested she toss them at the scrawny fellow and dash off. But the sag in his posture while he focused on the spit-stained ground made her take another step forward.

She took a calming breath. "Hello."

The man flinched.

"I'm sorry for disturbing you, but I have something that may help." She held out her hand, and the man's gaze softened. "I'll set them here on the walk if you're interested."

He gave a frail smile.

She pivoted toward the road, ears sharp in case the man intended to make his move.

"What's your name?"

Turning, she cleared her throat and acknowledged him with a small smile. "Elissa."

He straightened and cracked his neck to one side then the other. "Thank you kindly, Elissa." He stooped and picked up the lozenges. "It's nice to know decent people exist nowadays. Especially around this place."

"Quite welcome." She offered another warm smile, contemplating. "Have you lived around here for a while?"

"Several months." His eyes lowered while his blackened fingernails worked to unwrap the medicine. "Can't say my lodgings are ideal." He jerked his head toward the doorframe from which he just stepped. "But, at least from my view, you witness a lot of dealings. Some good." He lifted up the lozenge as a reference. "Some not so good."

Her pulse quickened. "Were you here the day of the explosion?" She pointed to the charred structure to her left. "Such a tragedy about Mr. Shelby."

"Maybe I was." He shrugged. "Maybe I wasn't."

So the nice old hobo wasn't as artless as he appeared. She

possessed only a five-dollar bill hidden in case of an emergency, and this qualified. "Any information you have would be helpful." She retrieved the cash from her purse.

The man's back straightened. Five dollars could feed him for three weeks. Four—if he was frugal and didn't waste it in seedy speakeasies. He sucked in air through his teeth, making him cough again.

She waited until his breath evened enough for him to speak.

"So happens that before the explosion, I saw a finely dressed man talking to a woman. She was a pretty woman from what I could see. I was camped over there." He pointed to the neighboring alley. "They argued a bit, and the guy let his temper out on her. Gave her a nice slap on the cheek. She called him a few ugly names and got into her car and drove off."

A woman? Mrs. Shelby? Elissa's brow wrinkled. The hobo had mentioned an attractive woman. Did that mean she was young? Mrs. Shelby was in her late sixties, and while the woman wasn't bad-looking, Elissa wouldn't label her a beauty.

And had the man she argued with been Mr. Shelby? Or someone else?

"What happened to the man? Did he leave too?"

The hobo's gaze slid to the money in her hand. She didn't want to get too close to him, but she didn't want the money carried away on the breeze either. A "No Parking" sign stood six feet away. Elissa folded the money and tucked it into one of the holes in the pole. There.

With a smirk, she stepped away. "Now. About the gentleman you saw? Can you describe him? Like was he tall or short? Old or young? And what became of him?"

He grinned. "Like I said, he was nicely dressed. His suit was all pressed, and he was wearing one of them fancy hats with a satin band. I couldn't see his face too well, but he didn't look too old. He was nice-sized. Tall. A bit on the thicker side. After he slapped the woman, he took off 'round the back."

Elissa tried to keep her heartbeat at a normal pace, but it spiked regardless. This was huge. Finally, a lead!

He stepped over to the sullied sign, withdrew the money, and stuffed it in his frayed coat pocket. "Fell asleep after that and got woken up by the loudest boom I ever heard. The place was in flames, and junk was everywhere. Then came the sirens, and I decided to move on out for a spell."

"Thank you, sir." Elissa beamed, and the man looked at her as if she'd sprouted five heads. "You've been most obliging."

He laughed. "Don't waste those fancy words on me, kiddo. But you're welcome."

She nodded and controlled her steps, walking a few blocks east in hopes of catching a cable car. The man's description eliminated Daniel Shelby. The inventor hadn't been tall and had definitely not been thick. More average height and lean. Could this mystery man have planted the dynamite? Set a timer to explode for when Mr. Shelby was inside the building?

High-dollar suits, a beautiful woman, and an irrational temper? According to the gossip column, all of those factors added up to one man.

Jeffrey Shelby.

CHAPTER 20

Elissa's community of Shadyside boasted charm and elegance, but its neighboring area, Jeffrey Shelby's turf, hosted millionaires. Andrew Carnegie, Henry Clay Frick, Mellon—all had lived in luxurious Point Breeze.

Slim were the odds of Jeffrey Shelby being home. Most wealthy families went south like Canada geese for these horrid winter months. But Elissa clung to the hope that Jeffrey might remain for his father's funeral Thursday. Hopefully, the socialite would find time in his busy schedule of wine and women to attend.

Her fingers, numbed by cold despite her wool gloves, rapped on the door. After Elissa waited a few minutes, the door eased open, and a butler appeared.

Elissa spoke up. "Miss …" Oh, she couldn't give her true name. "Freedy to see Mr. Shelby."

The butler waited for her card, hand outstretched, palm up.

"I'm afraid I left all my announcements in my other purse." Not a full lie. Her cards were indeed in her black clutch, but the butler did not need to know they read Tillman and not Freedy.

He nodded and opened the door wider, allowing her admittance to the stately house. Ornate, carved wooden panels lined the entryway, surrounding an enormous staircase leading to the second floor. The heels of her T-straps tapped the marble floors.

Her house was larger than most, but this, this was grandiose.

Elissa shed her gloves, and the butler received her coat and hat.

She ran a hand down her burgundy dress and followed the older gentlemen, who turned left and shuffled down another hall lined with paintings. How did Jeffrey get this kind of money? Yeah, his father could afford such a home, but did his father pay for all of this? The Mr. Shelby she had come to know through Cole had been a simple man, preferring mutton to steak and synthetic fur to fox fur.

The butler opened a carved door with an "S" etched in the center of the fancy woodwork. "Please wait in the study while I summon Mr. Shelby."

"Thank you." Elissa smiled, but the man was already out of the room.

The study wasn't as large as what she would've expected in a house like this, but the fire crackling from the hearth gave it a cozy aura. A mahogany desk crowded the space to her left, and two tall bookshelves stood behind. Books. Elissa's weakness. While she hardly expected a man like Jeffrey Shelby to own a copy of *Jane Eyre*, she investigated the spines of possible book-friends.

Hemingway, Dickens, and Melville filled the middle shelf, but most of the works were poetry. Cole would love this collection. Her fingers itched to pull out Wordsworth and find the works Cole had read to her many summers ago—when life had consisted of moonlight kisses—when she was supposed to be home tucked in bed. Instead of reading by the gas lamp, she had been listening to Cole's deep timbre reading of stars, seas, and her favorite fields of flowers.

"See something you like?"

Elissa's spine snapped straight.

Pittsburgh's playboy leaned against the doorframe, his arms linked across his chest as if he'd been there all day. The velvet robe over his suit and hair styled better than Elissa's said this man valued appearance as much as his lofty bank account.

He flashed a smile, exposing dimples that probably charmed more women than Casanova. "Hopefully, you find something to your liking." He dipped his chin and moved toward her like a hawk swooping in on his prey.

Oh, what a flirt. Shouldn't he be mourning? His brows weren't slumped in grief but arched in interest.

"Allow me to express my sympathies on the recent death of your father."

His gaze shifted to the fireplace behind her. "Thank you." After several crackles from the hearth, he returned his attention to her. "And to what do I owe the pleasure of your company, Miss Freedy?"

"I'm from the women's club. The one your father donated to. I've been tasked to inquire if you'd supply us with some kind words about him. Your comments would be placed in our quarterly letter along with those from others who've had the benefit of knowing Mr. Shelby. It's a memorial letter, you know?" The spiel she'd practiced on the trip over flowed without a hitch. She trained her focus on him, hoping to catch a reaction. If he disdained his father, she'd detect it.

"I see." He sunk his hands in the robe's pockets. "How much time do you have to spend with me?"

"As much as needed, sir." His lips twitched, and she caught her mistake. He'd viewed it as an invitation. "That is, I'm so glad you have ample amounts of generous words about your father. Perhaps this could help in your grieving."

His shoulders sagged slightly. "Yes, that."

She retrieved a notepad from her pocket. "Is this a good time for you? Or would you rather have time to reflect? We can meet again."

His brown eyes twinkled. "But the question is, have we met before?"

Elissa fought against an eye roll. One would think the well-seasoned aristocrat would be more skillful in his schmoozing. "I don't believe so." Because Shelby had been several years older than she and had attended an all-male, private school in Point Breeze, there was little chance of him knowing about the Shadyside Slob.

"That's splendid. I've always been fond of forming new acquaintances. Making friends."

Elissa took a step back. Jeffrey wouldn't be getting *friendly* today. Not with her. But she had to sway him into talking about his father. Up to this point, she hadn't sensed any emotion besides eagerness, unnerving her. No guilt. No anger. No trace of loss or regret. What kind of relationship had these Shelby men had?

Flipping open the notepad, she tightened her grip on the pencil and braved a weak smile. "May I ask what your favorite memory was with your father? Or perhaps you'd like to begin with what his legacy means to you? Either one."

He cleared his throat. "You may be seated, if you like." He gestured to a wing-back leather chair. "I may need a few moments to gather my thoughts."

"Of course." She sat in the plush seat, her nearness to the fire increasing her warmth. She expected him to sit behind his desk, but instead he paced the rug behind her.

"I will say my old man had a vigorous work ethic." Agitation lathered his voice. Or maybe it was hurt. Cole had relayed that Mr. Shelby had missed several of Jeffrey's ball games because of job deadlines. Perhaps that had caused the strain between them.

"That's notable." She jotted it down. "Thank you. Anything else?" Time to poke the bear. "Loyalty to family, perhaps?"

He scoffed. "Mother, maybe."

Sympathy softened her disgust. Wounds cut deep always rose to the surface. But did Jeffrey possess enough anger to kill his own father? Such an extreme measure. Warmth from his hand pressed into her shoulder. He towered over her, the look in his eyes hungry.

"Do you dance, Miss Freedy?" He removed his hand and walked to the other side of the room where a Victrola stood. He fingered through some records.

Her phonograph looked paltry compared to this one. Gold parts and fancy milled hardwood. "Um, I don't dance with strangers."

"Like I said, I have my ways of becoming acquainted." He

slipped a record on the turntable and wound the crank. "After all, I think it will take me a length of time to accurately relay my sentiments about my father."

Woodwind music crooned from the phonograph, and the light in his eyes glinted brighter than the sizzling fire. Elissa needed out of this place before the man deluded himself into imagining her interest. She launched to her feet. "I'll be more than willing to scribe your words. Can we meet at a coffee house next week?" A nice crowded place, where his hands could hold a mug and not her.

His brows furrowed and then lifted. "I'll be at The Steel Fountain tomorrow night. You could meet me there."

The Steel Fountain was a swanky speakeasy supposedly protected by city magistrates. Her stomach soured. Integrity died when graft money fattened the pockets of the honest.

"Or here." He shifted closer. "We can dance here. Privately."

Oh no, she wouldn't. "Thank you for the invitation, sir, but I am already engaged for the evening."

His hand slid across her back. "Why waste this moment?" He scooped her in his arms, and she did everything she could not to stab her heel into his shoe.

"Please release me."

He laughed. "I'm not used to rejection, Miss Freedy."

Then she would knock him over the head with the brass candlestick on the mantel. She wasn't sure she'd need to resort to such measures, but her eyes found something enlightening beside her could-be weapon.

A pipe.

And by its carvings, a significant one.

Jeffrey nuzzled her hair, and she pulled back. "What a remarkable item." She broke free and gestured to the mantel. "Those markings and the lettering."

His gaze darkened. "It's nothing." He snatched it from the wood plank and shoved it in his robe pocket. "Only a family heirloom." The recording had ended, and the ticking of the needle on the record filled the room. He rushed over and plucked it up.

"I should leave, Mr. Shelby. I do have an engagement to attend."

His manner softened. "Forgive me if I was too forward with you. I sometimes act impetuously, especially during difficult times."

Was he trying to tell her something deeper? "Of course, Mr. Shelby."

"Please call me Jeffrey." He reached for her hand and kissed it. "Remember an invitation for dinner and dancing is yours. You tell me the day."

She forced a smile. "I'll be sure to inform you when I'm free." Which would be never. "Good day. I believe I can let myself out." And with the knowledge she'd just gained, she was going straight to the newsroom.

After seven o'clock, the newsroom fell vacant. Elissa had approximately an hour before she met Cole for dinner. The butterflies invading her stomach flew north, making her chest tight. Within the next moments, she'd know if the story's lead would prove fit for the typewriter or the trash bin.

She opened the bottom drawer, and her jaw unhinged. Her articles. The ones she'd penned about the Cartelli case had been moved. The order at her secretarial station had always been the *Review* paperwork to the left and her personal projects to the right. And currently, the Cartelli articles were mingled with the advertisement log. Not only that, but the pages were not in chronological order.

She fell back in her chair.

Who would tamper with those articles? Why? Maybe she should put a lock on the drawer. Not that the writings were anything but a pretense—a futile attempt to prove to herself she could write noteworthy editorials.

Sighing, she rummaged through and found the flyer which included an image of the identical pipe she'd spotted at Jeffrey

Shelby's. Perfect match.

Maple Grove Lodge.

Nestled across the state in the Poconos, the resort offered an escape for the well-to-do. After contacting the place, Elissa had decided since Maple Grove benefitted only the rich, it wouldn't make a sensible spotlight for the society column. But her favorite feature had been the honeymoon package, including a stay at a secluded cabin and offering a luxurious tea set for the bride and an engraved pipe for the groom.

Jeffrey Shelby had been secretly married.

CHAPTER 21

"I'm going to propose to you in tomorrow's spread." Cole leaned over his Delmonico steak, wanting to hear Elissa's warm voice more than the rich tones coming from The Regent's string quartet. "I need you to proofread it first. Will you do that for me?"

Elissa pushed her peas about her plate with her fork. "Sure, leave it on my desk. I'll—" Her head snapped up, and the glow from the candle danced across her features. "What did you say?"

"Just checking to see if you're listening." Cole chuckled. "But that's not a half-bad idea."

"Not a sound one either." She grimaced, her gaze following a waiter walking past with a tray of food. "This is technically only our second date."

He leaned back in his chair with a shake of the head. "No. It's more like our thousandth."

"The previous ones don't count." Her smile slipped from her face, and the pain struck him afresh.

"No more injuries, and no more running." He reached across the table and covered her hand with his. A gesture he'd done a million times before, but this was different. He held it like he would her heart, with protectiveness. "Just so you know. I'm not going anywhere."

Her lashes lowered with a sigh, disturbing the lace on her collar.

He hadn't proven himself yet, but he would. "So tell me, what has you distracted?"

Elissa fidgeted with her napkin, hesitancy marking the deep hues of her eyes. "I ran some errands today, and they've been weighing on my mind. That's all."

"Such as?" He motioned for her to continue, but she sampled her tomato bisque. "Have you started working on the article for your father yet? Any leads?"

Her fingers faltered, spilling a spoonful of soup on her ivory blouse. Her skin blanched, matching the napkin she scrambled for. "I can't believe I did that." She vigorously swiped at the crimson stains.

"I can hardly see it." Slight lie.

Deep creases bracketed her frown. "Everyone will notice."

Why did she care so much? "No. People will be too enthralled with your pretty face to notice anything amiss."

"That's a little much, Cole." With a frustrated huff, she lowered the napkin to her lap. "I'm aware of your pretense. You don't have to spare my feelings."

"What pretense?" Since when was complimenting a beautiful woman an insult?

"You *said* you never returned because of your father, but I can't help but feel there's more to it. I can handle the cold reality. In fact, I'll speak it for you. You never returned because I couldn't measure up. If you're wanting a perfect woman like Kathleen Stigert, I suggest you look elsewhere."

"Why would you mention her?" Then it hit him. The picture on Mom's wall. The falsehoods surrounding their non-existent relationship. From the cemented frown on Elissa's face, the gossip had reached Pittsburgh. "Kathy and I are just friends. There was nothing between us."

Elissa gave him a knowing look. "Not sure how you expect me to believe that. The woman is gorgeous and flawless."

"Untrue. She had a flaw. A major one." He latched his gaze on hers. "She wasn't you."

Elissa turned her face away, but not before he saw the lone tear coursing along her cheekbone.

"I've only ever had eyes for one girl, and she's sitting across from me."

She scoffed. "You think this now, but the ending will remain the same. Because I still don't measure up."

Her words sank in with hooks, unrelenting. How could she feel that way? "Ah, but you do."

"No. You don't understand."

"I want to."

Elissa trained her focus on the burgundy tablecloth. "I feel as if I have a deep gash in my soul."

"That's the best place for light to enter." Cole pointed to the cracked kitchen door, where a golden sliver shone through. "Scars may be present." He glanced at his knuckle. "But it's how we view them which makes the difference. They can be a reminder of defeat, or that our failures weren't bigger than our God."

Ice clinked in glasses. Silverware scraped against plates. And Elissa Tillman sat stoically.

"I'm sorry, Spark. Here I've been the cause of your pain, but now it's my desire to be the reason for your happiness. I'll prove it."

"It may take a while."

He shrugged. "As I said, I'm not going anywhere."

The maître d' approached their table, a telegram in hand. "For you, Miss Tillman."

Elissa thanked him and read it, eyes widening. "Father's in the hospital. Problems with his heart."

Elissa pushed open the hospital room's door, stomach queasy, nerves taut. Mother sat in a chair beside the bed, holding Father's hand. Her parents looked over as Cole and Elissa stepped inside.

"What happened?" Elissa rushed to her father's bedside,

brushing the tears from her face.

He raised a veined hand. "It's okay, Lissie." The weakened rasp of his voice hardly confirmed his words.

Cole's palm pressed against her lower back, a reminder of his supporting presence.

"Heartburn. Not a heart attack." The lines bunching around her mother's mouth relaxed as if the news just sank into her as well. "He'll be fine. Only needs to have less stress."

Father grunted. "If the doctors can loan me several grand, then maybe I'll be more relaxed."

Mother worried her bottom lip, patting his hand. "Don't think of it. Not now."

The paper's financial situation crowded her father's brain more than anything else. Elissa had to find a way to increase revenue. Father couldn't bear the burden alone. She leaned over and kissed his brow. "I love you, Old Block." She hadn't called him that since grade school when he'd introduce her at parties as the chip off the old block.

"Right back at you, Chip." He smiled, eyes glossy.

"We should let him rest." Mother stood and kissed his cheek.

Father grinned at Cole. "See, my boy, all you have to do is feign an illness, and beautiful women kiss you."

Cole's deep chuckle trickled in her ears. "I'll remember that, sir."

"No, you won't." Elissa nudged his side with her elbow.

Her father and mother stared at them with raised brows. She'd forgotten her parents weren't aware of the renewed relationship. If she could call it that.

Cole wove his fingers in hers, earning a wink from her father and a graceful smile from her mother. "We'll be praying for you, boss."

After one more kiss to Father's cheek and an understanding smile to Mother, Elissa exited the room, Cole following.

The fatigue tangling her thoughts must have appeared on her

face, for Cole wrapped his arm around her and practically upheld her as they made their way down the empty hall.

"I have to find a way to rescue the paper."

Cole stopped, his grasp on her hand jerking her to a halt. "Why does the weight fall on you?"

How could she explain? Not only did she want the *Review* to succeed for her father—to help him escape the pain of failure—but for herself as well. Her dream might appear selfish, but the paper had belonged to the Tillmans for two generations, and she'd hoped to be the third. A woman publisher.

Her gaze wandered over the beige walls to the glossy floors. The smell of antiseptic filled the air, the harsh scent bringing her back to reality. Maybe the time had come to wake up. Fanciful illusions had deceived her before. She glanced at Cole. Maybe she was falling back into the same snare she had five years ago. Her dreams had slipped through her fingers then, but with the *Review*, she could control the outcome. She'd save it.

Cole downed the meager remains of his coffee and tossed some coins on the counter. He cuffed the back of his neck, rubbing a knot. Sleep had eluded him most of last night as concerns for Elissa plagued him. Her expression in the hospital hallway haunted him. Desperation had etched lines framing her pain-filled eyes. He knew that look. One where the pressure to rescue a loved one, to ease the burden, bombarded the reasoning, forcing action. But the question was—what action would Elissa take?

Cole stood and slapped his hat onto his head.

Elissa had busied herself all morning, poring over financial ledgers in between proofreading articles and answering calls. Then she'd received a telegram which had prompted her to leave without so much as a goodbye. Cole was thankful he'd have all evening with her. They needed to have a long talk.

He checked his watch. Two o'clock. Three hours until the

wedding. Cole had plenty of time before he had to be at the church, but he should return to his apartment. Mother had been jittery since the last break-in.

He turned to exit the modest café but stopped. Mrs. Shelby sat alone in the corner booth, picking at a sandwich and sniffling into a handkerchief. Cole approached her, but she never glanced over.

"Good afternoon, ma'am." Cole removed his hat and held it over his chest.

Startled eyes met his. "Oh, excuse me." She frantically dabbed her nose. "I wasn't aware of your presence."

"I wanted to convey my sympathies over the recent passing of your husband. He was a good person."

"Thank you, young man."

"I had the privilege of being tutored by Mr. Shelby when I was younger. Because of him, I passed in ninth-grade science."

Her mouth pinched for a second then relaxed. "Are you Cole Parker?"

"Yes, ma'am."

"Please forgive me for not remembering. I'm better with names than with faces." She gave a feeble smile. "Dan was fond of you. Always mentioning how bright you were even if you couldn't comprehend the periodic table."

He chuckled low. "I still can't."

Her slow gaze traveled around the room and settled on him. "This place was his favorite café."

"Really?"

"They served fried catfish with cayenne pepper just for him. I don't know how Dan could stomach it, but he'd dump half the bottle on his food. That was always his preference. Spicy things."

Cole fingered the brim of his hat. "I hope the good memories you shared will bring comfort."

Her eyes brightened behind the glossy sheen. "Thank you."

Cole dipped his chin and said goodbye. His chest ached. What confusion and agony Mrs. Shelby endured. To ardently love someone whom you'd believed felt the same, only to be deceived in the end.

He froze.

Was that how Elissa had felt the day he'd failed to return on the train? No wonder she remained guarded. His resolve strengthened. He had no idea how to save a newspaper, but maybe he could rescue her dreams.

CHAPTER 22

Cole adjusted his bowtie for the fifteenth time since arriving at McKees Rocks Christian Church. Family and friends of the bride and groom filled the cedar pews. On the platform, the minister rocked on his heels, humming "O Perfect Love." Mom, fidgeting with the buttons adorning her sleeve, sat beside Sterling's mother, just in from Virginia. The woman shined brighter than the emerald brooch pinned to her collar, a gift from Sterling's late father.

From the lowest step, Cole craned his neck and peered through the glass window behind him, grimacing at the outside view.

No Elissa.

Had he told her the wrong time? What if her father had another episode? He rubbed his brow, heat coursing his veins.

"What have you to be nervous about?" Sterling stood on the top step, his large frame stuffed into a tuxedo making him resemble an Italian crime boss more than a groom. "I'm the one getting hitched."

"I'm happy for you, cousin." Cole smiled. "Though I can't help but pity Sophie."

Sterling chuckled.

Yep, his cousin's mood scaled higher than the steeple. A contented smirk replaced Sterling's routine, chiseled scowl. His narrowed eyes widened in expectation of seeing his future wife.

Yearning birthed in Cole. A bride. A family. Maybe a curly-haired daughter who mirrored her mother. He scanned the crowd again for any sign of Elissa. His chest deflated. Where could she be?

The organ's steel pipes belted the fanfare to "The Wedding March," and every pew creaked as guests turned in their seats. Attendants opened the wooden double-doors. Candles flickered. Sterling sucked in a sharp breath.

Nothing.

The organist crumpled her brow and replayed the fanfare. Sterling shifted behind him.

A messenger boy dashed through the doorway, sprinting down the aisle toward the minister. The child, puffing his cheeks with heavy breaths, handed the minister the telegram, but Sterling intercepted it. Cole's cousin tore it open, and his face hardened like the stone cross behind him.

"What's wrong?" Cole stepped closer and eyed the telegram before it crinkled in Sterling's iron grasp.

I can't marry you. I'm sorry.

His cousin glowered at the door the messenger boy retreated through, his nostrils flaring, masking his hurt with anger like when he'd been younger.

"Go find her. I'll take care of everything here." Cole placed a hand on Sterling's shoulder, and the gesture seemed to snap him out of the daze. Sterling gave a tight nod and strode out the back, leaving a confused mass of people in his wake.

Cole moved to the center step. "Ladies and gentlemen, thank you for coming, but there won't be a wedding today."

Gasps and murmurs echoed off the wood-paneled walls.

Wherever Elissa was, Cole sure hoped she was having a better time than he.

Of all the bad choices Elissa ever had made, this could be the worst. But what other option had she? She adjusted her faux pearl headband and stepped into The Steel Fountain Club. The bouncer at the door hadn't required a passcode or even a membership number. Purchasing passes into speakeasies for a high price had been on the rise lately, but no, all she had to do was slip the man some cash and follow the white painted arrows to the correct doors.

Pathetic.

Prohibition seemed valid only on paper.

The fringe of her dress tickled her knees with every step into the smoke-thickened club. Jeffrey had said he'd be here tonight, Wednesday, and she hoped he'd kept his word. The telegram in her purse forced this extreme action.

Slot machines lined the paisley-papered walls. Couples littered the dance floor, and Pittsburgh scotch soiled the fancy linens. A band gathered in the corner. Some musicians sat on stools, while others stood, swaying to the jazz melody. She gulped and willed her legs not to wobble like chilled marmalade.

She took in the vast area, perusing the plush red sofas and several tables. Approaching her from the right side of the room with a grin as thick as the cosmetics lining her eyes, Jeffrey Shelby captured the attention of every female within a twenty-foot radius.

"I see you came for me after all." His dark eyes focused on her.

She gnawed her bottom lip, tasting the grit of her lipstick. "Evening, Mr. Shelby."

With a wry smile, he tapped her nose, the drink in his hand swishing with the movement. "I thought we decided that you'd call me Jeffrey. Or Jeff, if you want to be more personal."

The rattle from the roulette table mixed with gleeful murmurs.

"I came to see if you'd remembered any more information for my women's club. The deadline is soon." Sooner than he knew. Four days and she needed to have an article on Father's desk and hopefully a sound plan to save the paper.

He laughed and grabbed her hand. Oh, the relief of wearing elbow-length gloves. She'd rather his oily fingers mar the satin than caress her skin.

"Is that really why you came here?" His gaze raked her body. "You look temptingly stunning to be concerned about a stuffy women's club."

"I confess I have a curious nature." Too curious. Would she be able to encourage him to speak openly? Maybe even admit to the accusation listed in the telegram? She inhaled a ragged breath and lowered her mascaraed lashes for a long blink.

"I'm fond of those kinds of natures." He sipped his drink, gaze locked on hers over his glass. "By the way, since you're calling me Jeff, it seems unfair to refer to you as Miss Freedy. How am I to address you?"

"Elissa?" A deep voice trickled over her shoulder.

She turned.

Adam.

Her gut sank lower than the three flights of stairs she'd descended to enter this place.

"Ah, Elissa, is it? Lovely name. Fitting." Jeff clapped Adam on the shoulder and lifted a dark brow. "And how are you acquainted with this gentleman?"

"I ... uh ..." This wasn't how the evening was supposed to unfold. What was Adam doing at a speakeasy, looking mighty comfortable breaking the law, sipping his wine? "We've known each other since we were young."

Adam stepped closer. "What are you doing here? And looking so ... so modern?" He spoke low in her ear and then pulled away to study her face.

She huffed. Elissa had combed her closet until she'd discovered a dress fit for raising the hemline and adding heavy amounts of fringe. What Adam had called modern, she called a tiresome endeavor. She shot the *Review* columnist a warning glare. At least she hoped it was one. Judging by Adam's smirk and the lazy way he eyed her, she feared he misunderstood.

Jeffrey observed the exchange with a bemused expression. Perhaps she should go home. Her strategy was failing, and the only way it could worsen would be if—

"I worked for her father." A waiter passed by, and Adam set his empty glass on the tray. "Before I got a job at the *Dispatch*."

Elissa's jaw slackened. "What? Since when?"

He straightened his suit jacket. "I leave for New York Monday. Care to join me?" The charming smile returned with the bonus of his dimples.

"So you're in the newspaper industry?" Jeffrey asked the question to both of them, but his penetrating glare sharpened on Elissa.

Adam laughed. "Her father owns the *Review*. Elissa's heart and soul is that paper."

Her gaze darted toward the exit. Now if only her legs weren't frozen stiff.

"The women's club, huh? I applaud your efforts, love." He lifted his glass in a toast.

The iron fist which had clenched her heart reached up and grabbed her throat, choking her from replying.

"Elissa, are you okay?" Adam looked between them. "What's going on?"

"This little scout is on the hunt for a story. Sorry your boyfriend had to ruin the ruse. We could've had fun."

A muscle ticked in Adam's cheek. "That's not the way you speak to a lady, Shelby."

"Lady? Maybe I should see how far she would go to get her scoop." Jeffrey grabbed her wrist and planted a kiss full on her lips.

She yanked back and slapped him, her measly glove lessening the impact.

"Don't touch her again." Adam shrugged off his jacket. "Or you'll have to answer to me."

A wicked smile crested Jeffrey's lips, and he widened his stance.

Elissa stepped between them. "Maybe I should just call Doris Green."

The spark of rage in Jeffrey's eyes extinguished into surprise.

"What?"

"The popular Ziegfeld Follies' actress." Her smirk held an edge of glee. "Or should I address her as Mrs. Shelby?"

His earlobes reddened. "How did you—"

"I'm a good little scout." She adjusted her glove, her fingers barely tingling from making contact with his arrogant face. "It's been reported that Doris recently visited Pittsburgh. I've also spoken with a witness who saw you and your wife arguing in front of the very building your father would be murdered in hours later."

"That's a lie!" His harsh tone garnered looks from other imbibers. "I was nowhere near the place."

"Just like that pipe is an old family heirloom."

His eyes darkened at her words.

"When it happens to be the honeymoon perk at Maple Grove Lodge." Her brows rose in a knowing arch. "The landlord confirmed your visit with Doris from the last weekend of December."

Jeffrey started toward Elissa, but Adam shifted in front of her and shoved him back. "I told you *not* to touch her."

"Woman, if you print that junk in your lousy paper, you'll be sorry." Spittle flew with his warning, his breaths heaving. He pointed a finger at her. "I'll see to it. I have many friends. Many."

Her heart raced at his threats. The rage in his dark eyes strengthened her case against him. This man was impulsive, deceiving, and possibly murderous. She stepped behind Adam, and her gaze snagged on a man in the corner, watching her. The intruder who'd wielded a knife at Shelby's office. Elissa's gut twisted.

Whistles pierced from the entrance, and uniformed men stormed in, billy clubs in hand. Federal agents.

CHAPTER 23

"How much did they offer?" Tillman's throaty voice penetrated through his closed office door, stopping Cole from his intended knock. He inclined his ear, trying to tune in over the frenzied noise of the newsroom.

"That's a decent price. Would they keep my staff? That's important to me if I were to sell."

Sell.

Cole stepped back, his heart sinking with each breath, and trudged to his chair.

Elissa would be devastated. But what could he do?

He elbowed his desk, leaning his forehead on his fists. Cole still had connections, maybe not with the *New York Dispatch*, but with other prominent papers. Had the conversation with the *Boston Globe*'s editor a while back been genuine, or was the man only feeding Cole small talk about welcoming writing samples for a possible position? Cole didn't desire the journalist job, but Elissa might. What other options would she have after the *Review* shut the press?

Cole glanced at his watch. Five till eight.

Most mornings, Elissa arrived before him. Not today. He frowned. What time was she coming in? He hadn't talked to her since yesterday morning. After the chaos at the church, Cole'd swung by Elissa's house only to be told she wasn't home. Where could she have gone? Whatever the reason, it must have been a serious, principled one. He may have broken promises in the past, but Elissa never had.

Cole eyed her desk. Only a minute or two would be enough.

He moved swiftly to her station. Cole had the habit of stealing pencils and typewriter ribbon from Elissa so it wouldn't appear odd to any onlooker. Instead of him opening the top drawer, he'd simply rummage through the bottom.

The wooden joints creaked, but not loud enough to attract notice. He grabbed a stack of papers, sifting through until one caught his eye.

"Women's Suffrage Stretches Beyond the Right to Vote."

He skimmed it. An article about equality in the workplace. Complete with facts about women getting lesser wages than men for the same occupation. Elissa had crafted this with brilliance, evoking emotion with powerful, deliberate words. He folded the paper and shoved it in his pocket.

Perhaps he should select a few more to provide a well-rounded take on her talent. Given the immense stack of paper, it'd take him a great deal of time to read them all.

"What are you doing?" Elissa's voice simmered with outrage.

His eyes slid shut against his wince. He attempted composure and hazarded a look her way.

"So it was you who's been going through my articles." Her tone, sharper than a razor blade, nicked his defenses.

"What?" He glanced at his hand, still clutching her work, and then back at her. "It's not what you think."

"You're trying to find my story for the contest." She grabbed the papers from him.

He'd forgotten all about that. "This has nothing to do with it." He stood from his crouched position.

"Really?" A perfect brow arched. "Evidence says otherwise." She flicked the corner of the stack of editorials and then put them back in the drawer, slamming it closed.

A few *Review* employees glanced over, Frank waving his pointer finger as if to say *shame-shame*. No, the shame lay in the fact that Cole couldn't relay the truth, not without exposing her father's plans. Tillman should be the one to break the news. Cole owed him that.

"Elissa, I can't explain. Not yet."

She pushed past him and took her seat. "Then let me explain something. I do not want to be near you. Talk to you. Even look at you. I should've trusted reason rather than heart." She motioned between them, a sheen filling her eyes. "This was all a hoax. Maybe acting is your true profession."

Cole placed a hand on her shoulder. "Sweetheart, let's go somewhere and talk. This isn't the place—"

She jerked from his touch. "I can write as well as any man, and you wanted to take that away from me. Stealing my article?" She slammed her palms on the desktop. "What were you going to do? Use it as your own?"

"I wouldn't dream of it." This was going south, fast. "I know you're only a secretary here, but your qualif—"

"Oh, that's right. You're the star reporter. Well, you may have been at one time, but now you're nothing but a destroyer. You destroyed your own career and now this relationship. Again."

Kendrew breezed in the door, clad in his driving duster, jogging toward Elissa. "I only have a second, but I wanted to be sure you recovered from last night. You were pretty shaken up when I took you home."

Elissa stiffened. "I'm fine. Thank you." Her panic-stricken gaze cast all around, settling on Frank. He eased back in his chair, brows raised in delighted interest, as though he was watching a nickelodeon. She narrowed her eyes at him.

"Last night?" Cole straightened, barring his arms over his expanded chest. "You stood me up for Kendrew?"

"Stood you ..." She jerked her glare from Frank and gaped at Cole, her fingers flitting to her mouth. "The wedding! I—I forgot."

Heat scorched through him. "Looks like distrust can go both

ways." His sharp words seemed to bleed the color from her face. Cole hardened himself against the flicker of hurt in her eyes.

"You know, Parker,"—Kendrew smiled, and Cole plunged his hands in his pockets to keep from pinning the man to the wall— "there are things about this girl that would surprise you to no end."

"Is that so?" The growl in his chest strove to break free.

"Mmm-hmm." He winked at Elissa, and Cole ground his jaw. "The offer still stands, darling. My train leaves from Union Station at ten, Monday morning. Love for you to be by my side." He didn't wait for her response but turned on his heel, stopping briefly to mention something to Frank before he strode out.

Cole should've given him a black eye as a souvenir.

"You went on a date with Kendrew?" Cole worked to control an even tone while fire sluiced through his veins.

"I apologize for missing the wedding." Her voice shook, and she avoided eye contact. "But anything else is none of your concern, Mr. Parker." She scooted her chair closer to the desk and withdrew a ledger.

"None of my concern?" He leaned over, grasping the sides of her desk. "Elissa, I'm not sure what game you're playing with me, but I don't like being two-timed." Better to discover this now rather than wait and experience Sterling's situation. His bride had skipped town. Cole had never witnessed Sterling so distraught. No, Cole would not be the next victim of female toying.

Her chin jutted, her gaze stormy, raging waves of blue. "That's quite the line coming from a man who just had his thieving hands in my desk."

He straightened. "I wasn't stealing."

"Hey, young lady." Frank scratched his belly, walking toward her. "Adam told me about The Steel Fountain. Didn't know you had it in ya." He gently smacked her shoulder. "Makes me proud."

"A speakeasy?" Cole's blood turned to ice water. The exact place Cole had been writing about this morning. The governor had ordered the raid as a message to the local magistrates who'd received graft money. All the while, the woman he loved had been carousing there, slaking her thirst with the forbidden liquid that had caused Cole's ruin. "You went with Kendrew?"

Her eyes turned sheepish. "Not exactly, but I did go. Adam helped me escape when the agents came."

"I've heard enough." Cole slapped his homburg on his head, yanked his article out of the typewriter carriage, and tossed it on the folder lying beside her. "Hope your every dream comes true, Miss Tillman."

The fragrance of vanilla normally brightened Elissa's spirits, but not even helping her parents bake Sussex Pond Pudding could cure the sadness. Cooking this dish had been a family tradition, marking the day Elissa's great-grandparents had sailed over from England.

She tapped the tines of the fork against the napkin, this morning's event weighing heavy in her gut.

Cole hadn't changed. She'd pegged him correctly from the beginning. Trample others if they hindered him from his goal. He'd burned Elissa once in pursuit of his career, and she'd been stupid enough to allow him to do it again.

Yet as much as Cole was to blame for their ruined relationship, she bore a sliver of the fault. She'd forgotten about her date with him. Missed the wedding. Well, the almost-wedding. When she'd heard about Sophie abandoning Sterling at the altar, Elissa's heart had splintered. Poor Sterling.

She released a gusty sigh, disturbing a few specks of flour coating the table where the pastry would be rolled out.

"Care to share, my love?" Mother stirred the eggs, the click of the spoon against the bowl scraping every one of Elissa's nerves.

She ran a finger along the counter, her silence pulling Father's attention from measuring the brown sugar. What could she tell them? How much of the speakeasy gossip had already reached Father? It hadn't been as if she and Cole had been quiet with their heated conversation in the newsroom.

Distrust can go both ways.

His words had serrated her heart. How could he have believed she would run around with Adam after what she and Cole had shared? Was his opinion of her that low? The pain glazing his eyes had seemed sincere. So had all those kisses. But his promise to prove himself? Ha! She clenched the dough, practically strangling the pastry.

"Lissie?" Father's voice broke through her anguished thoughts. Drat. She hadn't answered them.

Elissa pulled in a heavy breath. "I visited a speakeasy last night."

Mother lost her spoon in the bowl.

Father's eyes widened larger than the tablespoon in his hand.

She reached for the dishtowel and wiped clean the splashes of egg on the counter. "Not for enjoyment. Believe me, I didn't take a sip." Might as well confess everything. "I also went to Bootlegger Alley chasing a story."

"Not again," Father mumbled and tightened the lid on the sugar canister. "I specifically asked him to watch over you."

Elissa shifted forward, stomach butting against the counter. "What? Who?"

"Never mind." He rubbed his brows, almost pinching them together. "You shouldn't be going to such places. I'm disappointed in you."

And it never ended. Her failures. Her faults.

"It's dangerous." Mother wrung her hands on her apron. "What if something had happened to you?"

Elissa couldn't process her mother's concern. Not when Father's obvious blunder gripped her heart, shoving her curiosity to high levels. "Who did you ask to watch over me?" For some reason, she didn't believe he'd referred to the patrolman she'd spotted near the house.

"Cole."

The burn of something she couldn't pinpoint seared the backs of her eyes. She blinked, but the fire remained. "Why?"

"I know, Lissie. I know all about it." He set the utensils in the sink and regarded her with that fatherly expression that told her she'd done something wrong. "I found your articles about the Cartelli case. You went to dingy bars and traipsed around in search of the scoop. You even interviewed a bootlegger."

Her jaw dropped. Mother gasped.

"How do you know this?" Elissa tightened her grip on the edge of the counter. "Did you snoop in my desk drawer too?"

His jowly chin dipped.

Both Cole and her father? The very men who should have encouraged her had gone behind her back. Invaded her personal space. "I know why Cole did, but why you?" Understanding pierced her chest. "It was all pretense. The contest. The opportunity to get my article above the fold. Cole's feelings for me. All a deception to keep little Elissa from harming herself." She glanced at her incapable hands. Hands that were only to answer phones, cook dinners, and stay tucked in pockets away from life's adventures.

Mother gazed at her with innocent blues. "Elissa, I don't understand. What's going on?" Her attention bounced between them. "What's wrong here?"

The truth pressed against Elissa's soul, forcing a hot tear down her cheek. "It's simple, Mother. You should've had a son. That's the qualification I lack." The thick air pinched her lungs, her breathing sharp against her ribs. "Perhaps Cole could fill that position. He and Father are like-minded."

She ran from the room, from the house, from the world that set itself against her.

The chill of the stone pressed through her tweed skirt, but the numbing had started long before she reached her favorite thinking spot. Her refuge. On the edge of Shadyside, situated in front of the massive Howe estate, Howe Springs might have only been a refreshing area for some, but to her, it'd become a place where she solved life's problems.

The open-faced building, with its carved pillars supporting the thick roof, had always reminded her of a Greek temple. Only instead of housing ancient rulers, it lodged three natural fountains. Nooks with benches bookended the structure, high retaining barriers on one side and stone walls framing the springs on the other. The cove on the right Elissa had claimed as her own.

In these waters, Cole had washed the soil and blood from his wounds. His torn cap had flopped over eyes too weary for his years. What if she hadn't come here to read that day? Their paths wouldn't have crossed. Their lives wouldn't have entwined. Her heart would've never been broken.

The clouds, a confining gray, blocked the sun, and the breeze rattled the bare limbs of maple trees behind her. Nature sighed its coldness, and her soul felt just as drafty.

Now she understood her place in life. Cole had only paid attention to her because Father had insisted, and he sure had taken advantage of the opportunity.

Not enough.

The chant which had echoed within her years ago returned, pulsing through her entire being. She hadn't been enough to make Cole love her for who she was. Not talented enough for Father. Not poised enough for Mother's expectations. Not refined enough for society. Not. Enough.

She fingered her yellow rose. Even her efforts for the women's movement had amounted to nothing. What was she good for?

Trapped beneath heavy pain, tears wouldn't surface, but the water from the spring gurgled, invading her ears, her spirit.

But whosoever drinketh of the water that I shall give him shall never thirst, but the water that I shall give him will be in him a well of water springing up to everlasting life.

The Scripture verse read by the minister the day she'd given her heart to Jesus whispered in her memory. But that same heart was now cracked and dry. Dehydrated from effort. She couldn't live like a talking manners manual anymore. Couldn't place her entire worth, her life's value, on the success of her dream.

A stitch of hope threaded through her. Was that enough?

She might never achieve above-the-fold status, but failure to attain that goal didn't mean she was a failure. She might never find a man who'd love her for who she truly was, but maybe she could live with that. God called her His own.

God's love made her enough.

A smile broke free as she leaned back against the stone wall. It had taken heartbreak to receive this revelation, but the fragments rested in His healing hands. She trusted Him.

Eyes sliding shut and soul at peace, she inhaled the brisk air.

A twig snapped not too far from her, and her lids popped open. Her fingers clamped the sides of the bench.

She'd been followed.

The man she'd seen last night, the one from Shelby's office, blocked her exit, his eyes colder than the steel blade in his hand.

CHAPTER 24

Elissa launched to her feet, but with the retaining barrier to her right and the stone wall edging the fountain to her left and stretching behind her, she had nowhere to flee.

"Been waiting for you to be alone." His lips pulled back in a warped smile, baring yellowed teeth. "Unless you want to find yourself in pretty little pieces, I'd hand it over. I know you have it."

The telegram. Her evidence against Jeffrey.

Was this man one of the *friends* Jeffrey had threatened her about? But why would he have been at Shelby's office? She hadn't known about Jeffrey's secret life then.

"I'm not sure what you mean." Her voice quivered. A bird squawked overhead as if mocking her.

The man stepped toward her, and she rocked back, the backs of her knees smacking the stone bench.

His eyes narrowed to fiery slits. "I don't have time to play games with a scrawny girl."

"Then how about with me?" Cole lunged from behind and tackled the assaulter, his hat tumbling to the cement.

The man staggered but kept a firm grip on the knife. He whipped around, and the blade snagged Cole's coat.

Elissa's heart pounded. How could she help? Her gazed darted about. No branches or stones to launch. No fake gun to point. Not even a purse to whomp him over the head with.

Cole threw a punch. The man dodged it, reeling toward Elissa.

She hugged the cement retaining wall. Trapped. The attacker lunged toward Cole, blade swiping through the air. Cole leapt back. The thug, unable to control his momentum, bent forward. Cole charged him, driving him in Elissa's direction as the men pummeled each other. She hopped onto the stone bench, escaping collision, inches from the assailant's back. Knee raised, she stabbed her heel into his spine.

He grunted in pain.

Cole punched him in the jaw, and the attacker fell against the nook's wall, finally releasing the knife.

A shout emitted from the direction of the road. A lanky man jogged toward them, followed by an older gentleman.

"Over here!" Still standing on the bench, she jumped and waved her hands. "Help!"

The thug glanced at the newcomers then struck Cole in the gut. With a muttered curse, he dashed away, escaping through the wooded lot across the street.

Cole doubled over, bracing his hands on his thighs. Elissa jumped to the ground and rushed to him, placing a trembling hand on his back, tears streaming.

The younger man puffed out short breaths, splotches of red dotting his cheeks. "Are you all right?"

Cole nodded and straightened, slowly.

Elissa retrieved Cole's hat from the pavement, taking the extra moment to collect herself.

"I saw the man had a knife." The other gentleman, who bore semblance to the long-legged stranger beside Elissa, pointed in the direction the attacker had fled. "Crazy, these muggings we've been having."

"I'm glad you two showed up when you did." Cole's gaze sought Elissa's, and she handed him the hat. He nodded his thanks and slapped it on his head. "I'll see the lady home. Again, I appreciate your aid."

The men exchanged handshakes with Cole and left.

A moment ago, her life had been in danger, and now her heart was. Again.

"Are you hurt at all?" Cole searched her face. Ivory skin shone with tears, but thank God, no marks. Yet bruises weren't always in open view. How long had the man harassed Elissa before he'd arrived? "He didn't touch you, did he?" The thought of that slime manhandling Elissa hollowed Cole's stomach.

He couldn't shake his scowl. Another man had escaped. First the intruder at his apartment, now this goon. Cole's confidence plummeted while his anger surged. How could he keep Elissa safe if he kept letting these jerks get away?

"I'm not hurt." Her voice was soft, a reedy whisper. "But I should be asking if you're okay."

He held up his arm to examine his sleeve where the knife had made contact. Thankfully, the cloth was all it had sliced. "No injury here." Aside from the blow to his gut, both literal and emotional.

She steadied her gaze on him, brows lifting slightly. "How did you know I was here?"

Cole withdrew a handkerchief and stooped, gathering the knife in the cloth and weighing Elissa's question. Tillman had phoned and explained that Elissa had bolted from the house after she'd discovered her father's intentions of having Cole watch over her. God knew what she'd been thinking. "I was told you weren't home. That you left in a hurry." He refrained from relaying her parents' concern. He didn't want her to think they'd chatted behind her back. He was in trouble for that already. "I remembered this was your favorite place to be alone. Wasn't sure if you'd be here, but guessed it was worth a shot." He mustered a tight smile and slipped the knife into his pocket.

"Glad you did." The statement offered the perfect balance of obligation and sincerity. "What are you going to do with that?" She inclined her head to the knife wrapped in his handkerchief, poking out from his pocket.

"Take it to Sterling."

"I'll be on my way, then. No need to walk me home." She secured a loose hairpin and smoothed a hand down the front of her coat. "I'll stick to main streets and avoid the alleys."

She couldn't be serious, but the hardened look on her face spoke otherwise.

"Elissa, there's no way I'm leaving you alone." Yes, a mountain of regrets lay between them, but he'd not abandon her side until he knew she was safe.

She sighed and walked down the sidewalk, staring into the distance at the massive estate behind Howe Springs.

Cole cleared his throat. "Do you still pretend that house is Longbourn?"

A smile teased her lips, but she didn't succumb to it. "It's Pemberley." She cut a quick glance his way and then focused her attention ahead. "And no. I've given up pretending. Entirely."

The resolute tone of her voice seemed to stretch further than her childhood fancy of *Pride and Prejudice*. "I noticed the man who accosted you was the same as from Shelby's office." Minus his chubby sidekick. Cole had identified Wiry the moment he'd rounded the corner.

Elissa nodded. "And the same guy from The Steel Fountain. I caught him … watching me."

The speakeasy. Every time he thought of her at a gin joint, his heart twisted in his chest. And with Kendrew, of all people. Betrayal stung, and jealousy was a tough monster to conquer. "Why hadn't you mentioned this before?" His clipped tone made her stiffen. He pressed his mouth together. Allowing his irritation to surface wouldn't solve anything. Only push her away more. "Did the goon bother you on your date?"

Her brows lowered. "I wasn't on a date. I was on the hunt for a story. Adam just happened to be there."

Cole stilled. "So that was the reason you didn't show up at the church Wednesday? You were chasing a headline?"

She ran a hand along the iron rails hedging the yards of fancy homes. "I had a lead, and I let it consume me. I'm sorry about the wedding. Everything about that situation." Her tone reflected her words, genuine with traces of regret.

Cole exhaled. He should've known she'd been chasing the story. Should he be relieved she wasn't two-timing him at a speakeasy, or throttle her for putting herself in danger for the sake of a crummy lead? He'd known that drive, though she'd always had it stronger. Yet the hitch in her step and the sag in her posture spoke more than her words. Could she be realizing the emptiness of ambition? "Did the thug give any reason for following you?"

She shivered, but he wasn't sure if it was from the memory of the man with the blade or the cool temperature. "He knows what I have."

"And what would that be, besides stunning good looks?" He attempted lightening the mood, but she rolled her eyes.

"A telegram."

He motioned with his hands. "Go on."

"No." She shoved her chin in the air. "It has to do with my article." Her shoulders slumped. "But then again, it was all a hoax. A deception for you to babysit me." Coldness crept into her eyes. "I hope he paid you overtime. You earned it."

Was that what she thought? That all his attention toward her had been because of her father? He squashed the rising groan. "I wasn't getting paid for any of it. Your father simply asked if I could …" How could he phrase it without sounding patronizing? "You father loves you and didn't want anything to happen to you. And I felt the same way."

Her step faltered, but other than that, she walked casually despite the fact that he'd essentially told her he loved her.

"I can handle myself."

He stopped. "This isn't a slight on your courage or independence. It's about the man who's tried to assault you. Twice." The knife weighed heavy in his pocket. "Another time we may not be so fortunate."

She winced.

"Listen, Spark, things could've ended extremely badly back there. What was on that telegram that the man wanted?"

"I guess it doesn't matter anymore." She sighed. "The telegram was from the landlord at the Maple Grove Lodge, confirming Jeffrey's marriage to Doris Green."

"The Follies' actress? She and Jeffrey are married?"

Elissa nodded.

Cole let out a low whistle. "Wasn't she married three times before?"

"Four."

If Shelby had been aware of this and all the scandals that followed Doris Green, he'd mostly likely not favored the match. "But why would Jeffrey hire a man to come after you for the telegram? You already know he's married. The only way to get you not to talk would be …"

"To destroy the telegram and kill me." Elissa bit her lip, her eyes glazing with the somber truth. "Just like Mr. Shelby."

Cole scratched his late-day stubble. Had Jeffrey murdered his own father? "Do you think the secret marriage was the cause for their argument? The one that was going to get Jeffrey cut from the will?"

Another nod, but no words. Was she still angry with him from this morning, or was the shock of the incident now settling in?

"Why would that man be in Shelby's office that night? You didn't have the telegram then." He adjusted his hat. "Unless he was hired by Jeffrey to find and destroy the new will. The one that excluded Jeffrey."

Elissa stilled. "If the latest will was never found, the former would be honored, right? Jeffrey would still inherit."

"Yes." Was the man who had invaded Cole's place one of Jeffrey's hired cronies, and not Shelby's lab assistant, as Sterling had assumed?

After the invasion at his apartment, Sterling had shown Cole a picture of Matthew Young. The image matched the description of the intruder with the dark hair and lean build, but why would one of Shelby's workers break into Cole's apartment?

"Honey." He put a hand on her arm, and she shirked away. "We need to go to the police. I know this is your lead, but—"

"Haven't you heard me? It doesn't matter anymore. I'm not crafting an article. This competition is over. You and Father won." Her rushed words and labored breathing tugged Cole's compassion.

"This is not about winning, it's for your safety. A man also broke into my apartment on Monday."

Blue eyes widened. "Your apartment?" Her forehead wrinkled, and as much as she'd deny it, alarm laced her features. "Who was it?"

"Considering the stolen case of ethanol a couple weeks ago, it's possible the man was just an alcoholic desperate for a drink. But Sterling tends to think it has something to do with the Shelby case. If they were hunting for the will, they didn't find it, because I don't have the thing." He fastened his gaze on her. "Your house may be next."

"My parents." Her bottom lip quivered, and he wanted more than anything to calm it with his, to pull her into his arms until all fear faded. "Sterling should know, then." She resumed walking, this time with a quicker pace. "Perhaps he can put this all together and make an end of it." Glancing over, her features softened. "How is he faring?"

Cole shrugged. "Not good. Sophie moved in with her sister in Massachusetts. Left a note for Sterling saying she didn't love him."

She blinked. "They seemed so right for each other. How awful."

"Maybe this case will help keep his mind off her." Though Sterling was like him—when he loved a woman, it was forever.

CHAPTER 25

He had nothing.

Cole glared at the blank piece of paper in Jane's carriage and scowled. No inspiration. No leadings of what to write. Just a headache the size of Mount Liberty. And a beautiful blonde beside him who hadn't mouthed more than seven words to him over the past four days.

Nothing had evolved from all the information he'd given to Sterling. Jeffrey denied ties to the man who'd attempted to assault Elissa. And furthermore, Jeffrey had released a statement informing the public of his marriage to Doris Green. What motive could he possibly have against Elissa and Cole, except for the will? A will neither one of them had.

Cole had tried to reconcile with Elissa over the course of the week, but she had been distant and cool. Not cruel. But closed like a flower in the rain. All connections with her seemed severed with no chance of renewing anything—not even a friendship.

Agitation pressed his lungs. He needed air. He needed … something. He slapped his hat on his head and stood. "I'm breaking for lunch," he announced to no one in particular. The wall clock read ten o'clock. He wasn't hungry. But he was extremely thirsty.

"Lissie?" Father's head poked out of his office like a turtle from its shell. "Can you come in here, please?"

She sighed and pushed back her chair. The half-completed ledger laughed at her as if it knew she couldn't concentrate with Cole's sudden disappearance. He still owed her father an article and had no business quitting for lunch so soon. Where'd he gone to? She shrugged the concern away. Cole Parker didn't need her. Didn't want her. He'd only shown interest in stealing her ideas and heeding Father's orders. With a frown, she gathered her notebook and headed into the office.

"What is it?" She spoke in her most polite voice. Ever since her time at Howe Springs, she hadn't been angry with Father, or really even Cole, but the hurt still scratched at her heart, and that would take a while to mend.

He closed the door and pressed a hand against the wood, his head lowering. "I found a buyer for the *Review*."

Her heart sank. "Can nothing be done?"

He shrugged, his shoulders barely lifting as though he carried an enormous weight. "We've not generated enough profit to cover the expenses." His scrubbed a wrinkled hand over his ashen face. "I've failed."

Compassion overtook her. Remembrance of Father weak and pale in that hospital bed clouded her mind. "You can't take the burden. It'll exhaust you." And he needed his strength. "I'm sorry for the outburst the other day at the house. I wasn't thinking, and … while I was disappointed you created the contest only to have Cole spy on me, I'm not angry. I should have considered your health over my feelings."

"Lissie." Father set a hand on hers. "The contest is not a hoax. I'm still expecting an article. And yes, I may have invented it as a means to keep you out of trouble, but I know your talent. I wanted you to feel as if you'd earned your place and not that your old man was throwing you a bone. Cole is a worthy opponent, but between you and me, I think you can take him."

She gave a faint smile. "I'm an adult. I don't need a man to follow me around. I can take care of myself."

"Believe me. Cole wasn't forced. He seemed all too eager to have any and every opportunity to be near you. And I confess, there may have been a bit of match-making on my part."

Elissa's jaw swung open. "Father!" Why would he take on such a role? He'd never meddled in her personal life before. Not like she had much of one. But then, "Did you want me and Cole to get together so Cole could run the *Review* in the future?"

His eyebrows spiked, and his head jerked back. "No. That wasn't in my mind."

"It's just that you've always had me write articles under a man's name. Why have you fought against me all this time? What's so wrong with being a female journalist?"

Father scratched his cheek. "Lissie, if I gave you that illusion, I apologize. I'm never against you. I think you are more than adequate for any position, including publisher." He sighed. "But I fear you won't have any opportunity to prove it."

Squeezing his hand, she inhaled a calming breath and forced a smile. He needed her to be strong. God would see them through.

"Sell the *Review*," she whispered, pain screaming from every word. Heartbreak was occurring in many forms this week.

Failure.

The word wrapped around Cole's heart like barbed wire and squeezed. How many times would he butch things? Hurt the people he loved?

He ground his jaw and pounded his fist against the cold retaining wall outside the apartment building. The brick allowed no mercy, skinning his knuckles, blood welling to the surface. But he welcomed the pain.

Elissa had never realized the love he held for her. She only thought he'd taken advantage.

He tightened his grip on the object he could get arrested for.

Did anything matter anymore?

His entire reason for returning to Pittsburgh was gone. He'd lost his second chance with Elissa. He wouldn't expect a person like her to offer him a third.

As for the *Boston Globe*? He hadn't heard a word from them concerning her articles. A lump formed in his throat, and he worked to swallow. Cole had wrecked the relationship over nothing. When, or even if, he would get the chance to explain, it'd be too late. The feelings she'd harbored for him would be extinguished. Ashes from a love they could have shared.

He tucked the bag under his arm and sprinted up the stairs to his apartment, his mouth parched, his heart heavy.

The whiskey peddler had informed him this bottle had been imported from Canada, undiluted. Strong. Exactly what he needed. By this time tomorrow, he'd be in oblivion.

He closed the door, locking it. Ripping the brown paper away, he gazed at the amber bottle. Torn.

Perhaps this one mess-up wouldn't pull him down that road again. What could one mistake do? He pressed a finger to his chin, the bruising from his fall no longer visible, but the memory hadn't faded. Waking up in his own urine and vomit. Chilled. The eerie awareness of the alcohol's poison invading his blood. Seeing Elissa's face in his mind's eye and wanting to tell her the words he'd never felt worthy enough to say.

Words he'd still left unsaid.

He tightened his grasp on the bottle. Why? Why had he left her in doubt of his heart for so long?

He sank onto the chair.

God.

Knuckles wrapped around the bottle's neck, he asked for help. Help to see beyond the moment. Help to overcome the pulsing desire to drink.

Not in my own strength. "God, I need yours."

He didn't feel a thing. Not an overwhelming force gripping his heart. Not even a shift in mood. Weakness and defeat clutched his brittle will. He could numb the surging emotion in several swigs. His hand tightened on the glass, thumb skimming the metal cap.

But this was where failure had reigned before. Maybe he needed to step out in faith, even when his senses screamed for satisfaction.

With a shout, he lifted the bottle and hurled the thing. It struck the fireplace, shaking the mantel, taking down Cole's science test. The glass shattered, and liquid spewed. He lunged across the room, rescuing the paper before the leaking whiskey destroyed it. The edges were wet, as was the back of the frame.

He withdrew the paper and turned it over, surveying the damage.

Writing—not his own—stared up at him. Shelby's.

CHAPTER 26

Elissa's fingers curled around the steel. This time, no drawing back. Darcy pawed her thighs, standing on his hind legs.

"I can give you one too." She pulled him onto her lap. "Trim the fur around your eyes. You're due for a groom, mister."

Darcy eyed the scissors and jumped to the floor.

"Not yet? I completely understand." She reached to pat his head, but he scurried from the room.

A laugh escaped. How many times had she run from problems? Closed herself in from the world?

Not anymore.

Peering at the mirror connected to her vanity, Elissa studied her image. One so carefully protected. Exhaustingly maintained.

Snip.

A chunk of hair flitted to the floor.

Her hand shook. The cut was ridiculously uneven but … freeing.

Snip. Snip. Snip.

The more locks shorn, the lighter her spirit became, almost as if she was shedding the labels. Shadyside Slob. Grace's awkward daughter. The Tillman spinster. Yet she wasn't finished. Society burdened her with demands, but the heaviest expectation was the one she'd placed on herself.

Perfectionism.

She clutched a handful of tresses, and with one long slice, it fell to her lap. She clipped the rest, cutting a good eleven inches until what was left framed her chin. Smiling, she ran her fingers through her bobbed hair. Curls, no longer weighted, sprang with new life. Just like her.

To others, cutting her hair might seem a silly action, but to her, it was an outward show of the inward liberation. She was God's child. The only label she would cling to.

The only one that mattered.

"Not a word to anyone." Sterling's hand clutched Cole's test paper, his red-rimmed eyes narrowing in warning. "Not even your pretty girlfriend. You used to squeal everything to her if I remember correctly." He picked up a mug from the coffee table and sniffed it, his nose crinkling.

Cole settled on Sterling's sofa, arching an eyebrow at the several ties draped over the back cushion. The frilly pillow was gone. "I've always told her everything, except what was most important." Tonight he'd fix that. She most likely wouldn't want to hear the words, but they needed to be spoken. She deserved to know. "And she's not my girlfriend."

Sterling raised his stubbly chin in question. Had the man not shaved since Sophie left?

"Long story." Cole raised both hands. "Tell you later. I have to return to my side of the building. Gotta clean up some liquor before Mom finds it. Mostly the glass from the bottle. I'd hate to step on it in the middle of the night."

Sterling straightened. "You just informed a cop that you have alcohol. Do you think the prohibition doesn't apply to you?"

"For a while I did. I didn't think any rules applied to me. But no, if you want to confiscate the stuff, you'll need to bleed it from the fireplace bricks. The bottle is in a hundred pieces."

Sterling nodded his understanding. "Keep dry, Parker. Or I'm obliged to turn you in to the feds." He said it with a smile, but in a world of crooked cops, Sterling was undeniably straight. A man of honor. Sophie had lost out by refusing him.

"By God's strength, I will."

"You better. Or I'll tattle on you to Uncle Wooly. He'll wallop you with his cane just like old times." Amusement glinted in his eyes. "Man never went anywhere without it. Now come on, I'll help you clean up."

Cole grabbed the doorknob and stilled. "He was without it."

Sterling's smirk flattened. "Huh?"

"I knew something didn't add up. Should've seen this before. Shelby's walking stick."

"What of it?"

"The day I met Shelby on the street. He was without it." Cole lowered his hand and propped a shoulder against the doorframe. "Yet at the Halloway Building, he had it."

Sterling stroked his neck. "His house and office were in the other direction. So he couldn't have picked it up on the way. Unless someone brought it to him."

"Exactly."

"Didn't Shelby need it for stability?"

"No." Cole pulled the door open and stepped into the hallway. "Just relied on it for the multi-tool. He designed a stainless steel topper that unscrewed and served as one of those Swiss knives. Complete with spring mechanisms."

"So the question is now, who returned Shelby his walking stick? The killer?"

"That's your expertise, cousin. You'll figure it out." Cole reached for the handle to enter his apartment. "But first, for heaven's sake, shave."

Cole had left his apartment door unlocked when he'd hurried with his discovery across the hall, and he thought he'd left the light on in his haste. It was off now. He flicked the switch.

"The intruder! He's back!"

As before, the man scurried to the opened window. Sterling

launched Cole's briefcase at his retreating form, knocking him off-kilter. Cole tackled him, but unlike last time, he held on, smacking the side of the thug's head on the corner of the fireplace as they fell. The intruder lay unconscious but recognizable.

With a growing smile, the mail carrier handed Elissa a stack of envelopes. The slender man must have been twice Elissa's age, but he was always ready with a flirtatious expression.

"Thank you." She regarded him with the customary nod, and he exited the newsroom.

Frank gave her a knowing smirk, and she rolled her eyes. Seriously, that man could rival members of her mother's needlework club for the busybody award.

Sighing, she flipped through the pile, mostly bills, some from clients who most likely were sending their latest ad, and one from … the *Boston Globe*. Addressed to her?

She tossed the other correspondence on her desk and stared at the manila letter, confusion spiraling through her. Why would the editor be contacting her? She slid to her seat and tore it open.

Dear Miss Tillman,

Hope this letter finds you well.

Mr. Cole Parker relayed that he acted on your behalf, but I decided to reply directly to you concerning the editorial samples he provided. Based on the work I've seen, you have talent and potential. I'd like to conduct an interview by telephone. If interested, please contact my secretary to arrange a time and date. I admit I was surprised Mr. Parker inquired about a position for you and not himself, but he spoke highly of you and your writing. Hope to speak with you soon.

Warm Regards,
Samuel Overly
Boston Globe Editor

Her heart pressed against her ribs. She'd shed the corset years ago, but her breath constricted just the same. Cole had acted on her behalf? She glanced at his empty desk. He should've been here already. Should be crafting an impressive article, making her pulse race without her permission.

The letter weighed heavy in her palm. She leapt to her feet, the chair behind her tottering, and dashed through Father's office door. "The other day. When you discussed selling the *Review* to that lawyer, was your door open?"

Father's eyes widened. "W-when did you do that?"

"What?" Oh, her hair. She'd forgotten Father hadn't seen her since she'd cut it. Sliding a curl behind her ear, she beamed at him. "Last night." She twirled, giving a full view of her bobbed head. "I'm going to keep it this way. It suits me." Natural and unconfined.

"I think so too." His cheeks puckered with a full smile. "Has your mother seen it?"

Elissa laughed. "Yes. She reacted better than the last time I cut it."

He nodded, expression aglow. "So no fainting?"

"A lot of fanning herself." Elissa mimicked her mother's frantic gestures. "A few yelps, but no collapsing on the parlor rug."

"We're making progress, then." Father winked. "What about the other day and the financial lawyer?"

Elissa clutched the Boston Globe letter. "When you were talking on the phone, discussing the sale of the paper, was your door open?"

He tapped a pencil against his thick chin. "Um. No. It wasn't. I didn't want anyone overhearing."

Father's gruff voice had often carried through his closed door, and she'd bet every dime she'd spent on novels that Cole had overheard.

"Thanks, Father." She blew him a kiss and glided to her station.

She skimmed her fingertips over the wooden handle of her desk drawer. Could this be why Cole wouldn't explain why he'd been rummaging through her articles? He hadn't wanted to divulge her father was making plans to sell the paper? Her lip twisted. Maybe he felt trapped between respect for her father and loyalty to her.

She inhaled, realization dawning. *That's why he was so adamant his actions weren't about the contest.*

He'd taken the samples to send to Boston. For her. If Father sold the paper, Cole would be out of a job too, but instead of promoting himself to the *Globe*, he'd recommended her.

Her heart could burst.

Like in high school when he'd protected her against Adam's slander and fought for her without her knowledge of it. Yes, he'd been wrong to leave her without a word, but even then, he'd felt it had been for her good—protecting her from himself. She understood now. All for her.

Tears threatened to escape, and her throat tightened. She glanced at his chair for the fiftieth time this morning. Where was he? She poked her head back into Father's office.

"Did Cole mention where he was today?"

Father's head whipped up. "Really, Lissie. This is twice you've startled me in five minutes." He smiled, not looking offended in the least.

"Sorry. Just curious about Cole."

Father's brows lifted with a grin. He stretched in his seat with a long, exaggerated yawn. "Let me think. He did mention something. Hmm."

"You enjoying my desperation is unnerving." She struggled to keep a frown in place, but a smile won out.

He chuckled. "He may have mentioned that he'd be at the courthouse today. Important legal business."

What would that be about? Another lead on the Shelby case? Or a new story altogether? Her lips pursed, and determination set in. "Thank you. I'm taking lunch."

"At nine o'clock?" His eyes twinkled. "Pretty early for a sandwich."

She teased back. "But not for a cup of coffee." A cup she would have right after she located Cole and apologized.

Everything was in place. Cole peeked through the crack in the door to the courthouse meeting room, feeling like a peeping schoolboy, complete with the racing pulse of getting caught.

Mrs. Shelby sat beside her son, Jeffrey. Shelby's lawyer, Paul MacAfferty, claimed the seat on Mrs. Shelby's other side, chatting with her in too-familiar tones. Was that man sweet on her? The secretary, Miss Kerns, sat across the table from MacAfferty, frantically tapping the chair's armrest.

"We should begin in a few moments." Sterling's bass voice echoed off the wood-paneled walls. "Just waiting for the executor of the will."

"What's going on?" MacAfferty's face reddened, more crimson than his awful tie. "I'm the executor. Have been for decades."

Cole couldn't see Sterling but could picture his stern grimace. "Not for the new will."

Everyone's gazes flew to the corner where Sterling stood.

"The new will?" Mrs. Shelby's voice quivered. "You … found it?"

"Surprised?" Sterling, that rascal. "It proved very interesting."

Cole rolled his shoulders, hoping to ease the tension. Didn't work. He'd stick with the calculated strategy. Wait for Sterling's knock and then start the circus.

A flash of gold passed the window, pulling his attention.

Elissa.

What was she doing here? And with short hair? His breath lodged in his chest. What should he do? Leave his post and meet her in the mezzanine? He raked a hand across his face. Most likely she wasn't here for him. Probably another court case arrested her interest.

Cole moved toward the window for a better view. Desperation

etched Elissa's features as she hustled down the walk. What made her distraught?

She approached the doors only about fifteen feet from where he stood. He glanced at his watch. He had five minutes, give or take, before his cousin gave the signal. Five minutes to see her.

As Cole bounded into the entrance hall, a jumble of activity equaling the chaos of Grand Central Station met him. A spattering of patrolmen scaled the stairways. Shoeshine boys, gripping their polishing supplies and contesting loudly for business, flanked men in homburgs, armed with briefcases. Women of different ages conversed with one another. Elissa stood beneath the limestone arch, lifting on her tiptoes, eyes searching.

Their gazes connected. Her shoulders lifted with a sharp intake of air.

With makeup smudged and hat askew, she snaked her way through the mill of people. Everything about her spoke dishevelment, but everything about her was stunning.

She stopped in front of him, the deep hues of her eyes more entrancing than a sea of starlight. "I'm sorry." Her words were breathless.

"For what, sweetheart?" He knuckled away a lone tear coursing down her flushed cheek. "I'm the one who should apologize. I've confused you. Brought pain. It wasn't intentional. I wouldn't purposefully hurt ..." *The woman I love.* "You."

She blinked and patted the pocket of her overcoat. "*Boston Globe.* Interview. I can't thank you enough."

He pieced together her babbling and didn't fight the grin. "They got back to you? Loved your work, huh? I knew it." Pride coated his voice. "You've earned it." He tugged a curl. "This hairstyle's my favorite. I loved it the first time, Spark."

She bit her lip, hiding a smile. "You could've easily snagged that position." She grabbed his hand, soft against his warm palm. "I know your reason. Father told me ... about his plans for the *Review*."

He wove his fingers into hers. "Your dreams have always been about that paper. I wanted to help."

"I know. I'm sorry I accused you. I should've trusted you more this time."

Time.

The signal.

He drew back and glanced at his watch. Thirty seconds.

"Sweetheart, I have to run." Literally.

"But why?" She tangled her hands in his lapel, pulling him closer. In the middle of the courthouse foyer. Surrounded by strangers. And hopefully amongst the crowd were some of Sterling's men dressed in casual suits.

"I was hoping we could discuss us?" She cupped his cheek, grazing her fingertips to his chin. "You know, I've always loved your cleft."

Man alive.

"Come with me." He grabbed her wrist and pulled her into the side room. This might not be the soundest plan, but he didn't want her anywhere but near him. Once inside, he pressed a finger to her lips and whispered. "You'll have to remain quiet. What you're about to see will probably make you want to scream, but you can't. Okay?"

With brows furrowed, her gaze bounced around the small space. She hesitated as Cole approached the smaller of two other doors that marked the wood-paneled walls then nodded her agreement.

Knock. Knock. Two-second pause. *Knock.*

The signal. Let the chaos begin.

CHAPTER 27

Pulse pounding in her throat, Elissa huddled in what she could only guess was a waiting room.

In the adjoining chamber, Sterling cleared his throat. Loudly. "The executor is here and will explain everything."

Eyes hardened and serious, Cole disappeared through a smaller door into another room, not the one Sterling occupied. What was going on? Elissa moved to follow, but the door swung open, revealing Cole and …

"Mr. Shelby," she whispered, her heart stopping cold.

Or was it? She squinted at the man who looked identical to the dead inventor but had black hair instead of gray and a bandage on his temple. No, she was definitely gaping at the real Mr. Shelby.

The supposed dead man tipped his hat to her.

Cole flashed her a dashing smile, snapping her back into reality, putting her feet into motion. No way was she missing any of this. Cole must've read her mind, for he grabbed her hand and tucked it in the crook of his arm, his muscle tight under her fingertips. He inclined his head to her. "Shelby was the *intruder* at my apartment. Apparently, I had something of his."

Before Elissa could respond, Mr. Shelby strode into the large adjoining chamber.

Mrs. Shelby yelped and then fainted, slumping in her chair. Cole rushed over, catching the woman before she collapsed onto the floor. Jeffrey launched to his feet. The woman Elissa supposed to be Miss Kerns gasped then threw a hand over her mouth. The broad man with the hideous tie—the lawyer, maybe?—blanched whiter than the papers he clutched.

"Father!" Jeffrey spoke first. "You're ..." A sob ripped free. "Alive."

Was the son's emotional declaration because of joy or guilt?

"Indeed, he is." Sterling nodded, eyes pensive and chest expanded. "Which is why you all have been summoned here."

Several men in suits brushed past Elissa and invaded the room, the air thinning and hot with emotion. Cole assisted Mrs. Shelby back into her chair. Though her body quaked, and her eyes blinked rapidly, the woman remained seated.

"Even though Shelby is alive, there is a murderer in this room." Sterling's gaze swept the space. "And the only man who can identify the killer is the intended victim." He set his intense stare on Mr. Shelby. "Now's your turn to explain."

Shelby gave a tight nod and gazed lovingly at his wife—now quietly weeping.

"It's okay, Anna." Shelby gave a tight smile. "I realize my presence here is a shock."

"But ..." Mrs. Shelby's quiet protest drew every pair of eyes. "Someone died. There was a body."

Sterling stepped forward. "Matthew Young was the unfortunate victim, ma'am. His real name was Marcus Jenkins. Not Shelby's lab assistant, but a man employed by the United States government."

"My project was top secret. I couldn't tell you, Anna." Mr. Shelby's face darkened, sadness creeping into his eyes. "Marcus was helping me determine who was after my propeller plans. The Halloway Building on Garson Street had been the meeting place for the thieves. The day of the explosion, they had intended to sell the last installment. Too bad the plans were falsified."

"Wait." Disbelief still registered on Jeffrey's features, and he blinked as if trying to make sense of it all. "You made *fake* plans? Why?"

"To catch them in the act." Shelby glowered. "I was to meet Marcus at the Halloway Building that night, but he arrived first to snoop around. He used my walking stick—I'd installed a lock pick on the topper just for that occasion. The killers thought it was me and believed since the propeller drawings were safely in their hands, they would dispose of me with a time bomb. The perfect opportunity to complete their plan." His stare turned flinty. "But let me clarify, there is *not* a new will. I was supposed to write one, but I didn't get the chance. The killer didn't want me to."

"You're not making sense, Dan." MacAfferty leaned forward in his chair, his neck mottled red. "One minute you're talking about secret plans, and now the will?"

Mr. Shelby glowered. "Let me clarify everything for you, Paul, but somehow I think you know the answers."

"What's that mean?" Mrs. Shelby spoke up.

"It means, love, that the will was intended to include a new member of our family, who is to arrive in about nine months." He leveled his gaze at Jeffrey. "I overreacted the last time we talked, son. You came to me in earnest with news about your wife." He pressed his lips together, flattening his mustache. "Yes, I was angry, but there was no chance of me disinheriting you or your family. Your wife is welcome in my home, and so is your child."

Child? Elissa swallowed.

Mrs. Shelby gaped at her son, eyes wide as Miss Kerns' had been a few moments ago. "Doris is with child?" She pressed a hand to her cheek. "So that's what the will was about, Dan? You weren't cutting Jeffrey and me out?"

"You?" Mr. Shelby smiled tenderly at his wife. "Anna, you're my very soul. I could never do such a thing."

"But your affair?" Her hopeful expression pierced Elissa's heart. "The divorce?"

Mr. Shelby sharpened his stare on Miss Kerns, whose complexion turned scarlet. "There was *no* affair. Miss Kerns was my secretary, possessing a character by which I'd been deceived." His cold tone enforced his words. "But she had help, didn't she, MacAfferty?"

"What do you mean, Dan?" The lawyer tugged his collar, face pinching. "I told you from the start not to hire her. There were questions concerning her morals."

Miss Kerns jerked her head toward the attorney, her finger slicing the air, pointing. "Liar! You're lying! You got me the job!"

"Enough!" Sterling bellowed over the clamor, moving behind MacAfferty.

"Enjoying the show?" Cole sidled beside Elissa. "I should've brought my notepad. You wouldn't happen to have yours, would you?"

Of course she did. She never went anywhere without it. She offered it to him, but he shook his head. "You do it, Spark." He whispered in her ear and then kissed it.

She quickly jotted the information and flipped to a fresh page.

Cole nudged her shoulder. "Note that Shelby's real propeller plans were scribed on the back of my science test. Clever, huh?" He winked at her.

"It was all a deception." Mr. Shelby spoke above the voices. "MacAfferty invented the idea of the new will involving Miss Kerns. To deflect suspicion. To provide a different explanation for the murder. Worked pretty well until you realized my plans were fake, right, Paul?"

"You're mad!" MacAfferty began to rise, but Sterling set a hand on his shoulder, keeping him seated. "There's no truth to what you're saying."

Sterling raised a palm, gaze sharpening on MacAfferty. "It's easy to clear up. All I have to do is escort you to Garson Street. There was an eye witness who claimed to see both you"—he slid his stare to Miss Kerns— "and you, near the time of the murder."

Elissa breathed out, thankful she'd told Sterling the other day about her visit to Bootlegger Alley and the hobo she'd encountered there.

"I may have gotten the wrong person at first." MacAfferty

launched to his feet, pulled a pistol from his jacket, and aimed at Shelby. "But I won't now."

The gun fired. Mr. Shelby crumpled to the ground. Screams pierced, and gunpowder hazed the air. Elissa jumped behind the door.

"Dan!" Mrs. Shelby reached toward her husband, but MacAfferty caught her by the arm, holding the gun to her head.

"Drop your weapon, MacAfferty!" Sterling aimed his pistol at the lawyer.

"Let her go!" Mr. Shelby shifted to a kneeling position, the bullet hole in his shirt revealing a tightly woven silk underlay.

"Japanese body armor vest, Dan?" MacAfferty sneered. "Too bad you didn't make one for Anna."

"I'll surrender the plans in exchange for her." He withdrew the paper and waved it frantically.

"Too late." MacAfferty pulled the gun's hammer back, the click chilling Elissa's blood. "The foreign power cancelled the purchase." He snorted, and a bead of sweat dripped from his brow. "Your plans are worthless to me now. Let me leave, and I'll let her live."

"Paul! Please!" Mrs. Shelby's cry echoed off the walls.

MacAfferty dragged his captive toward the exit, his back toward Elissa.

Elissa held her breath, crouching behind the door. Should she run for help? No doubt the brute would notice her then. Her trembling hand slipped inside her bag, sliding out the gun lighter she'd swiped from Mr. Shelby's office.

MacAfferty stilled in the doorway, only a couple feet from Elissa. "I'll set her free as soon as I'm sure of my safe getaway."

The cops approached him with their guns pointed.

"Drop them, or I'll squeeze the trigger. Who's to stop me?"

Elissa shoved the barrel into MacAfferty's vertebrae. "Me."

He cussed and turned his gun on Elissa.

Cole lunged at him, taking them both to the ground.

A shot fractured the air.

Sterling's men piled onto MacAfferty, and Cole rolled to the side, covered in blood.

His.

CHAPTER 28

Sterling's men cuffed the writhing lawyer and escorted him out the room, Miss Kerns following with her own set of constraints. Mr. and Mrs. Shelby reunited.

Elissa fell to her knees beside Cole, his crimson-stained hands clutching his right shoulder, his face twisted in anguish.

"We need to get you help." Her tears streamed almost as fast as Cole's blood gushed. What had she been thinking? Pulling a phony gun on someone with a real one. Cole had recognized her bluff and saved her, the bullet marked for her now lodging in his pain-stricken body. "I'm so sorry."

"Seeing you cry … hurts worse." Cole's gaze pierced hers, his husky tone strained. "It's … nothing, Spark." He sucked in air through his teeth and sat up, the entire area around his shoulder soaked with blood.

The gruesome flow had to be blocked. She fished her handkerchief from her overcoat pocket and pressed it against the wound.

Cole winced.

She whispered another apology, staring at the flimsy piece of cotton—a poor relief against the pulsing surge.

Sterling crouched beside her. "Let's take a look."

She removed the handkerchief, and Sterling's thick fingers tore the fabric of Cole's shirt, exposing the gashed flesh.

Elissa gasped.

"It's deep." Concern threaded Sterling's voice. "Gotta get you to Mercy. Can you stand?"

Cole nodded. Sterling slid a hand under Cole's good shoulder and helped him to his feet.

Mercy Hospital stood only a mile away, but how much more blood would Cole lose between here and there?

"I'm going to pull my squad car 'round front." Sterling assisted Cole to lean against the wall. "Don't faint in front of your girl, Parker. I won't let you live it down." His words were playful, but seriousness flooded his eyes. He assessed the injury one more time and bolted from the room.

"Elissa." Cole's weak drawl pulled her closer. "I need you to do something."

With her left hand steadying his good side, she used her right to push the hair from his forehead, fingers trailing to cup his jaw. "Anything."

"Leave."

Her hand dropped from his face. "What?"

"Get to the newsroom." He mashed his mouth together and swallowed. "Write the scoop."

Her gaze snapped to the notepad she'd dropped when the turmoil had started. This would be an exclusive for the *Review*. A story of this caliber would pull in revenue. Get national attention. A journalist's dream.

What if this headline could save the paper from being sold?

"All set." Sterling reappeared, rain dotting his suit, umbrella in hand. "It's a torrent out there."

"Here's your chance, Spark." Cole winked at her, pain bunching the corners of his eyes. "Show the world what you've got."

Sterling stepped between them, allowing her no chance to respond to Cole's words.

He leaned into his cousin and ambled away. She stood in the doorway, gaze lingering on Cole until he disappeared from the mezzanine. The handkerchief moistened her palm, reddening the cracks of her skin. A couple of weeks ago, Cole had stolen her golden opportunity, and now, in the exact same building, he handed it to her with his gracious blessing.

A sob rocked through her.

She nabbed the notepad from the floor and scurried out of the room, praying with all her soul she'd made the right decision.

"Are you here for my Last Rites prayer?" Cole struggled against the searing fire in his shoulder and forced a smile at the nurse who'd introduced herself as Sister Mary Monaca.

The nun softly chuckled and shook her head. "The only blessing I'll be saying is the one over your dinner."

His stomach protested. Because of his history of addiction, Cole had declined any use of opium, choosing over-the-counter pain relievers which had done nothing to calm the raging burn. "How long do I have to wear this thing?" The sling not only looked pathetic but didn't do much good limiting the movement.

"For a while." She gently prodded the area around the gauze. "Has the anesthetic worn off?"

Cole slid his eyes shut against the pain.

"Guess so. Be careful not to move too much. The concern now is infection. We need to keep the wound clean." Sister Mary Monaca's white habit swallowed her frame, leaving only her oval face and plump hands visible. She motioned another nun, holding a tray, into the room. "The doctor said you must eat. Set the food in front of our patient, Sister Ferdinand. If he eats, allow the officer in for questioning."

The nun must be referring to Sterling. But what was all that about questioning?

"That includes your vegetables." Sister Mary Monaca raised a gray brow at Cole, her chin upturned.

Cole would laugh if he could be sure his stitches wouldn't burst. There wasn't much room in this antiseptic-laden cubicle, but Cole wouldn't decline a familiar face.

He shoved a bite of potatoes in his mouth. With a nod, Sister Mary Monaca left, the smaller nun following.

A rolled newspaper edged the dinner tray. Cole grimaced at the masthead.

Pittsburgh Post?

And they expected him to get better? He grunted and, with his good arm, opened the competitor's evening spread.

Daniel Shelby Alive, Exposes His Assailants

Cole gaped at the headline, the potatoes in his stomach hardening to brick. He scanned the article. *Pittsburgh Post* had gained the exclusive. Where was Elissa? Why hadn't she—

"Do you have enough to share?" Sterling removed his hat and entered the room. "Missed lunch in all this excitement."

"I can't believe this. *Pittsburgh Post* got the story." He tossed the paper aside, his shoulder throbbing.

"Careful there. Don't want to aggravate anything."

Cole didn't understand. Her dream was right there. So close. "She lost the opportunity. Again."

His cousin swiped the roll from his plate and shoved it in his mouth, lips smacking as he chewed. "She couldn't very well be two places at once."

Cole's brow lowered. "What do you mean?"

Elissa appeared in the doorway, eyes wide and stunning. "I came here instead." A Mercy Hospital blanket wrapped around her, the bottom of her dress rumpled and discolored. Had she walked from the courthouse in the downpour?

Their gazes melded, the silence speaking clearer than words. She came to the hospital instead of going to the newsroom. Chose him over her long-cherished dream. His chest swelled with love for her.

Sterling cleared his throat. "I'm ... uh ... going to wait outside. Guard the door against Sister What's Her Name." Glancing between them, a twinge of sadness marked his eyes. He focused on his hat in his hands and then strode toward the exit. "Don't be too long. I convinced the nun I was here for police investigations and needed Miss Tillman to accompany me."

Ah. Smart. Otherwise, Elissa wouldn't have been able to see Cole because she wasn't family. "Thanks, cousin. I owe you."

"You've done enough." His eyes locked on Cole's like a firm handshake, and then he stepped out.

"How are you feeling?" Elissa moved farther into the room, a cautiousness marking her steps as if she was unaware of her welcome.

Cole shifted, straightening against the five pillows Sister Mary Monaca lodged under his back. "Never been better." He shot her a smile. "Got my consolation prize in a jar and my favorite girl for company."

Her nose wrinkled when she caught sight of the bullet on the side table. "They put it in a jar for you?"

"Much better than tonsils, don't you agree?"

She bit her lip, fighting a smile. Another step, but not near enough for him to reach her. Her gaze traveled to his shoulder. The amusement in her eyes disappeared. "I'm sorry, Cole. I was so foolish. You could've been ..."

Killed.

He moved his hand, palm up, beckoning her.

She glided closer and slipped her fingers in his.

"When MacAfferty turned his gun on you, in that flickering second, my world died. For me, there is no tomorrow without you in it."

She sniffed, eyes glassy.

"But so you know." He squeezed her hand. "I'm confiscating that silly gun lighter."

"I'll gladly surrender it."

"Just like you surrendered your chance at the golden article? Being placed above the fold?" He raised a brow. "Spark, that was your dream."

Her lashes lowered. "Somewhere along the way, my dream and my heart blended."

This blasted injury. Crushing her in his arms seemed the only appropriate response. "There's something I want to tell you. Words you need to hear." His gaze settled on her, and he stroked her index finger with his thumb. "But I'd rather not be in a hospital gown, smelling like ether, when I say them."

She nodded, exhaustion framing her smile.

"You need to get some rest, sweetheart. I'm sure you'll see me soon." He flicked a glance at his bandaged shoulder and then to her. "As you can tell, I'm not easily gotten rid of."

"I'm glad for that." She bent low and placed a lingering kiss on his cheek. "And as much as I would love to return home, it's off to the police station for me." She feigned a frown, but excitement ignited her eyes. This woman loved adventure. "Thanks to Miss Kerns, the two thugs from Shelby's office have been arrested. She ratted out her own husband and brother, hoping to get a lighter sentence. Sterling needs me to identify them."

"Which was the wiry one?"

"Her husband." She smoothed the ripples in the blanket draping the side of the bed. "MacAfferty hired them all. He was the mastermind. The object was to get the plans and then get rid of Mr. Shelby."

"Poor Shelby. Some friend, huh?"

She twisted her lip, eyes thoughtful. "But I still don't understand the idea behind the perfume. Why did Mr. Shelby let her douse her fragrance on him, when he wasn't having any relations with her?"

"Simple. He'd lost his sense of smell."

Her jaw dropped. "What? How did you know?"

"Remember the cayenne pepper you found in his desk? Apparently, Shelby dumped the stuff on his food. It reminded me of my aunt who had done the same thing. She had dulled senses, and the only way she could taste anything was with a strong spice. I told Sterling, and he verified it with Shelby's doctor. Shelby was embarrassed about it. He told no one. But the doctor and MacAfferty are friends from college."

Elissa's mouth made an O.

Sterling rapped on the door. "Hurry it up, you two. Sister Mary is coming down the hall."

With one last squeeze of his hand, Elissa voiced her goodbye. Cole eased his head back on the pillow. No sling, no hospital room, and no Sister Mary Monaca could keep Cole any longer than necessary from her. Three unspoken words separated them, but not for long.

CHAPTER 29

"The *Pittsburgh Press* wants to shut us down." Father's voice cracked with the admission.

The ledger Elissa had been reviewing in Father's office fell to her lap. "The *Pittsburgh Press*? They're the buyers? The one who gave you the offer?" Her father had never mentioned the name of the intended purchaser. Her gut sank. No doubt the high-dollar paper would want to stop the *Review*'s presses. How could Father not have known that?

"Yes. I was deceived." He collapsed onto his chair and sunk his face into open palms. "They convinced me the *Review* would be an extension of their brand."

Elissa's shoulders curled forward with an exhale. "I thought you said the buyer planned to keep the staff. That the paper was simply going to change hands." She glanced out Father's office door window to the vacant newsroom. Dozens upon dozens of employees, from a top editor to the twelve-year-old newsie, relied on their employment at the *Review*. "Nothing like eliminating the competition."

"It was tough news to discover." His heavy shrug equaled his weighty stare on the loan agreement. "The *Pittsburgh Press* has offers on two other papers besides us."

"Did you sign the contract yet? Did you officially sell?"

His chin raised. "No. Not until next Tuesday."

"What are the names of the other two papers? The ones the

Pittsburgh Press wants to shut down too?"

"The *Evening Post* and the *Weekly Sun*. Neither can afford to run their presses."

Papers that ran a nightly edition and a Sunday-only one.

"Times are tough. Competition is fiercer than ever." He tossed a pen onto his desk.

Guilt stung, nestling in her mind about her decision to reject the initial coverage of the Shelby story. But her heart knew the right choice had been made. Cole was supposed to be released from the hospital tomorrow, but sadly he wouldn't have a job to return to.

He sighed. "Maybe we should consider it a blessing we stuck around this long."

Elissa allowed the news to sink in, but instead of grasping defeat, she embraced an idea. "What if we've been going about it all wrong?"

"That's kind of the point, Lissie. If we'd been doing things right—"

"No, I mean our thinking. Here we are, believing everyone is our rival, when we could be joining forces."

Father leaned forward in his seat, pinning his stare on her. "What are you suggesting?"

"We're done with our press by four. After that, the place empties. And since our weekend edition goes out on Saturday, the press is open Sunday." She straightened as the vision took form. "What if *we* print the *Evening Post* and the *Weekly*? We can do both without inconveniencing our operating hours."

Father stood. "That may work." He commenced to pacing while scratching his neck—his deep-thinking practice. "If they sold their press, they wouldn't have the overhead cost of running it. Therefore, they could pay for us to print it for them. Keeping them alive and going."

"With that extra ongoing revenue, we could chisel down that loan in no time."

Her father gaped at her.

"What?"

"You astound me." He bent over and kissed her forehead. "Chip off the old block."

Grinning, she grabbed the phone receiver and held it out to her father. "The papers may not accept this offer, but it's putting forth our best effort, right? Now's the perfect time."

Father took a step back. "I would like you to make the call, Lissie. If this works out, I'm thinking about slowing down, handling less responsibility." He patted his heart. "This ticker is going strong, and I'm going to keep it that way. Besides, I've always wanted to travel more with your mother. After all these years of sharing me with the paper, she deserves it."

She lowered the receiver, setting it on the desk. "What are you saying?"

"That starting now, you're in training for publisher. Out of the handful of Tillmans that have managed this paper, I think you're the strongest of the bunch." He winked and grabbed his hat from the wooden rack then held out his office keys. "Do you mind locking up?"

The significance brought tears to her eyes as she received the keys. "It's an honor, Father."

He smiled and left the room.

Her heart was full, not only because her lifelong dreams could come true, but because she had a God and a father who believed in her ability. Maybe it was time for her to believe in herself as well.

She withdrew the note from the *Boston Globe*, her gaze toggling between it and the phone. Indecision had ruled her long enough. With a ragged inhale, she dropped the letter in the trash bin.

Pittsburgh was where she belonged.

Elissa buttoned her overcoat, a million possibilities dancing in her head. The *Evening Post* and the *Weekly* had seemed interested in the plan. Because Father had the meeting with the buyers Tuesday, Elissa had requested their final answer on Monday.

Hope and unease wrestled for prominence, but Elissa believed God had dropped the idea for the solution in her heart. Her only effort now was to trust.

She pulled her purse from the desk drawer and stilled.

Cole's pen lay centered on her desktop, as intriguing as the man who owned it.

How did it get there? She perused the empty newsroom. Everyone had gone home.

Heart pounding, she reached for it, unscrewing the barrel like she had hundreds of times over their years together. Her breath jammed in her chest.

A note.

Cole was in the hospital. How had he managed this? Had he paid for someone to deliver it?

Fingers shaking, she pulled the paper from its home around the ink cartridge. Seconds into reading, she dropped her purse and sprinted toward the newsroom exit.

Back pressed against the wall, Cole jittered his leg, eyeing the iron monster.

Had Elissa noticed the pen, or was he going to be locked in the *Review* building all night? Why he took risks like this, he hardly knew, but when Sister Mary Monaca had allowed him an early release, all Cole had thought about was Elissa. He had to see her. Talk to her. Hopefully, kiss her senseless.

Heels against the metal steps snapped every cell to attention. She'd found it.

Gliding toward him, she smiled with a brightness that warmed his heart. He'd never tire of being a recipient of those nose-crinkling grins.

"I thought you were still at Mercy." Her gaze landed on his

shoulder, the sling. "How are you feeling?"

Most of the day, like ripping his arm off, but … "Right now, all is perfect."

She bit her lip. "I got your note."

"I see that." He wrapped his left arm around her waist and pulled her close. "Do you remember the last time I asked you down here?"

She rested her head on his chest and nodded, the lemon scent of her hair engaging his senses. "You kissed me."

"Did you know I had planned that for months, and even that day I'd considered backing out?"

Pulling slightly away, her upturned face bore confusion. "You never told me that."

"I was scared." That moment had pushed their relationship from casual to serious. "What if you rejected me?"

She scoffed. "I don't think you understood how much I was in love with you."

"I can say the same about you." He angled back to peer into her eyes. "Even now."

Her mouth parted, a perfect invitation. The urge to smash his lips against hers coursed through him, but something else took precedence. He swallowed and released her.

"I was wondering if you could assist me."

Her brows lowered. "Anything. How so?"

He reached into his vest pocket and withdrew an envelope. "I never turned in my article to your father for that competition. I was wondering if you could proofread it. You're the best around when it comes to copyediting."

"Is that what you called me here for?" She huffed, and her cuteness reached new heights. "But there's no contest. The Shelby case is closed."

He clucked his tongue, and she frowned. "I promised him an article. As did you." Flashing a smile, he waved the editorial. "I'm going to keep my word. Just need your pretty blues to look it over."

"Okay." She held out her hand, and Cole placed the article on her palm.

Elissa sliced a fingernail through the envelope, probably a little harder than necessary. If Cole had wanted her to proofread his article, he could have asked in a less dramatic fashion. She thought he'd summoned her to the basement for something romantic. Like last time.

She swallowed her disappointment and conjured a smile. At least he was near. The past few days had been acute torture with Mercy's visitation rule of family only. She stepped closer, brushing against his healthy side, and unfolded the paper.

Spark,

Your soft heart, your ambition, your zeal to help those afflicted by injustice are what make you a woman like none other. You've held my heart since that day at Howe Springs, and now I'm asking you to keep it forever. Would you give me the honor of a lifetime and be my wife?

Cole

Her tears fell onto the letter. His wife?

Cole dropped to one knee.

Her heart thrashed louder than the press behind her ever could.

"What'd you think?" He dug in his pocket.

She glanced at the note again. This was what she'd longed for five years ago. To be by his side. To be united in the most holy way. But something was missing from the page. Eight letters seemed a trifle, but to her, they meant everything. "I confess. It seems … incomplete."

"Indeed." He retrieved the box, opening it, revealing a ring.

Her hand went to her opened mouth. When did he have time to purchase that? The stunning diamond winked at her as if it knew something she didn't.

"You're exactly right. A couple of words were purposefully left out. I wanted the privilege to voice them."

Her breath fluttered in her chest.

"I love you."

The shards of her heart poured as tears from her eyes.

"You should've heard those words long ago. Just because I hadn't voiced them, didn't mean it wasn't in my soul. You've always been the girl for me."

"I love you too." The first time she'd spoken that, it'd been a disaster. This time, it was beautiful.

He cleared his throat, eyes hopeful. "So what do you say? In response to my letter?"

"Editorial-wise, it's a bit short." She laughed, her smile as bright as her future. "But content-wise, it's perfect."

"What place does it have in your heart? Above the fold, or in the funny papers? The decision is yours."

He talked her language, and she loved him even more for it.

"Above the fold." She bent lower and pressed a kiss to his lips. "I will marry you."

He slipped the ring on her finger. "Finally, where it belongs." He brought her hand to his lips, kissing each knuckle. "I purchased this ring the night before I left for Columbia."

"What?" She stilled. "You've had it for that long?"

"Mmm-hmm." He stood and reached around her, drawing her to his chest.

She angled as to not bump his sling, but Cole didn't seem to mind about his wound. With his eyes intensely on hers, he dipped his chin, lowering until he was a touch away.

"I was a fool for not returning sooner." He sighed against her lips. "My love for you had caused me to believe you were best without me, but now I see God put us together. And He doesn't make mistakes."

And with that, his mouth pressed against hers, tender but sure. His one arm held her with the strength of two. The whispers of their stormy past faded from her being. His warm touch carried the promise that matched his loyal heart.

Cole Parker had pledged himself to her. Her heart swelled with adoration for the only man who'd held her hand, kissed her lips, and now, said "I love you." Suddenly, a lifetime seemed too short.

ONE YEAR LATER

"It seems you're well qualified. A degree from the University of Pittsburgh. Articles published in *Ladies' Home Journal*." Elissa skimmed the resume Miss Graham had provided and glanced up. It still seemed strange being seated on this side of Father's desk, but it was a peculiarity Elissa relished. She focused on the young woman opposite her. "My main question is, why do you want to be a journalist at the *Review*?"

Miss Graham straightened in her seat, her large brown eyes peering at Elissa from under her stylish cloche hat. "It's always been a dream of mine." Her smile blossomed. "I've enjoyed writing articles. I truly have, but there's something about stepping out from the confines of my desk and working in the field. The adventure of finding that one story. It's thrilling." She folded her hands in her lap and dipped her thick lashes. "I apologize for being starry-eyed. I have a weakness of getting carried away when discussing journalism." Her rosy cheeks matched the piping on her long-waisted dress.

"I know the feeling, Miss Graham. Too well." Elissa smiled and ran a thumb over Cole's pen. "What you believe to be a weakness, I consider a strength. *Never* lose that drive."

Miss Graham gave an enthusiastic nod. "I won't."

"And *always* arrive at your station promptly at seven a.m.," she said with a wink.

The young woman lifted her head, mouth slanting in a gracious smile. "Thank you. I'll work my hardest."

Elissa rose and shook Miss Graham's hand. "I have no doubt you will. You start Monday."

With a bounce to her step, the new scout reporter exited the office.

Elissa slid the resume into the filing drawer and glanced at the clock on the window sill. Father should arrive any moment. A smirk curled her lips. Just because the former publisher had resigned hadn't meant he wouldn't swing by for several hours throughout the week. When Mother allowed, of course. Laughter bubbled in her chest.

"Mrs. Parker." With a hip cocked against the doorjamb and arms crossed, her husband regarded her with a crooked grin. "Got some news for you." He stepped forward, closing the door with his foot.

They'd been married eight months, and butterflies still invaded her stomach when Cole walked into the room. She hoped that never went away. "That reminds me, I have something for you too."

"Oh really?" His smile hitched, and that gleam in his eyes brightened. "Is there a lip-locking session in my near future?"

Laughing, she playfully smacked his shoulder. "I'm not talking about kissing." She scooped up a folder from the desk and handed it to him. "Here's the latest financial statement. Can you check over it for me?"

"I will, but you're the genius around here. It was your idea to rent out the press, and we've been gaining momentum ever since." He hooked an arm around her waist. "We've always made a great team, Spark." He kissed the side of her head.

"But you trimmed our expenses and brought in more advertisers than we've seen in decades."

"I'm a natural-born salesman." He winked and snatched his hat from the rack. "If I could convince a woman like you to marry me, then anything's possible, right?"

"It's a privilege to be your wife." She adjusted his tie and slid her hand to cup his handsome face. "I love you, Cole."

His dark eyes zeroed in on hers, stealing her breath and warming her heart. "I love you too." He took her hand in his. "Now back to business. I got us a whopper of a lead." He released her and retrieved her burgundy overcoat.

She bit her lip, excitement gripping her bones. "This better not be another one of your tricks to get me alone."

"I wish it were." He wagged his brows and assisted her with her coat. "But no, this is a verified tip from our favorite private detective."

"Sterling?" Her pulse kicked up another notch. Cole's cousin no longer worked for the police force, but he'd remained close with several officers whom he'd hoped would eventually slip information. "Is it a substantial lead?"

He snagged the belt of her coat, reeling her to him. "Heart-stopping." He pressed a kiss to her neck. "And so are you." His lips trailed her jaw until claiming her mouth.

She wrapped her arms around his neck, and Cole deepened the kiss.

Someone rapped the door.

Cole groaned. "If it's Frank, I'm going to kick him in the pants." He adjusted his hat, which had been knocked askew, and opened the door.

Father stood there, brows raised and eyes suspicious. "Do I have to separate you two?"

Elissa laughed and bussed his cheek. "Not necessary. We're off to check out a story." She grabbed her purse and flashed a cheeky grin at Father. "You think you can hold the fort while we're gone?"

"I'm pretty sure I can handle it." His words were flat, but the twinkle in his gray eyes gave away his delight. Alfred Tillman remained a newspaperman through and through.

She snatched her gloves from the drawer and met Cole by the door.

With a wave to her father, Elissa slid her hand into Cole's, a prayer of thanks filling her heart.

Her dreams had been elusive like a breath of wind, but her value wasn't found in triumphs. Or failures. God's love defined her. Cole's love embraced her. Her life's story remained unfinished, but blank pages no longer meant insufficiency. Just the privilege to fill the bare spaces with adventure, excitement, and living her days to the fullest. While her future remained to be chronicled, the narrative was His to pen.

AUTHOR'S NOTE

Dear Reader,

Thank you for taking a chance on a debut author. I sincerely hope you enjoyed Elissa and Cole's story. If you're curious about which factors of this book are true, I'm happy to provide details!

While the *Review* is a fictional paper, fierce competition between newspapers existed during this period. There'd been morning, afternoon, and evening editions of newspapers available, but the introduction of radio—and with it, the expediency of current news updates—caused newspapers to struggle to keep their presses running.

The views displayed in this story concerning Prohibition in Pittsburgh are sadly accurate. At one point during the twenties, over five hundred speakeasies operated within its borders. Bootleggers paid police officials for protection. One illegal establishment operated directly across the street from a police station! Because the local police wouldn't uphold the law, the state government stepped in and conducted raids.

The Allegheny courthouse, described at the beginning and the end of the book, is truly a work of structural art, boasting rusticated granite and massive archways. The "Bridge of Sighs" was colloquially coined because convicted criminals were escorted from the courthouse to the county jail via an enclosed stone walkway hovering over Ross Street. The courthouse and its walkway remain, but the jail had been closed and renovated to become a court of common pleas.

The William Penn, the location of the gala, is an actual hotel complete with a lavish ballroom. If you visit this hotel, you'll notice there is, in fact, a speakeasy. The lounge is still tucked beneath the lobby and has been restored to its former historic decor.

Howe Springs is another real site. While the lavish estate which was situated behind it has been replaced by other buildings, the stone fountain still stands.

My favorite historical location mentioned in this story is the Duquesne Incline. The incline during the twenties was only viewed as a convenient means for locals to safely and quickly travel Mount Washington. Today, the incline is noted as a must-see tourist spot in Pittsburgh. The once pocked and barren mountainside now flourishes with vivid greenery, and the steel factories and smokestacks have been replaced by a crisp city skyline. The view is truly breathtaking.

Those familiar with the area will recognize street names such as Forbes Avenue, Cherry Way, and Fifth Avenue as well as the areas of Shadyside, Oakland, and Point Breeze. I aimed to keep everything geographically correct.

Thanks again for reading this story of my heart. If you're interested in more of my writings and the latest news, you're welcome to visit me at RachelScottMcDaniel.com or on social media.

Blessings,
Rachel

CPSIA information can be obtained
at www.ICGtesting.com
Printed in the USA
LVHW011607081219
639822LV00002B/336/P